JASPIERRE

Mixi J Applebottom

Printed in the United States of America

First Printing, 2015

ISBN 978-0-692-29572-4

www.MixiJApplebottom.com

Life is crazy.

JASPIERRE

CHAPTER

ONE

Something was wrong with the car. It was obvious as she lifted her foot from the gas pedal. Nothing happened, nothing slowed down. The Lexus kept flying forward, faster and faster. Fifty-five mph. Fifty-eight mph. The engine whirred and spun. She cringed, her heart pounding. The woman slammed her foot onto the brake pedal. Nothing happened.

"Are these pedals even attached to anything?" Her mind exploded with irritation, as she grabbed the black emergency brake handle and pulled up. Nothing happened. Sixty-three mph. She glanced around, she had just flown through a quiet town and was now at it's outskirts. She needed to get farther away from everyone while she sorted out what to do with her Lexus. Her car skidded and slid as she turned, following the road, and almost smacking into a telephone pole.

She glanced at the gas tank. Full, of course. She hated an empty gas tank; she rarely allowed it to get below three-quarters of a tank. At least now she was on a long, straight country road. Farm after farm flew past her windows. Seventy mph. Her back tensed as she swerved around a slow-moving tractor. No other cars on the road. How was she going to stop?

She would have tried turning the key and shutting everything off, but she had a key-less car, with a push start. She pressed the button, but nothing happened. The dealer's voice rang into her ears. *To turn the automobile off, shift into park and the car would automatically shut down the engine.* No key, no problem.

She braced herself and tried to shift. It wouldn't budge, preventing accidental shifting into park, or worse, reverse while going highway speeds. She ran her frustrated fingers through her long tangled brown hair.

Lights flickered far behind her, and she heard a faint siren. "Shit. That farmer must have called the cops." She cursed her fate and then did the only thing she could think of to do.

"Call 911." Her dashboard responded to her after a brief ring.

"This is 911. Please state your emergency."

"My car is accelerating uncontrollably. I am on a small country road, going eighty-five mph. I tried to brake, but it won't stop. Also, there is a cop behind me now, so please tell him not to shoot me." The lights and siren were gaining on her, but he was still far enough away that he probably couldn't shoot her tires yet.

"Okay, hold on." The 911 operator sounded nice. A strong male voice. She frowned as she saw a truck up ahead. Far ahead, but at this speed, it would be all too soon. She moved to the left lane, trying not to swerve. Her black shiny car swayed at the lurching movements.

"Are you still there? What is your name?" Mr. 911 was back.

"Uh, yes. My name is... Jen." It was the first name she thought of that started with J. "I don't know what I should do. I am now going ninety-five mph."

He paused. "Okay, I spoke with the cop; he won't shoot you. Please try the brake." She pressed it hard with both feet; nothing.

"Nope, no response."

"Okay, do you have an emergency brake? Try that."

She pulled up again, even though the lever was still raised where she had left it. The sirens were closer now.

"Not working."

"Well, the next thing to do is to put the vehicle into neutral. I have to warn you, the power steering may or may not turn off. So try to stay straight on the road. It might take more strength than normal to turn the car."

She pulled the shifter and it did not budge.

"I don't know why it won't work. I can't seem to move the shifter." Her heart pounded harder and harder.

Mr. 911 was so calm, and reassuring. "Okay, the next option is to use the key to turn the vehicle off. Don't bother taking it out of the ignition; just twist the key, turn the car off. Keep your hands on the wheel and apply the brake."

Jen snapped, "It is a key-less car! *I don't have a key*." Her voice sounded angry and rattled against the black interior.

"Take a deep breath Jen. I am here to help you." Mr. 911's voice poured over her anxious body like sweet chocolate on ice cream. "Press the start button and hold it in for one minute. I'll time it."

She hesitated as she saw what was ahead. "The road is closed," she whimpered. One hundred ten mph and the road was closed. The barriers were across the road like orange beacons of doom. She scanned for a way to turn, a place to go. And she saw it. A sparkle up ahead: A lake. She was going in the lake. *Stay buckled, airbag, then get out and swim. Wait for it. Wait for the airbag. Then get out and swim.* Trees flew past her windows as she zoomed faster and the sparkle drew close.

"Jen, calm down and press the start button.

It's okay, you are gonna be fine." Mr. 911's voice seemed far away as she looked for a decent spot to drive in. She cut right, and her car tipped up to two wheels and then smashed back to the spinning squealing tires. Her engine was roaring with the effort. The tires skidded on the sand as she plunged into the water.

The crash was painful, like charging headfirst into a brick wall. She had imagined the liquid would be soft, and gentle, and her automobile would sink down like a leaf through the air. It was not like that at all. Her whole body cried out with pain, and the airbag pummeled her. Her nose bled. *What was happening?*

The ringing in her ears was loud. She looked around and saw lake creeping in the floorboards. *Get out and swim.* Her brain was screaming with pain and she tried to open the door, but the water pushing on it stopped her. The water was already at the windows. She tried to move to the other door, and realized her seatbelt held her. Water had crept inside up to her ankles. She turned back and struggled to unbuckle, panic rising inside her. As soon as she was free she tried to open the window to get out. The electronics clicked once, and then nothing. The window failed like every part of the luxury vehicle so far had failed her.

She tore into the glove box as the car sank further, submerging her knees. She found the window breaking device. Water now covered the windows outside. The stupid little pointed hammer was pathetically light in her hands. She slammed it into the window, and a satisfying crack of glass starred across. Again, and again, and water poured inside. She paused, terror washing over her. *Think.* Spotting her backpack and purse, she grabbed both with her left hand, and took deep breaths as the seat filled up with liquid. As soon as the flooding slowed, she shoved herself out the window and into the lake, struggling toward the shore. The cop stood there on the beach, slow clapping with a hideous smile. She turned back to look. The front half of her car was submerged, but the back was dry. If she had moved to the back seat and not shattered the window she would have been fine.

He did not come closer. Or offer her a towel. Or ask her if she was okay. She heard other sirens far, far in the distance, coming closer. He aimed his gun at her. "So, Jaspierre. Are you going to resist?"

Her head was ringing and her heart pounded. She wiped blood and dripping water from her face with her left hand. "What?"

He fired a shot into the lake near her foot. Jen froze, her wet, cold body trembling. She raised her hands above her head. Her black leather pants hugged tight against her ass, and her black leather vest had come open. Her big breasts felt exposed with the wet green shirt pulling snugly against them. "Walk."

She walked closer, her backpack and purse hanging across her back on her left arm in the most uncomfortable way. Her nose bled, dripping into the lake. He grinned, and his eyes burned into her nipples. As her torso shivered, she realized her right hand still had the tiny hammer in it. Even with her aching, pounding head, she knew this would be fun. She stumbled and her breasts bounced. As he stared laughing nastily the hammer flew from her fingers and slammed into his arm. His gun fell out of his hand and he screamed and curled into a ball. His stocky body shuddered, pain ricocheting through it. Jen walked over and picked up his gun. He rolled to look at her and gave her the finger. She laughed and pressed her foot into his arm, crushing it into his chest, and grabbed the little window hammer yanking it hard out of his bone. He screamed. "You bitch!"

"I'd stick around and play, but I have a headache. Chance, you bastard, I'll be back for you later." The sirens sounded closer. She straightened her wig and climbed into his still-running cop car and drove off in the other direction. If she had her head screwed on straight she would have killed him.

Two Weeks Earlier

Russell Holmes was having an average day. His father had been begging him to come back and work at his mechanic shop. But Russell didn't care to do more oil changes. A boring, average day, he stuffed groceries into a bag over and over in an endless cycle. Bread last, milk first, blah, blah, blah. A trained monkey could do this job. Though, he had his favorite customers, not that he knew any of their names. Purple Sweater & Wrinkles always slipped him a five when he carried her bags out while she pushed her walker. He shouldn't take tips, but he didn't care. Mommy with Infant, always gave him hope the baby would cry and she would spring a leak. The teens who wore little clothing were always a favorite.

He did, in fact, have least favorites; Anyone who smelled, good or bad, it didn't even matter. Scents were obnoxious cocktails running past his nose as frequently as the groceries. No perfume, fart, urine, hair spray or deodorant went past him without disgusting his precious nose.

As he listened to the *beep, beep* of random piles of food being scanned and slid toward him, his eye caught someone special. She was a little bit heavy, and not too tall. Not too bad; along with her rounder belly came a nice round ass and large, pretty titties. Her hair was short and dark red. She looked close to his age, twenty-six or so. But she didn't wear a band. Maybe she'd be a good pick for a sweet lay.

Her groceries slid toward him and the *beep, beep* continued. He checked out her food. It looked like food for one; a half gallon of milk, one small loaf of bread, chips, and lunchmeat. But then, a long stream of canned cat food; not a good sign. "So, cats?" He smiled his prizewinning smile.

She turned and looked at him. "Yes, I have two. But, they aren't cats. They are servals; big, eat a ton."

Two. He rolled it around in his head. She didn't look like a crazy cat lady. He had no idea what a serval was, though. "Can I carry these to the car for you?"

She looked startled, but then grinned. Her teeth were straight and her smile looked tasty. No horrible odors poured out of her. A good start. "I am sure I can carry them..."

Russell flashed back his own pearly whites, trying to clue her in. "Oh, no doubts you can, but why would you when I will do it for you?" She blushed then. A stir of excitement fluttered through him. Would she say yes? He seemed to always strike out.

"Well, when you put it like that..." She coyly waved him along, tossing her red locks, and he loaded up her cart and pushed it out with her.

"I haven't noticed you in the store before. Do you live around here?" He asked.

Her dark eyes looked so intense. "I recently moved into town." She lied.

"Well, let me give you my number in case you need someone to show you around." He grinned.

She paused and turned to him. Her body looked fabulously soft. She didn't look like she would say yes.

"Do you like Chinese? We could meet up for dinner..." He hesitated. This wasn't working. It didn't often work. He stared at her black Lexus and whistled, "Wow, that is a nice car. I thought you'd be driving a beater." Regret struck him. He was a jackass.

"A beater? Do you think I am a broke-ass high schooler? Pssh." She tossed her short red hair with annoyance. "Fine, Chinese food would work, I guess. But I will pay because you have a lame-ass job and drive a beater." She bit her lip in this expression of annoyance and pleasure all at once.

"Heh, okay. The place is right over there." He pointed across the street to a blinking sign of a panda bear. The restaurant was a rundown, dingy place. The paint that might have once been blue was flaking off. There were two neon signs; one said Open and the other was a panda. There was no name of the store posted anywhere outside.

"That place?" She hesitated.

"Er, it's better than it looks. I swear! Meet you there around six?"

"Okay."

Russell set her final bag into her black, over-sized trunk. She closed it and he stepped back taking the cart with him. "See you later!" He flashed his bright smile and waved. She smiled and nodded and got in her car. As the Lexus backed out of the parking spot, he trudged the cart back. *Crap, I didn't get her name*, he thought.

CHAPTER

TWO

Jaspierre pressed the gas and zipped down the road at a nice clip. Mother would likely approve of a boy toy, but not a grocery bagger. After all, the CEO of Kyller and Co should only date someone of her level. Men were too hard to figure out, though, so she wasn't much for dating. Mother had mastered emotionless affairs, and Jaspierre hadn't even mastered dating. An hour along the highway, she took a turn onto a small, abandoned, looking street. After a while, she came upon a rock fence, tattered and weed covered. She slowed as she pulled up to a large, metal gate. As soon as it saw her, it glided open and her Lexus slipped through.

The tattered and unappealing outside had never met the inside where a manicured lawn awaited. The perfect, extra-wide driveway held not a single crack or pothole. Along the hill behind a large, tall row of trees, the road led to a perfect garden complete with marble cat statues. Two large feline bushes stood mirroring each other right at the foot of the marble staircase. The house was gorgeous, expensive, and dripped with luxury. Marble pillars, sky-high windows; the whole kit and caboodle. Everything drug money could buy. The legal kinds, diabetes medications, antibiotics, boner pills, she ran the largest distribution center for hundreds of miles. The car pulled to a stop right in front of the stairs, and she stepped out of it, her heels clicking on the smooth pavement. She popped the trunk open, and picked up the four bags of groceries. She walked inside onto the smooth, polished, glistening floors.

"Tessa!" Jaspierre called and a furry, soft head poked itself over a high ledge. Yawning and stretching, the large, spotted serval leapt down six feet from its perch. Purring, she swished around her legs rubbing up against her. "Ikali!" Her voice rang out, and her big male serval descended the large staircase. She kissed and petted them both, then carried the bags into the mammoth kitchen. It was a professional kitchen, designed for a live-in chef. She had no chef. It never was pleasant having strangers walk around your home, spying on you.

After she set the groceries in the organized cupboards, she grabbed two plates, and pulled two cokes from the fridge. She made two turkey sandwiches, shooing the magnificent cats away as she worked. Carrot sticks and a handful of chips. She folded two white linen napkins into little swans, and set them atop the sandwiches. The plates sat on her crisp white serving tray.

She glanced at the clock. 1:30 pm; plenty of time for experiments before her date. Carrying the tray, she walked into the massive library with a huge fireplace. The carved, white, glistening marble had two servals carved into each side. She walked up and playfully petted one, tugging on the right ear until she felt a soft click. It might be rather predictable to have a room underneath the fireplace, but it was too much fun to skip. The fireplace slid back, revealing the dungeon-like stairs. The two servals came running at the sound of the door opening. "Let's go play, my dears." Down the stairs they went; a girl and her tray of food, and two excited felines into a dark, dark room.

Clicking on the lights revealed a large wall of computer screens and a massive observatory. Past the computers was a long glass window on the left, and on the right three large windows. Jaspierre walked around gazing through the long window. Inside was a massive maze, both vertical and horizontal, easily as big as a football field. It was stark white. The house was a mansion but compared to the basement seemed small . The maze was built entirely underground and snaked under the perfect driveway. A black rabbit hopped through the maze. The smooth walls and platforms were crisp and clean. She turned to check the other rooms. Behind her were three windows. She looked down into the rooms and two were empty, other than a set of black metal rings trailing up one of the crisp white walls in pairs. She walked past them to the room that held an occupant. He seemed a bit depressed.

In the third room, she viewed a sad-looking fellow sitting on a sanitary bed. He wore plain bleached scrubs and crisp white socks. He sat there, watching his hands. She pressed against the glass from her spot way up high. Staring at him, as he stared at his hands, she ran her fingers through her short red hair. Lately, it seemed all he did was look at his own fingers in a miserable way.

"Hello Lucas." her voice rang out, and the blond, skinny man jumped to his feet. She opened a tiny box in the wall and set his plate into it. She pressed a lever and a little dumbwaiter lowered down. The box was so small the sandwich, coke, carrot sticks and chips filled it completely. It was not an escape route; nothing was an escape route. He had been in here for ten years. He took his captivity better than most would have.

A small opening appeared and held his lunch. He walked over and took it quickly. He didn't want his fingers anywhere near the door when it shut. As soon as the plate and soda had moved, the door snapped shut, its razor-lined edge clicking sharply together. "Thank you for this tasty lunch," he said not even bothering to lift his blue eyes, but she heard him through the microphones just the same.

She smiled. "No problem." He did seem depressed. Maybe she should get some Mountain Dew. Would he like that more than a Coke?

"Are we doing experiments today?" he asked as he nibbled at the edges of a single chip.

"Oh, yes. Ikali and Tessa will play find the rabbit, as always. Who do you think will win today?"

His hands trembled, and he fumbled and nearly dropped the chip. "Is it a wager?"

She laughed. "You want to wager today?" *A wager could cheer him up!* "Oh, oh yes we shall. But not about the bunny." They had already wagered about the bunny too many times. It had gotten boring. He cringed and ate faster, though his anxious stomach would barely allow food past his throat.

Ikali pressed his fur against her and yowled. "Into the box," she said, and the two cats raced to their doors. With a quick flick of a switch, the doors slid open and each cat stepped into its own glass box. The glass, vented with slots across the sides and top, held the servals. They sat, ears twitching as they stared into the maze. The rabbit didn't have a chance. They both closed their eyes, allowing their huge ears and tiny noses to hunt while they waited for the doors to open.

Jaspierre already knew they would wait as long as she asked them to. She also had learned the longer she made them wait, the faster they found the rabbit once released. But today, she tested something else. The game was always find the rabbit. Hunt the rabbit. Eat the rabbit. But today, there would be another animal in the game. Mice-- ten entertaining, tasty mice. Would they forgo the tiny bites of squeaking food to eat a whole rabbit? Would they even remember the game was to get the rabbit?

When she pressed another button, a tiny little box opened on both sides of the maze, and five small grey and brown mice began peeping out each side. Another small yellow button and four tiny platforms lowered from the ceiling. Each was different. Pelletized food, water, cheese, and a fresh can of cat-food.

"Are you gonna guess today, Lucas?" she bubbled. "Lucas? Lucas! Who will get the rabbit? Ikali or Tessa?"

He stood. "I'm sorry Jasp. I think Tessa will win today." He then curled into his bed, under his blanket, quivering. His empty plate sat on the floor with the empty coke can set upon it. He was unable to watch. He had no windows to the maze. The best he could manage was to climb the pairs of metal rings up the wall and stare into Jaspierre's observatory. He wasn't up for it, though. He curled under his blanket and hoped for the best. Hoped this wouldn't turn into a wager.

She glanced at the clock. Hmm. Already 2:15. She threw several levers and the machine purred while the room sprang to life. All the platforms and walls shifted positions creating a new maze the cats had never been in. At the same moment, the doors opened for the big cats, but neither moved yet. She moved away from the screens, buttons, and levers, and perched on the railing. Watching through the long glass was always more pleasant than staring at screens. Her legs crossed, and her heels tapped at the glass as she sat there, munching her chips and staring at the cats.

The tiny brown and grey mice ran. They were hungry. Some would go for food, some for water. The bunny hopped along. Ikali stepped out of his box and leapt from platform to platform. Tessa sat motionless, eyes shut, ears twitching.

Ikali paused as he saw a tiny brown mouse. Three platforms below him, it ran across the ground. Ikali descended, pouncing and crunching. When he lifted his paws the crushed carcass lay still. He was clearly disappointed; playing with his food was the best part. He swallowed it and leapt back up to a higher platform, and sat watching.

Tessa charged out of her box. She leapt from platform to platform, moving higher and lower. Then she landed smack on the rabbit, and it let out its shrieking, squealing cries. She let go and it ran. Her tail twitched as it went around a wall. She leapt straight up and landed on the other side of the wall, directly on the bunny. It screamed again. She lifted her paw to let it go, and Ikali jumped on top of her. Tessa rolled underneath him, kicking repeatedly, smacking him with her paws and baring her teeth. He jumped straight up and landed on the running rabbit. It shrieked as he bit into it and carried it off.

Tessa followed and they both ran, racing around, up and down platforms, jumping and hissing. Ikali leapt into a small corner, intending to eat the screaming bunny in his mouth, only to find two mice in the same corner. He paused, undecided, as Tessa leapt next to him. They both stared at the mice, nibbling on crumbs. Ikali dropped the rabbit and swiped up both mice, one with each paw. He crunched one's head and let the other sneak off, smacking it back with his paw. Tessa snatched the bunny and ran off, hiding behind a wall panel. She crunched into the rabbit enthusiastically, dismantling it so it would stop shrieking, lest she attract Ikali's attention again.

Jaspierre stood up, grinning. Tessa had won. She dropped her heels off her feet and walked to Lucas's glass window. "Well, you won. Tessa caught the rabbit." His blond hair poked out of the white blanket. "Shame it wasn't a wager."

He did not want to wager. It wasn't a game he could win. He couldn't think of anything to say. "Aren't you pleased?" her insistent voice pestered him.

"Yes, yes. She is a smart serval. I'm glad she won." His flat voice tried to sound enthusiastic.

"I have a date," she said. Her dating anyone made his stomach turn. "So, what should we wager? How many times he looks at my breasts? If he pays for my dinner? If he invites me home for the night?"

Please invite her home. Invite her to move in and never come back. He paused as he had an idea. "I will wager he won't come home with you."

Jaspierre hissed, smashing her Coke can with her hands. "Nobody can come here!"

"Does that mean you forfeit?" His mind spun. Could he win one?

She burst out laughing. "Oh, I see. So if I decline to bring him here, then you will win? And if I bring him here, then I win?" She rolled the idea around in her head, amused. "Deal."

His voice trembled."But I have to see him to believe it happened."

She paused again, considering. "You know if you see him, he'll end up in the room next to you."

He nodded and it was a bet. They both knew the stakes. The wager was always the same.

She spun around and walked back to the massive control bay. When she pressed a button, a whistle rattled. Both cats leapt to their feet and raced to the box. She opened the doors and they came tearing out, up the stairs and off to nap. They hated the next part. She turned and looked at her white maze; bloody footprints, and a half-eaten rabbit carcass. *Disgusting*.

She placed headphones over her ears. They stopped all noise except for the soft music. She pulled a large lever and told the remaining mice to hold on. Or not. They'd float away with the rest of the mess. Dozens of nozzles sprayed; the noise was incredible, not that she could hear it. Lucas covered his ears tightly and closed his eyes, trying to block out the deafening racket. Ten minutes later, the maze sparkled, glistening wet and shiny, and sterile.

She took off the headphones and placed them back on the hook. 4:30. A half hour left before she had to leave. Popping her heels back on, she told Lucas goodnight and hustled up the staircase flipping off the lights. She walked through the library, clicking the ear and sliding the fireplace back. Up the marble steps to her bedroom. The closet was magnificent, almost as large as the bedroom. Past all the wigs and shoes were her dresses. She dug through them, finding the one she wanted. It was a vibrant teal color, hugging her breasts and curving around her ass, without making her stomach look too much like a round pumpkin. She picked out sparkling silver shoes and massive, dangling silver earrings. She looked in the mirror. Why had she worn such short hair today? She looked for a silver headband to pull the hair back out of her face. Screw it. Like he'd even notice. She went to the wig wall and looked at all the shorter, red options. Jaspierre switched her short, red, straight hair out for a longer, curlier hair. It looked like she had spent hours curling and prepping her hair to get such a dramatic wave. *Fabulous*. She glanced at the clock: ten minutes left. She made up her face with skin smoothing products and dark, vibrant lipstick. Next, she added a light silver color to her eyes, and stood up. "Juniper." Satisfied, she grabbed a simple silver purse.

She came teetering down the stairs in the tall shoes and she strutted out the door, calling out, "Tessa and Ikali, be good." The cats did not respond, and as she stepped outside, she could see why. Ikali lay sleeping on top of the black Lexus, looking contentedly warm. "Ikali, off the car." He opened one eye and yawned. She shook her head and walked around to get in. Tessa was sitting in a nearby gazebo, napping in a hammock.

Her car started up with the push of a button. The metal roof rumbled underneath him and Ikali leapt off, wandering away to find a better spot to nap. Jaspierre pressed the accelerator and sped along the street, she was in no hurry. She wasn't late, the hour drive would be a breeze, but driving fast was her favorite. She smiled, and her red curls shook around her. She turned on the radio and enjoyed the drive.

As she pulled up to a parking spot, it was a quarter to six. The Chinese restaurant did not look more appealing in the dusk. Bright neon said "open," though it flickered because the bulb was starting to fail. The panda bear sign was in better shape and gleamed bright. There were three other cars in the cracked and uneven parking lot. Jaspierre waited in the car for her grocery bagger, amused she hadn't asked his name. Delivery drivers hopped in and out of cars, a steady stream of food-filled bags leaving the restaurant.

* * * * * * * * * * * *

A rattling, yellow, Volkswagen bug drove up, backfiring a few times. He drove a beater. He parked and turned off the engine, using the little mirror in the sunshade to check his hair. Russell ran his fingers through, coaxing it into a pleasant shape. *I should get a haircut soon*, he thought to himself. He stepped out of the car and looked around for a shiny black Lexus. She sat there, watching him fussing at himself in the mirror. *Great. Just great.* Her door swung open, and sparkling silver heels clicked out, her teal dress following in such a nice way. Her short red hair curled. She must have spent hours getting ready. His body loved hers all over again.

He choked on his words. "Hi, you... hi, *cough* Well, shall we eat?" He blushed like a child. "You look amazing," he said with a soft whisper.

She flashed a bright smile; perhaps she didn't even hear his compliment. "Yes, let's eat." They walked together, and he got the door for her.

The restaurant was small. One other table had someone sitting at it. No staff greeted them at all. He led her to a small dingy booth, and regretted suggesting this place. He wondered with a hint of fear if the seat might stain her dress. It looked old but wiped down; perhaps they would be lucky...

She sat without a single care about the dress. Her mind had one thing on it. Winning.

He sat across from her and said, "I swear the food is good." The kitchen clanked and crashed and the chef sang to foreign radio. *The food is good,* she thought as she watched delivery driver after driver leave carrying order after order.

"I, uh, get it delivered. I haven't actually been inside here before, sorry."

She raised an eyebrow. "So, I didn't catch your name."

"Oh, yes, uh, it's Russell," he replied. She wrinkled her nose. *Russell. Seriously? I can't believe I am out with a name like Russell.*

"I am Juniper." She smiled as she lied.

"Juniper! What a nice name." He leaned in and stared into her eyes a moment. She stared back devilishly. She looked so full of secrets.

A short, crabby Asian waiter walked up. "What do want?"

"Dinner for two special, please," Russell blurted out. He felt the tension build; he hadn't even asked her what she liked to eat. "Also, can we have two drinks?"

"Two, two," the waiter said, then left.

"Sorry, I... they sell the dinner for two special and lousy egg drop soup." He looked sheepishly at her, her irritation burning his cheeks. Juniper didn't respond. "Anyways, what do you do?"

"Anything I want." And it was true.

He laughed, thinking she was being coy. "Well, uh, I bag groceries, obviously. But I am a student. I have been going to school for my computer engineering degree." Truth was, he hadn't taken a class in three years.

The food was plopped in front of them: One plate of fried rice, one plate of chicken and vegetables, one plate of noodles, one plate of beef and broccoli, two sets of chopsticks, and fortune cookies, nothing to drink.

"Hey, uh, drinks?" Russell mimed a glass to his lips. The waiter glared and walked off.

She looked at the four plates of food. *How awkward*. No empty plates to serve herself. She slid the steamy fried rice in front of her; picking up the chopsticks she selected a delicious bite and tasted it without spilling a grain.

He took the noodles and picked up the chopsticks. No idea how to eat using them. He watched her daintily pick up the rice, and he tried to pick up a noodle. After several attempts he switched to the chicken and vegetables, stabbing one with the stick, he finally took a bite.

She smirked at him. "Tasty?'

"Uh, yeah. Normally, I eat using a fork. I don't know how a civilization can last so long without making an eating utensil better than a stick."

She laughed. He was in the zone. *She loved him*. Maybe she would even come home with him.

The food wasn't bad; tasty even. She ate the rice and beef and broccoli and did not offer to share, shaking her head when he tried to take a bite from her plates. The waiter reappeared and set two drinks on the table. "We out, make do," he said and disappeared.

One was neon blue. It was a thick liquid, and cold. A smoothie? A milkshake? The other one was neon yellow. It was a thin liquid. Soda? It stunk.

She took the blue liquid and sniffed it, then took a small sip. Blue raspberry... something. Milkshake or smoothie. She didn't know which, but it was a strange drink to be coupled alongside this meal.

He stared at her drink. Then he took his and sniffed it. The scent he recognized. "I... he... this is the egg drop soup!" He burst out laughing at the absurdity of it. "Why would they serve this?"

She laughed. "This is a weird restaurant."

* * * * * * * * * * * *

They ate and neither of them sipped any more of their strange drinks. *The date was going well, and it was gonna get more fun,* she thought to herself. She sparkled, laughed at his jokes. Listened to him coyly and leaned forward so he could see her cleavage. She stared into his eyes and knew he was hooked. Then she paid for dinner, twenty-two dollars, eight for beverages. She left no tip.

Her heels clicked across the floor as they walked out together. She giggled and slipped her fingertips into the crook of his arm. She pressed her skin up tight against his and whispered into his ear that she wished she had more of the soup drink. He laughed and turned to her; their faces were close, and he had an impulsive urge to kiss her.

Before he could try, she stepped back, sliding her hand down his arm until their fingers were touching. "Want to come over for a drink?"

He said yes before he even registered what she had asked. She pressed her skin up against his; his heart pounded. She leaned in close, he felt a click, and realized she had opened the car door. Stepping away grinning, she held the door, and he sat in the passenger seat. His heart was pounding and his face hot and red. She sat beside him in the driver's seat, pressing the start button and soon they were flying down the road. *Nailed it*, she thought to herself, grinning as she drove. She had never tried to take a man to her house before. Who knew it would be so easy?

After about fifteen minutes, his heartbeat settled and his brain returned. He wondered how far away her apartment was and regretted leaving his yellow bug behind. Of course, he could stay until morning, and she'd drop him off for work. His car would sit right there, safe and sound.

Little did he know he would never see his car again.

"You must live way out here, Juniper."

She grinned. "Oh, yes, sorry, I'm about an hour out."

"Should... Maybe..." He paused, thinking. Should they go back for his car? That might end this exciting rendezvous. He settled on, "I can't wait to see it."

She laughed, trying to decide what would happen next. "Oh, it'll be fun."

They pulled up to the beautiful house. Her heels clicked up the marble steps. He tried to take it all in: cat statues, cat bushes, and massive mansion. She was a rich, crazy cat lady. He thought he saw one of her over-sized cats, but she offered no introduction. That should have been his first clue something was wrong, but it wasn't. She dropped her heels off in the entry, shrinking what seemed like a foot. He followed her into the kitchen, like a mesmerized puppy. The house was enormous. She must be *flipping* rich.

She mixed him up a drink, making nothing for herself. It was blue and yellow. She giggled and leaned forward as she handed it to him, letting him see her sexy cleavage. "I made you a blue raspberry and lemon drink in honor of whatever it was we were offered at the Chinese place." He took a sip. It was strongly alcoholic but sweet and delicious. He drank it faster than he meant to while they walked to her library. There was a massive fireplace, surrounded by marble cats. She put on music, laughed, and took his drink. "Let me go get you another." He almost told her to stop, but he was busy staring at the place. It was spectacular to look at: the serval carvings, the fireplace, and the books...

Jaspierre slipped back in, her bare feet and teal dress looking better than ever. This time she came carrying two drinks. He took a small sip, reminding himself to slow down. Her drink was pink and strawberry. His was a repeat-- lemony, blue raspberry-- and his head buzzed light and fluffy. *God she looked good.* He grabbed her hand and twirled her around to the music. She giggled and he pressed close to her, trying to steal a kiss. Against her better judgment, she let him, her leg curling up around him. Her heart pounded and her body responded. She hadn't enjoyed sexing anyone yet, but still, her body wanted to try again. It had been eight years.

But then she remembered. *Russell.* She couldn't have sex with such a stupid name.

"Juniper," he whispered into her ear what he thought was her name, and she snapped back into game mode. Shutting off her emotions like Mother, she clicked the ear on the cat and the fireplace swung open.

"Come and see." She slipped down the dark stairs and flipped on the light.

The white room sparkled and still smelled of bleach. Lucas stood up with a mix of terror and excitement as the lights came on. Did he win? Would she let him win? What if she was angry?

The cats came running in hopes of a rabbit.

Before they even came to the stairs, they heard her command, "No kitties." It was not loud, but it was a forceful command, and neither of the cats even glanced at the fireplace stairs. They both settled into the library, grooming each other and waiting in case of rabbit.

Russell looked around the white room. "What is this place?" He swayed while he walked. She turned to him, and thought about kissing him again. "Come meet Lucas!" she squealed, giggling and taking his hands. They walked across the observation area and looked down into Lucas's room. Lucas was on his feet, staring up. Two bodies. He could see their outlines. Fear overwhelmed him. He had lost.

Russell stared, his fuzzy brain not processing. "What is he doing down there? Where is the door?" She laughed, and Russell slumped against the wall.

"Russell, dear, he's my prisoner. You are too." She walked over to the wall and held her hand on it. A large box opened in the wall. Russell was too confused and drugged to understand. She led him like a lamb to slaughter, pushing him into the box as he fell unconscious.

Jaspierre was grateful he got into the box with so little effort on her part. The wall shut and was smooth again. She shouldn't have made herself a drink. Giddy delight danced within her. Mother would never understand these emotional swings. She shouldn't have kissed him. Her body begged for more. She had an idea. No, no, she couldn't. Could she?

She turned and pressed her hand on the wall, and a panel door slid open. A small spiral staircase was behind it, and she descended humming to herself. At the bottom of the stairs was a hallway access to the basement layers. The maze maintenance rooms were on the left. She walked to a room on the right and pressed her hand to the smooth wall. The door led to an empty room except for the rings on the walls. She looked around for Lucas and his bed. But then she saw Russell stuffed into the box in the wall. Wrong room. Ha.

She laughed and stumbled out, shutting the door. She moved over to the other room and pressed her hand into the wall. The panel slid open, and Lucas looked terrified and surprised. "Jaspierre?" Before he said anything else, her breasts pressed tightly against him. Her mouth kissed at his neck. Bewildered he stood frozen. She had never made advances toward him before. In fact, he couldn't even remember the last time she was in his room, years at least.

His body responded even when he begged it not to. Her soft, warm flesh, pressed tightly against his. Nobody had touched him in so long. He had been here for years. He didn't know how many, but he was sure it was many years. Alone in a box. Even his hatred and his fear of her was not enough to hold back the demands of a lonely man. He kissed her and found her to taste like strawberries. She broke away and giggled, and walked over and shut the door. He couldn't help but stare. Her booty was hugged by the teal dress in so many delicious ways. She slipped her hands beneath the teal and her panties were on the ground. *Holy hell she was serious.*

CHAPTER

THREE

Lucas lay on his white prison bed, his nearly naked body still holding her sleeping form. *Was this Stockholm Syndrome?* he wondered to himself as he sniffed her hair. Yesterday, he worried she might forget to feed him, and he would wither and starve and die like a houseplant. Today, he was her lover. He loved her. He hated her. She was terrifying. She was stunning. He dared not move as she slept, her soft breaths moving in and out of her. Maybe now he'd escape. Or he would be upgraded to her room. He should try to strangle her. He stared at her bare soft neck. Could they do it again? Lost in confusing thoughts, he heard a thumping scraping noise. Terror rushed over him. "*Do not wake her!*" his mind hissed. "*This is the best day I have had in years! Do not wake her!*" But the noise did not care. The noise did not know.

Russell half-fell and half-climbed out of the

box in the wall. It closed behind him, but since he wasn't watching, it seemed to him it had vanished. His head was pounding. "Hello?" He turned and looked around the room. It was smooth and white. Three white walls. At the top, about a story upwards, there was a single glass window. The final wall had pairs of black metal rings dotted up it like yellow stripes on a road. He called again, "Hello? Hello? Where am I?"

"Sssh," Lucas tried to whisper, but he knew it was too late. She stirred and fluttered awake against him. Terror washed over him. What if she woke up full of regrets? He had to convince her it wasn't a mistake. He would make a wonderful lover. Maybe, just maybe, they wouldn't have to wager anymore?

Russell heard. "Hello?" His voice echoed in his room, and it hurt his already aching head.

If I could kill him I would. Lucas thought to himself as she rolled over from how they were spooning and faced him. She said nothing as she stared into his eyes. She looked like she might have regrets. The thought terrified him. So he did the only thing he could think to do. He kissed her.

"Hello?" Russell's booming voice echoed again. He climbed the metal rings to see if he could get out the top of the room through that window. His bones groaned and creaked as he complained and whined. "Where the fuck am I?" He grabbed for the next ring. "I am too fat to climb shit." He was grunting at the effort. "Shit, shit, shit."

She kissed him back. Jaspierre kissed him back! At least for a moment they kissed, until the shouting in the other room got too obnoxious. Lucas's momentary relief broke with the kiss. He held her close, but she stood up. He whimpered and tried to find words to make her stay. Her naked body bent down and picked up her dress and panties. He lay on his bed, so close to tears. She slipped the panties on, and stood there, holding her dress. "Wait, don't go," he whimpered. "Don't leave me down here!"

"Fucking shitface!" Russell slipped. His arm slid down into the ring. He dangled there, his feet running in the air. The weight of his body hanging on one mere arm caused his bone to crack. His feet scrambled and scraped along the wall, missing the rings. "Fuck-Fuck-Fuck! *Motherfuck!*" His arm kept cracking at his struggles and the pain shuddered down him. He pulled with his remaining arm, lifting his body, and his feet caught the rings.

Jaspierre dropped her dress, looking pissed. She slammed her hand onto the wall, the hidden door slid open, and she stepped out. The door stayed open as she fumbled out of Lucas's sight, and he started to get up. The door was teasingly open, tempting him. He thought about the razor-lined dumbwaiter that brought his meals. Being sliced into pieces would be an unpleasant way to go. A few days ago, he had contemplated trying to hang himself from a ring on the wall, but today he wanted to live.

He heard a loud, hissing noise and a pause, then a crashing thump. She reappeared, standing in nothing but her panties in the open doorway. He smiled at her and held back tears again. Life had improved.

"You lost, you know." She referred to the bet, and he knew he owed her. He stood up, letting the blankets fall, socks being the only clothing still remaining. "If this is losing, I don't want to win." He said and ran his eyes across her. She burst out in a delicious laugh. He was so pleased, he made her laugh. His body was begging for hers again.

She picked up the dress, and turned, but paused. She dropped the dress and spun back kissing him, and pressing her breasts against his naked chest. He let out a soft cry as her skin met his. He ran his hands down her back lifting her up, hands on her ass as he carried her to his bed.

* * * * * * * * * * * *

Chance breathed a hot, steamy whiff of air onto his badge. He shined it with his shirt and then pinned it back in place. He didn't feel like being a cop today.

But, then again, being a cop had its privileges.

He drove down to hooker alley in his personal car, not his cop car. The sluts wagged their tails around. He waited until one walked up to his car.

She had brown hair. Just like Jasp. She was too skinny, though. Her breasts looked all wrong. They were too small, too pointy. He missed her big, round jugs.

Not that he'd seen them in a while.

He already had a boner thinking about her. It was time for a transfer. Back home. Betcha she was still living there.

The chick hesitated when she saw his badge. She backed up and tried to walk off. He got out of the car and grabbed her by the hair.

"Do you fucking think you get to pick who to fuck? You're a fucking whore! I pick if I want *you* not the other way around."

He pulled her up and pressed himself against her ass. His free hand tiptoed down to her crotch, and slapped it. She yelped. Her tiny knit shorts didn't soften the blow much at all. He slid his hand up to her stupid ugly breasts and grabbed one, squeezing it. He wondered if he pulled hard enough if he could pop it off of her. Now he was ready to fuck her up.

She trembled in his arms. He meandered his tongue up her face. "You're gonna get in my fucking car and give me a free one. I deserve it after the fucking disrespect."

He always got a free one. Who the hell would tell on a cop?

He dragged her into the back of his car and shut the door. He got back in the drivers seat. Tears ran down her face while she cowered in the seat. She reached for the door handle so she could make a run for it. But there was no handle.

"You're coming home with me Jaspierre. You're gonna give it all you've got. Hell. You'll even stay the night. Or the week." He grinned at her and drove home. "Maybe we'll even start a motherfucking family."

She didn't last a week, but he did get her breast off.

CHAPTER

FOUR

Jaspierre sat straddled on top of Lucas, her heart still pounding. *Vigorous* was the word that came to mind. She leaned forward and kissed his forehead; his hands gripped her hips with such strength. She got off his spent body and he held her still.

"Don't go," he whispered with longing eyes.

She smiled at him. "The cats need fed."

"Later," he whimpered, running his fingertips up her side.

She stood anyways, looking around the room. The door still open, she realized.

"You are trying to escape!" She snatched her dress off the floor with a snap, fire blazing in her eyes.

Lucas leapt off the bed, grabbing her hands, trying to stall her temper. "I don't want to escape. I want to hang out with you." Her angry eyes still burned into him, and he blushed. "That was the best day I have had in years and you know it." Her glare changed. "Jasp, please, I..." He couldn't find any words. Begging was not helping him, and he knew it. "I..." He collected himself. "If you need me again, you know where to find me." He kissed her hands and went back on his bed, sliding his white, wrinkly scrubs back onto his pale skin.

Her spark of anger faded a little. She didn't need him. Just... well... whatever it was, it was over. How did Mother remain so detached?She stared at his sad little self getting dressed, then walked out. Jaspierre felt so strange.

She walked up the spiral staircase, trying to remember where she left her high heels. She pressed a button as she left and Lucas received clean bedding and scrubs, and a granola bar. He changed the bedding and his clothes, carrying the used items to the empty box in the wall they had come from. He found her silver panties tangled in the sheet, and kept them under the mattress, smiling to himself.

Jaspierre emptied four cans of cat food, plating them neatly, two cans per plate. She set the plates on the ornate stand, and both felines came over and ate. Jaspierre picked the dress off the counter and started up to her room. Seeing her silver heels, she grabbed them and walked up the stairs. She tossed her dress into the laundry chute, and the heels went back into the closet. Her wig was removed, brushed, and then pinned to reset the curls. She slipped on a long, soft, striped maxi dress and clean panties. She paused at the mirror. Her hair was dark brown and short. Her temples were already showing hints of grey. It was a nice pixie cut, and it suited her.

"What the hell just happened?" she whispered to herself. Yesterday, she was a towering, powerful scientist, experimenting like Mother. Today, she was feeling emotions about him. She couldn't imagine this ever happened with Mother. Also,the sex didn't seem to hurt like the other two times. Maybe this was because she was older? Was this Lucas's plan? To trick her into inviting a date over, and then trick her into sleeping with him? How could he have guessed his name was Russell? That bastard! She should starve him a few days to punish him.

But the thought made her stomach turn. He was already so thin. What this situation needed was more experimentation. She would have to plan the experiment, and test the results. Mother would approve. Mother had always been skilled in a clinical way. She'd slice off a man's head just to see how it bled. Jaspierre didn't have that kind of guts. She only could muster up that kind of skill when she was furious.

What to do with Russell? She didn't really have a plan. Maybe she could kill him properly.

Take him apart in that emotionless way Mother mastered. She froze mid-thought, and it came to her. Why not test Lucas with Russell? What a fabulous idea! She grabbed her leather notebook and went to her office.

Midnight came, and her book was full of sketches and plans. Most of them had Russell eviscerated. She had never killed a man before, but it could be time to start. There was, after all, no particular reason to have another Russell in the world. Besides! Lucas would do the real work. It saved her the squeamish feelings. Mother would be so pleased. Jaspierre was becoming a proper scientist. Delegate if needed. It was a skill she had learned for business quite well. She felt a tiny pang that Mother wouldn't be proud that she couldn't seem to do it herself. Why couldn't she slaughter a man on command?

She glanced at the clock and walked back to her bedroom, whistling. Two beautiful felines came running. Her bed was massive; the four wooden posts were each servals in various positions. One was licking its paw, the next sat stately. The third one stood on its hind legs, its paws lifted as if ready to bat at an invisible fly. The final cat had its teeth bared in the most terrifying scowl. Jaspierre climbed into the crisp white linens, lifting the sheet, and both cats crawled underneath the blankets. The three of them curled together in the magical way creatures do when they have slept together their whole lives.

Lucas did not have the same night. In fact, his night was downright awful. Russell had awakened and he was screaming again. He screamed and moaned and fussed and cried and sobbed. *God it was irritating.* Lucas tried to recall his first night, and he couldn't remember it being so loud. If it had been quiet he would have spend the night reminiscing how sweet she smelled. But he couldn't. He couldn't think of anything with the blubbering, screaming racket. He hadn't bothered to respond to Russell's nonstop noise. First off, there was no point; he couldn't help him. He couldn't reassure him. What was he supposed to say? Welcome to your new home? Can't wait for your first wager? You might get to bone her in a few years if you are good?

The thought struck him with irritation. She better not let him bone her. *Sigh.* Not that he had any choice. What he should figure out was a way to keep her climbing on top of him. Touching another human after all this time was so blissful. He played her over again in his mind, how she confidently dropped her panties, but a scream interrupted. It would be nice when Russell passed out.

* * * * * * * * * * * *

Jaspierre awoke as the cats stirred and squirmed. She hopped out of bed and tossed her rumpled maxi-dress in the bin. No wig, but she slipped into a silky gray jumpsuit. No time to leave the house today. Down the stairs she went, grabbing two oranges as she passed through the kitchen. She couldn't wait to get started. With a quick click, the fireplace swung open: she almost told the cats not to come, but it didn't matter. To the steps they went.

The lights clicked on and the crisp white room held no scent of bleach. She walked to the observatory and stared down at Russell. He was lying, crumpled on the floor awkwardly. Hmm, maybe the sedative was too much? It shouldn't have lasted all night. She looked at his room. Blood smeared in little streaks across the floor to his torso. One of the rings from the wall was lying near him. He looked so dark against the bright white floor in dark blue jeans and a dark t-shirt. She wrinkled her nose with annoyance. Filthy. Uncontrolled experiments. Mother would never allow her subjects to be like this. Russell stirred. She rolled her eyes, pressed a button, and the gas poured in.

The gas hissing brought Lucas to his feet. Was she up there? Would she come to his bed again? He was almost giddy; it was a blessed relief from the guilt, and misery he normally carried. He stared up at the glass a whole story up, and wanted to climb up the rings and peek at her. What was she doing? Well, besides gassing the idiot in the cell next to him? Her silhouette appeared.

She stared down at him, surprised. Normally, he cowered on his bed, eyes downcast, staring at his hands or feet. Usually, he curled under a blanket and looked miserable. Today, he was standing and staring up at her eagerly, like a sweet, delicious puppy. *Oh my.* Her plans changed as her heart beat fast. She bit her lip. Her inside spun. Pitting Lucas against Russell was no longer an option. Mother would never understand this, these emotional decisions. Mother had sex all the time, but she never seemed to *care.* Jaspierre hadn't killed Lucas in all these years, and now, with sex, he began to matter even more to her. She placed her hand on the wall, and the door at the top of the spiral staircase slid. An orange in each hand, she waltzed down the stairs. Her palm pressed to the wall and Lucas's door slid open. Juggling her colorful fruit playfully as he stared, she tossed one to him. He flailed and missed the throw, then scrambled and grabbed the orange off the floor. His face was red and bright.

She smiled devilishly at him. "You wanna help me out with that dipshit?" she asked, cocking her head to the silent neighbor.

"Yes." He didn't hesitate. He didn't care. Anything. Anything other than this room. Besides he felt like he owed her.

"Good. First job is getting him ready. I think he'll be heavy." She grinned and Lucas, for the first time in years, set foot out of his room. His heart fluttered. It was a hallway. Smooth walls and a spiral staircase, door open. He walked to the staircase, but she made a disapproving click, and he froze. Her hand pressed against the wall and the panel slid. Inside was a mess. She cringed. The scent was disgusting. That man had pissed himself. He needed changing, like a baby, and yet Lucas was still so pleased to be out.

A soft tickling between his thighs froze him in his tracks. He hoped it was her. Ikali shoved between his legs pressing forward to sniff the strange, stinky, room. Tessa yowled from the top of the spiral staircase, uncertain of this small hall.

"Ikali! What the heck! You can't be down here. You'll shed on everything." Lucas had heard of the cats and bet on the cats a few times, but had never seen them.

"This is Ikali? So she must be Tessa? They are so beautiful!" He ran his hands on the soft fur--he tried to and was met with a piercing bite.

Tessa leapt down from the staircase, refusing to walk on it.

Jaspierre burst out in a grin. "Oh you kitties. No rabbits here. Lucas, put his clothes in the bin. I'll hose him off later."

She turned and walked up the stairs, both

cats following her. Pausing halfway up, "After you are done, come upstairs." Freedom rolled off her tongue like it was no big deal. Excitement surged through him. After ten years of imprisonment he could go upstairs.

Lucas went into the room. He stared at Russell. Had she undressed him his first night? He supposed she had, since he awoke in his room with the white scrubs in place. That was how he remembered it. An empty room too. The bed was an afterthought added after the first... month. Russell's t-shirt was soaked in blood. He was wearing those ridiculous cargo pants with many pockets. Lucas wondered if those pockets held anything useful.

He first took off the shoes and socks, stealing the laces. He tore off the wet pants, trying to avoid touching any wet spots. But it could not be avoided. He scrunched them up tight, feeling them for anything useful --a set of keys, a pocketknife, a wallet. Lucas trembled when he pulled each item out. Life had gotten much better. He checked the wallet. An ID and a bunch of cash. He didn't count it because he had nowhere to shop. The keys he pressed into the wallet, folding it as shut as it would go, hoping it would keep them quiet. The knife went into his sock. He tied the strings together in a makeshift belt for the wallet holding the keys. This was a stupid plan, and he changed his mind, wrapping the string around the wallet to hide under his mattress. He should hurry lest she shut the doors and leave him down here. He did not want to touch the man's underwear, seeing how wet and brown they were. Russell stunk so much worse with his pants off. Hopefully, she wouldn't mind if he left the soiled underwear.

He pulled off the t-shirt, exposing Russell's hairy chest. As he pulled his arms up, the left arm clunked and twisted. The left shoulder appeared to be dislocated. There was a lot of skin missing on his left arm; blood pooled underneath it. He pulled the t-shirt off. Then he grabbed the arm, and braced his foot against the man's shoulder. He pulled, and he felt several snapping pops. Well, maybe it would help, though the upper arm appeared to be broken. It didn't seem to be dislocated now. The t-shirt went into the bin, and Lucas took his stolen wallet into the hall. His prison contained the only hiding spots. The hall was empty. It terrified him to go in, lest he end up with the door shut behind him. But he didn't know where else to stash the wallet. So he raced in, shoved the wallet under the mattress, and raced back. He caught his breath for a second, and then walked up the stairs.

Jaspierre sat perched on a railing munching on an orange, wedge by wedge. She was staring at the maze, her two cats jumping and charging around, crunching mice. Lucas stared.

He had no idea the maze was so huge. "What are you testing?" She turned to him.

"I gave them thirty mice. I haven't released the rabbit yet. Who do you think will get it today?"

Lucas stood next to her behind the railing, leaning on it and looking deep into the massive maze. "Who has eaten the most mice so far?"

Jaspierre laughed. "You are thinking like a real scientist!" She clapped her hand on his back in merriment.

She finished her last wedge of orange and spun around on the top of the rail, standing up and waltzing over to the giant command center. Lucas looked at all the levers, buttons, and screens. He saw the cats, the mice, his bed, and Russell lying in his messy underwear. She pulled a lever, and a faraway hissing sound started, and Russell appeared to stir. Another button and a big brown rabbit hopped out into the maze. Lucas could hardly contain his excitement. He was out of his room!

"I am increasing his oxygen so he will wake up sooner. Aren't you ready to play?" The cats paid no attention to the rabbit and continued chasing, crunching, and playing with mice.

Jaspierre reached over to a lever, pulling it out of the wall. The shiny metal swung to Lucas's throat before he knew what was happening. The flat of the blade hit him, and he tripped backwards and fell flat on his back, smacking his blond head into the floor. Dazed, he said nothing while his eyes watered. Jaspierre straddled him, her thighs pressed tightly on each side of his hips. Then she pressed the tip of the sword against his chest and she sat on his confused aching body.

She is going to kill me, Lucas thought with depressed resolution. He didn't even try to stop her, or beg for his life. It was time. He deserved no better. He had two deaths on his hands.

"Did you think you would kill me with this stupid fucking knife?" She pulled his sock off and let the knife fall out of it next to his hand.

Lucas's eyes grew wide with fright. "No! No, I... no. I thought I might need it." The tip of the blade pressed harder into his flesh, cutting his shirt and piercing the skin. "In case you made me fight him."

She leaned down, one hand on the blade piercing toward his heart, and her lips against his. "You are a fucking liar."

Lucas cried. The best days were the worst days. He couldn't hold back; tears poured out of him. He made no effort to stop, silent tears running. Why did he have to take the knife? "I don't want to kill you. I don't want to be in my room anymore. Please. You can have the knife back. I am sorry."

"I can have it back?" She laughed the angry laughter of a terrifying woman. *"I already have it!"*

The blade shifted deep down into his skin. He cried out with pain.

Her nose touched his, her right hand on top of the blade. Rage pounded inside her. She stared into his eyes with fire and ice. She should kill him right this second.

He closed his wet eyes, waiting for inevitable death. His heartbeat pounded through the handle of the sword into her fingers. Her body stirred and she pulled the blade out and stood up.

"You still owe me the wager." She turned to his bare foot. It was missing all the toes except the big toe and the pinky. She lowered the sword, prepping for a golf swing. His white shirt stained with a spreading bloody circle.

"Wait!" Lucas burst out, not moving his foot, lest she swing and eviscerate him for flinching. He used every ounce of courage for his plan. "I already paid my debt."

She paused, eyebrows raised. He tried not to shiver with fear as he grabbed his cock and said, "You got your digit. Twice if I remember right."

She dropped her blade and laughed brightly. Her thighs pressed on his as she climbed on top of him, and kissed him. Her hand slid into his pants. He couldn't give her a boner that fast. Not after being stabbed and threatened four seconds ago. Hopefully, she wouldn't kill him for it.

She frowned at his inability to get it up in the breath of a moment she gave him. Was she not good enough? *Fucking ass.* She kissed him again, harder, gripping and stroking at him. *Fucking ass.* He rose to life inside her fingers, but it was too little too late. She stood up and grabbed her blade, slamming it back into the console slot. Then she kicked the little pocketknife to him. "Time to play."

He was bewildered, but he could grow used to her wild swings. She was unpredictable, but if he could keep her from getting out-of-control angry, he could survive. Escape wasn't important; surviving was. Besides, anything was better than being locked in that room. He snatched the knife and his sock and put it back on. She was pressing levers and buttons. He checked his chest; it was bad, but survivable. He didn't even think she quite nicked his ribs. There was a loud whistle, and the cats came tearing out of the maze and up the stairs.

"The experiment was a total bust. They didn't even kill the rabbit." She slipped on the headphones and handed Lucas a pair. He hesitated to put them on. She pulled more levers and before the power-washing sprays turned on, he heard a yell from Russell. He slipped the headphones on and it was quiet except for the sweet classical music. He looked out the window and the sprays washed tiny mice footprints away, and a soaking wet rabbit looked miserable and scared. Lucas saw Russell, apparently screaming bloody murder while water pummeled him. He curled into a ball, covering himself as much as possible. Blood dripped off his left arm.

Jaspierre threw a switch, and he heard her voice, clear as a bell through the headphones. "That dumbass is never gonna get cleaned up sitting all curled up like a kid." She pressed a button and said, "The sprays will not stop until the shit is cleaned off your ass, Russell." Then she released the button. "What an idiot." Lucas watched the screen showing Russell, and he stayed curled into a ball. The maze finished spraying, and the antiseptic permeated the room. Jaspierre took off her headphones.

"He has no sense between his ears!" she exclaimed. Russell lay curled up tight into a ball, making no effort to clean himself. Lucas watched with a pang of despair.

She said, "*Hey dickwad.* Wash your ass or you are gonna be sitting there in the hurricane for days."

Russell moved; he was sobbing and yelling, but he couldn't be heard over the spraying sounds in his room.

"Oh dammit, I forgot to have you hook that ring back up," Jaspierre said. Russell threw it angrily at the wall. "You hungry?"

"Yes."

"The cats need to be fed too. Do you want to watch him, and I'll go get food for everyone?"

"Yes. That sounds wonderful." He tried to sound warm. But anger flickered within him. Jaspierre hesitated.

"No, you are coming with me. No funny business."

He smiled to himself. *She thinks I am always out to kill her, I guess. Maybe I am. How would I know?* "May I hold your hand?"

Jaspierre was surprised. This was getting so weird. Scientists shouldn't let their pet monkeys out of the cages. It made them less fun to experiment on. Don't play with the rats or the rabbits. Mother knew. She rolled her eyes and grabbed his hand. Up the stairs they went, out of the fireplace. "Do the cats eat much after the rabbit and the mice?"

"Oh yes, they eat. Thirty mice is a snack. If I fed them bigger rabbits, they would be much less hungry. But I don't. I have many animals for them to eat. Rats, mice, rabbits, chickens, doves, pigeons, chinchillas, ferrets, foxes, prairie dogs, etc. Live food is best for them, but I like to feed it to them in the maze where it can be tidied. Mother has... well, I have a large breeder barn out back."

He stared at the room and the great servals carved into the fireplace they had climbed out of. She tugged him along and he dutifully followed, his eyes inhaling everything. He felt so overwhelmed after being in the small, white room for so long. The kitchen was magnificent; every piece was a statement. The oven was a massive, six-burner professional oven. The fridge was as dramatic with a carved front and multiple doors. Both cost more than most houses. She swung open one of the fridge doors, unimpressed by the splendor. He stared and held back the painful memory of the last time he saw this room.

"I realized how tired I am of making lunch." She snapped it shut. "Your turn."

He looked in the fridge. It was color coordinated with each drawer filled with a fruit or vegetable. A delicious rainbow. He took out strawberries, pears, and spinach.

"Oh God, stop that." He froze. She walked over and took his bloody shirt off his torso. His chest was still dripping. She grabbed a bottle and sprayed his chest with it. "Liquid band aid will keep you from getting blood into my food. Go wash your hands."

Obediently, he did. "Do you have um, sugar and pecans? Oh, and a pan." She grinned. Their usual fare was sandwiches and chips and coke. She pulled a coke from the fridge and sipped it, pointing at the cabinets. He grabbed a new pan, and dumped in a small scoop of sugar with a large handful of pecans. A pinch of salt, and he paused. *Butter?* He didn't remember. *Does it need butter?* He decided against it, and swirled the pan over the heat. The sugar melted onto the nuts, and the nuts roasted. He prepped the strawberries and pears into neat little slices. Washed the spinach and chopped it too. For a half second, he envisioned stabbing her with the knife and making a run for it. No. What would be the point? The crumbly cheese smelled about right. He sprinkled the warm pecans and the cheese on top of the fruit and spinach. The tiniest bit of oil and vinegar to moisten the dish, and then plated it artistically.

Jaspierre waited. He had a certain art to his movements that was quite pleasant to watch. She tossed her empty coke can.

"What makes you think I eat salad?" She frowned.

He paused, terror striking him. He was cooking for his life. "No no no, it's... a dessert salad. Candied nuts and fruit?"

"If this sucks, I'm gonna take all your toes." She smirked and took a bite.

Please, oh please be kidding.

She smiled. "Well if you stop trying to kill me, you are now my chef."

Sure, if I stop trying to kill you, he thought to himself.

"The cats get two cans each, once a day. They all must be the same flavor on the same day. Don't be wasteful and open a can when I don't have four of them." He nodded, got them out, and slopped them on the plate. "You have *got* to be kidding me." He froze. She took the plate and dumped it in the garbage. "What the hell is wrong with you?" She grabbed a clean plate and plated and garnished the food with a piece of spinach. "Presentation counts. They aren't stupid dogs."

"I am so sorry, I was..." He chose his words lest she have another sword hidden somewhere. "I should have been more careful."

She was pleased with his reply and said, "Grab something for Russell if you feel like feeding him." Lucas grabbed a small apple, and they both slipped back into the fireplace. Russell was screaming, but the loud spraying muffled him. He was naked, and his underwear was lying in the corner. He looked clean. The water turned off as Jaspierre pressed a button. "Russell, toss your gross underwear in the bin." Her command was fierce and demanding, threatening almost. The wall slid open and a small hole appeared.

"**Fuck you.**" His voice rang out so loud and clear, Lucas realized his microphone had been off the entire time it was spraying.

She laughed, and the water turned back on. Lucas stared, as Russell looked like a naked, soaked kitten. She turned and stared at Lucas. "You okay?"

His face twisted. "I just, I--" He choked back a cry and started to laugh. "I just am so glad

I'm not down there." His insides jumbled with relief and terror. Quickly he changed the subject."What do all these things do?" He pointed at the control panel.

"Oh, uh, lots of things. Like this whole panel moves the maze." She pulled a lever and pushed a few buttons, and the walls and platforms shifted shapes. Then she did it again, and it formed a perfect circular track. Then one more time and the maze became taller, with higher platforms.

"Oh wow! May I?"

She laughed and let him touch her controls. She did rather like Lucas; she supposed that's why she had kept him around for so long. He learned the controls, shifting all the panels to the left, clearing the maze entirely. "How is it the basement is so much bigger than the house?"

"Oh, it goes beyond the house, under the driveway and the garage."

Russell kicked his underwear into the bin. The panel snapped shut with a crisp click, and another one popped up, with clean white scrubs. Jasp turned off the sprays. Russell grabbed the scrubs and put them on. She turned to Lucas, "Didn't you grab an apple?"

The maze had been dancing in front of his hands. It was beautiful. The controls were fabulous. He held out the apple, and she nodded toward the wall. A box opened, and he set it inside. In Russell's room the apple appeared in the wall. It was strange to watch him there in that room. Would he be down there for ten years? Guilt was creeping in, but Lucas tried to shake it off.

Jaspierre was orderly and full of plans. She thought of her notebook and how she had intended to pit Russell against Lucas in the maze and let them fight. But now she hesitated. Lucas seemed like an asset. And, truth was, she was lonely.

Plus, she'd kill him if it didn't work out. She had never killed a man before, but it was probably about the same. Now, Russell; what the heck was she going to do with him? She yawned. Time for a break.

"Come now, Lucas." They walked upstairs, no hand holding this time. He followed her like a nervous puppy afraid of the curtains. They went up the marble staircase and she showed him around a little. The large, barely used workout room with every piece of equipment imaginable, her bedroom with the massive wooden bed. "Go in my closet and I will kill you." He nodded respectfully. The hall had so many, many doors. She led him to the one next to her bedroom. "You may sleep here. Things will be different from now on, I think. Though, regretfully." She paused and wrapped her body tightly around his, holding him still. He closed his eyes a moment, hoping this would be pleasant. Her hand slid up his shirtsleeve, and then a painful prick as she stabbed him. A sedative. He was careful not to move. As she released him, he lay on his new bed, and smiled. "Lie with me until I sleep?"

She smiled and curled up with him. "I have to do stuff..." Her voice trailed off.

"You can sedate me when you want. But even if you don't, I won't do a damn thing to mess this up." His lungs grew heavy. "It's been a lot of years you have kept me. Where would I even go?"

"Ten. It's been ten years." She paused. "You can't ever leave. I'm sorry, but you can't."

"I know. I don't mind it. Please let me be useful at least. Don't make me go back into the box..." He tried to lift his arms and hold her, but he found he could barely move them.

She smiled and climbed off his bed. Her workroom was the only room in the entire building not clean and organized. It was the only spot where chaos reigned. Deep in the storage facility, she rummaged through boxes. In the first box, she found them despite the piles of stuff. She had gotten the set for Ikali and Tessa, but instead changed the fence. But this was a brilliant idea. Tracking devices. The only question was how to modify it. A bomb? An injection? She looked at the monitor in her hands.

Then it came to her. She would not make it fatal. She could add a bomb or poison, but frankly, she liked Lucas. And if he ran away, she'd rather kill him herself. Plus, it had a GPS locator in it, so it was a simple thing to find him. Come to think of it, if tracking was the most important part... She dug around another box and found the vet box. An under-the-skin GPS locator made sense too. She didn't know why she hadn't thought of it before. After she sterilized and cleaned each piece, she carried it up on a white crisp tray and up the marble stairs.

"Welcome to a little bigger world," she whispered as she stabbed the injection gun into his unconscious back. She checked his chest and regretted pressing so hard on the sword. The wound looked rather deep. Happily, she realized it was an excellent chance to practice stitches. She tightened the ankle monitor on his leg with the special screwdriver, and walked into her room. Thread and needle in hand she doused the thread in alcohol, and stabbed through his skin.

It was much more difficult than she expected. The needle wasn't sharp enough, and somehow, her second stitch was too tight and tore straight through the skin. The wound was getting larger and dripping blood again. Mother's furious disappointment weighed on her mind. Mother would have beaten her or torn out her hair by the handfuls. What an embarrassment she was; twenty-seven and still unable to do stitches. She stopped and threw away the needle and the thread, leaving one lousy stitch in his skin. Stitches would have to wait.

She cleaned off the gun and reloaded it and went down to her other prisoner.

CHAPTER

FIVE

Lucas woke up to the screams of a woman. He stood up; his back had a spot throbbing, and he wondered if she had stabbed him, again. Then he felt the odd weight on his ankle. It was a monitoring bracelet. It was the most wonderful thing he had ever seen. He would get to walk around!. She screamed again, and he pulled out his tiny knife. Maybe Russell had gotten out. He couldn't let Russell kill her. He was the whole reason they were in this mess.

He crept around into the hall and heard her in her bedroom. He opened the door and saw she was sleeping. Were her nightmares of him? Of what he had done? Those were his nightmares. Did she have them too? He stepped closer and realized it was a mistake.

Tessa curled around Jaspierre, purring, licking at her face. She was trying to wake her or ease her terrified cries. But Ikali was standing on the bed, his teeth bared. He stood over his family, ready to fight to the death for them. Lucas raised his hands stepping backwards. Battling the cat, he knew, would mean his own death. These were her prized possessions. He dropped the knife. If she saw him holding a blade at her feline he couldn't imagine the consequences. Frozen in terror, he realized this could be the end.

*** TEN YEARS EARLIER***

Lucas was driving down the road in his ancient tan Wagoneer. It wasn't in good shape, and he sometimes wondered if it would get him to college. It was his freshman year. He was going to be a computer science major. He loved computers and hacking into places as a kid. He was good at it too. Once, he hacked Facebook and made every post about a Powerball ticket.

The day it happened, the lottery sales went bonkers--Even though everyone knew it was a hacker. There was something so powerful about seeing lottery ticket numbers in front of your eyes. What if it was a sign? Almost everyone bought a ticket, and many got two or ten tickets. It created such a chaotic buzz. Hilariously, his Powerball he picked was correct, though none of the other balls were, and there were massive crowds of people who won four dollars. Anyone who picked the Powerplay won twenty bucks. That was fantastic.

He bought himself a ticket, and won twenty dollars. It had more winners then any lottery had ever had before. Everyone knew someone who won twenty bucks. The jackpot became the highest ever recorded. The record high jackpot was $653 million, now it was $2.1 billion.

Lucas was so proud. It would have smart if he had hacked in and made *himself* billions, instead of the lottery. But he was seventeen at the time; he wasn't thinking big. Now he was nineteen, ready to think big, ready for millions or billions.

He was contemplating things he'd hack to make himself piles of money when he turned on a strange dirt road. This was the wrong way to school. He didn't see a spot to turn around, so he turned up the music and enjoyed the drive. Driving was always so pleasant. He grinned. Life was his oyster. A beautiful, new start to a lovely new world. Anything was possible. He would meet a girl, have kids, and hack money into her accounts until she owned everything she could ever think up.

He was right on one account. He would meet a seventeen-year-old girl.

These next four minutes of his life he would play over and over and over in his head, analyzing every second. If only he had made any different choice.

A cougar jumped out on the road; standing

there, teeth bared. It was a color he hadn't seen before, striped and spotted, with big ears. But it was a cougar. In a fit of teenage wisdom, he accelerated. The crunching impact against his bumper, and then the quick *thump thump* as it went under his tires. He grinned. Nailed it! That thing won't be eating children or pets or maiming people. For the good of the country! He laughed at himself.

A hint of remorse --but it was a cougar! It was an enemy of mankind. Like killing a wasp nest or stomping out a biting spider. He should shake off the lingering regret in the back of his mind.

He saw a girl with long, brown hair standing at the end of a driveway. She was in a white dress, and her skirt was dancing around her with the wind. For a moment, he thought he saw her panties. She looked upset. He slowed down. "Hey, are you okay?"

"What did you hit?" Her eyes were wide, and there was terror in her voice like he had never heard before. *What did the front of his car look like?*

"I don't know..." He hesitated, dread sinking in like an anchor. "I think it was a cougar." She gasped, and he saw tears well up in her beautiful eyes.

"Where is she?"

"I'll take you to her, I..." His voice weakened and he saw her pain. He said nothing as she got in, and he whipped around in the driveway she was standing in.

As they pulled up to the great feline, she leapt out of the still moving car. She curled around the cat, holding it in her arms, sobbing.

He got out and stood there, his own body full of grief. His parents had died a year earlier, in a car wreck. Grief and loss were good friends of his. He wouldn't have hit it if he had known someone loved it. Guilt took hold of him. How could he have caused this horrible tragedy to this young woman?

The cat let out a soft yowl.

Oh shit, it's not even dead. Hot tears ran down his cheeks.

She scooped the cat up and climbed into the seat. "We have to get Rainbow home." He climbed in and drove back to the driveway. She focused on the cat not noticing him.

He drove up to the most spectacular home he had ever seen. It was massive. There were gardeners everywhere; planting things and building pieces. She carried the cat and walked up the large, marble staircase. The front doors opened for her like magic, and he followed her inside.

"Jaspierre?"a maid said, standing with the door in her hand, her mouth hanging with shock.

"Get everyone out," Jaspierre hissed, and the maid sprang into action, the house shuffled and people disappeared out the door.

Jaspierre carried the cat to the kitchen where lunch was in the middle of being assembled. The maid followed, and the chef disappeared at a word. The maid shoved all of the food and plates and dishes to the floor, and they shattered and clattered. She set the cat on the island counter, kissing its forehead, examining it.

Lucas stood there, lost and watching the beautiful young woman tending her pet. He was now rooting for the cat he tried to kill moments earlier. This was his fault.

"Katie, get the med kits."

"Which?"

"All of them," Jaspierre said.

"Her legs are broken, her ribs are broken. Her skull is fractured." Jaspierre didn't even mention one eye was swelling and popping out of her head. Blood was pooling behind the cat. The breathing was raspy and miserable. Blood dripped out of her ear. Jaspierre grabbed a small slender knife. "I am so sorry," she whispered, and she laid her hand on the cat's stomach and drove the knife into the skin.

Lucas yelped in horror. "Don't!" he cringed.

Jaspierre looked up with such hate in her eyes, blood already smeared on her face like war paint. "Shut the fuck up."

She turned to the crying, dying cat, and

dug her hands in farther, slicing and digging. She pulled out organs, laying them on the counter. Lucas cringed, turning away. Katie was back setting the boxes she was holding on the table. She pulled out a pair of surgical scissors and handed them to Jasp.

Jaspierre cut into the first organ, and Lucas understood. The tiny limp kitten lay there, and Jaspierre handed it to Katie, who dried it with a towel, and rubbed it, warming it and trying to wake it.

Jasp cut out the next kitten and it squirmed, and she handed it to Katie to be dried. Her hands covered in blood, and her hair kept falling in her eyes. She wiped her hair, smearing blood on her face. She cut the third kitten out, and it too squirmed. The fourth organ was just an organ. No kitten inside.

She turned her attention to the three kittens, one limp and two moving. Gently she washed them each with warm water, and Katie scrambled off and returned with a heating pad. Lucas and Katie stood and watched as Jaspierre kissed and dried and petted each kitten. The limp one never moved. Jaspierre eventually set it back with its mother.

Katie held Jaspierre as she broke into sobs. "I am so sorry for your loss." She turned to grab a rag so she could wipe off Jaspierre's blood-soaked face. Her foot slipped on the many liquids pooled on the floor. She tried to catch herself, and her hand landed on the edge of the small heating pad with the two tiny kittens. The pad flew off the counter, while Katie slammed into the floor face first.

Jaspierre cried, out racing for the kittens. Both smashed into the floor with a sickening smack. One was still moving; the other one had its neck snapped. Jaspierre clutched the two kittens; the live one, and the dead one. She stared at them, her body trembling. She set the live one in the lid of an open med kit box sitting on a corner counter. Her eyes were burning into Katie's groaning body. Fury had taken over. She threw the dead kitten at its dead mother and picked up the surgical scissors, and stabbed them into Katie's back over and over.

"You fucking idiot!" Jaspierre's voice rang out with such rage and hatred.

Lucas froze as he watched the scene, trying to process what was happening. The scissors plunged into Katie's back again and again as she gurgled and shuddered. He was witnessing a murder. Jaspierre looked up at him with hate-filled fire in her eyes and left the scissors in Katie's bloody back. Sliding on the pools of blood underneath her, she tried to charge him. Her body slid into the counter top next to him as he ran. He tripped and smashed into the pile of dishes. Skating and sloshing through food, shattered dishes, and blood, he ran out of the room.

He tried to run out the front door, but it was locked. He didn't see a way to unlock it, and he heard her scrambling after him, so he ran up the big marble staircase, screaming for help. Was anyone here? He didn't see anybody. Maybe he could reason with her -- maybe not. She killed that girl. He shut up and ran.

His legs pumped with the effort as he raced down the halls. The power to sprint left him and he tried the nearest door. It was a linen closet. He crawled in next to a mop and closed the door, waiting, trying to regroup and come up with a plan. He had watched her murder someone. His heart was pounding, hands sweating. She was a murderer. Fighting a murderer terrified him.

The door was solid and he regretted getting in this closet. He couldn't see where she was. If he opened the door, then she would know where *he* was. Her light footprints tapped past the door. He froze, holding his breath.

* * * * * * * * * * *

She walked the hallway, listening. She stopped, there wasn't much farther he could have gone. He was here, in this hall. She waited another minute. Then she heard the tiniest click of a latch and turned around. The closet door was barely open. She tiptoed behind the door and readied herself.

He peered out the tiny crack into the

hallway and waited. Nothing. He waited. Not a sound. He waited. The front door surely was able to be unlocked from the inside. That was where he would head. He debated, sneaking or running, or worse, if it came to it, fighting her. Sneaking was his best choice, and he swung the door and stepped out.

She drove the knife into the crook of his back. The blade pierced his skin and tore into his muscle as her hand wrapped around his throat. "Make a sound and I will kill you right here." He gurgled a scared scream and nodded.

She escorted him down the hall, and then into a small bedroom, and then into a smaller closet. Exhaustion washed over her; the adrenaline had worn off. Did she have the energy left to kill him tonight? Mother would have had the energy. She tied him to a column post and scurried away for a moment. When she returned, he saw a tired, weary girl, her dress soaked in blood. Tears streamed down her face. "How could you kill her?" She sobbed with a hoarse miserable noise. He tried to answer, but she pressed a chloroform rag into his mouth and he was out.

She descended the stairs, dejected and sore and sad. It had taken so much energy to kill Katie. That bitch. She would have to fire everyone, she supposed. She looked at the mess in the kitchen; blood, dishes, four dead bodies. Rainbow, her only friend, lay on the table, bones broken to bits and her guts all torn out. Her best employee was lying with scissors sticking out her back. This was a bad day. A soft cry awoke her mind. Ah yes, the lucky little leftover. She turned to check him. He was cold. She took the blood-soaked heating pad off the floor and wrapped it around his tiny furry self. "I have to clean up, but then I will hold you, my love."

She turned and picked up Katie; too heavy. She dropped the carcass on the ground and grabbed the food cart. She pulled and tugged Katie onto the cart, and wheeled her over to the fireplace. She dumped the body into the huge, marble mouth and covered it with wood. The pile she doused with starter fluid. *This fireplace is big enough to walk in,* she thought to herself. Someday, she would add a room behind it. She tossed her dress on top of the pile. This probably wasn't a great idea, but she didn't have a better one. A strike of a match lit the pile and, with a woof, Katie burned.

The dampers were opened wide so the smoke would swirl outside. *Like a pig roasting,* she thought to herself. She came back to the kitchen and picked up her remaining kitten and took it up to the shower. They showered together in the hot steam, and she petted and caressed the kitten, singing to it and kissing it. As soon as they were both clean and dry, she slipped into bed, naked with her kitten, and they slept for a few hours.

Soon, the squirming kitten's cry for food woke her. She kissed it and slipped on a robe, carrying the kitten in her pocket. The kitchen, it seemed, had grown more horrifying. The blood was crusting over and it stunk, in part because of the roasting carcass in the other room. She tiptoed around everything and grabbed a bottle for the kitten. She was well stocked because they were due to arrive at any moment. The house was warm from the fire, but other than charring her skin, Katie was still intact. Roasted and ready to eat if she had been a pig.

Jaspierre sat, rocking the kitten in front of the fireplace, humming as it suckled a bottle. *What to do next --what do I do next?* It came to her.

She'd put him in Mother's room until she was ready to kill him. How did Mother have such a strong stomach for such things? Katie's carcass was gross. She threw more wood on the fire until it was massive and roaring. It was a bad place, Mother's room. But he could stay there a few days until she was ready. She shut the library door and locked it. The kitten was safe in her pocket, staying warm. She climbed upstairs and went into Mother's room. The bed was covered in spider webs. The room looked so sad. She looked into the closet at her mother's clothing, hanging, coated in dust. She pushed them aside, trying not to shake any on herself. Deep in the closet was a panel; she slid it aside and pulled the lever.

Mother loved levers.

She walked into a tiny observation area with three big windows. The observation glass was gloomy and dirty. Each room was white and crisp with dark metal rings lined in pairs up the back wall. Twenty pairs of metal rings hung in the wall, like a playground ladder. The floor of the rooms was in the basement. The rooms were otherwise dusty and empty. Mother would be so irritated to see this. She pulled the power washer out of her mother's closet and attached it to the little hose. She sprayed down the windows and then each room. The water drain was clearly still working. She shook off memories of the last time she was here. They didn't matter now.

The kitten protested the whole time. But she had work to do. And tears were good for the soul. She was seventeen and finally a murderer. Why did she feel so bad about it? Mother had made her first kill sound transcendent, not sad.

As soon as the grime had gone swirling down the drain, she trudged over to the bedroom. Lucas was sitting against the column, groggy and confused; his arms were still above his head tied to the column. She untied him, and took his hand as he staggered where she led him. *Hurry before he comes to. He'll try to run.* Her mother's white scrubs were stacked neatly on a shelf in the closet as they marched. The least dusty pair was on the bottom and she grabbed it as they went past. His clothes were gross; bloody and smeared with food from when he fell into the dishes. She escorted him down the small metal staircase and into the first room with the rings. He fell asleep before she could tell him to dress himself.

She pulled his shirt off his head. His skin was smooth, with only a few blond hairs scattered about. She blushed, pulling the white shirt on over his stomach, covering up the skin she had been staring at. His shoes she took, remembering her mother said nobody ran far without shoes. But she left his socks. No reason to take them. His pants slid off easier than she expected. His legs were white and hairy. She had an urge to take off his underwear and see what was under there. Her seventeen-year-old body gave her complicated signals she barely understood. She hesitated.

She took a peek. The underwear slid down as her curious fingers examined him. He made a noise and stirred a little. Embarrassed she pulled them back up and left the scrub pants. Scooping up all his other clothing she left, kitten still in her pocket. After she locked the door she climbed the staircase and looked down.

The skinny blond boy she had captured lay in his socks, underwear, and a white shirt. He looked so beautiful to her. How could she possibly kill him now? The kitten in her pocket meowed, and she glared at the boy. He had killed her friend, the bastard. He should be murdered tomorrow, as soon as she was up for it. She walked off to feed the kitten yet another bottle.

Newborn servals need to nurse every two hours. She threw more logs on the fire again before she sat and let the kitten suckle the bottle in her arms. Maybe he would make it. She stroked around his eyes and ears, and he drank until he slept. She kissed the beautiful baby slipping it back into her pocket. It was five a.m according to the clock. Chef was coming at six a.m.

She stared into the flames. Katie was getting crumbly. She poked her with the fire poker and her body crumpled a little. Satisfied, she put the rest of the wood she had in the house on the fire. Her corpse was buried under the tower of wood and in such ash. The fire was hot though. And the house had warmed to a nearly unbearable level.

She trudged to the kitchen and stared at the never-ending mess. It was too much to handle so she went outside. She stood on the porch and watched the sun start to peek. It was so easy to forget important things, like his car. Sitting there, a massive red flag; both doors were open. The keys were sitting in the ignition. She closed the passenger door and sat in the driver's seat. Her feet couldn't touch the pedals and she had to scoot up the seat quite a bit. It squealed, the battery weak, but finally started. Then she pulled up to her garage. Inside her parking garage, there were fourteen vehicles, all Mother's. Dust coated the tops of them all. She parked his car in the middle and left it. It was so disgusting leaving her best friends blood on the front of the car, and then leaving it there with Mother's cars. It was a horrifying shrine.

She called up her maintenance crew and chewed them out for leaving the cars dusty. They said they would be washed today. She started to dial Katie, but remembered it was pointless. Irritated, she called Chef and complained Katie didn't show up, and explained that she had done surgery in his kitchen, and he was in charge of clean up. Chef did not sound pleased, despite the 10k bonus. She wondered if Katie had brought her car. She looked over and saw her pink bike on the bike rack. Easy fix. She picked it up and tossed it into the dumpster.

Later, she would set up a steady stream of money and cards "from Katie" to her mother about how she moved to Paris. Her mother was a notorious drug addict, and couldn't care less if she heard from Katie again, as long as the honey flowed.

Jaspierre sat in the rocking chair at the hot fireplace. The wood burned brightly and the smell of roasted human flesh faded into an oak musk. The fire had been burning for at least six or seven hours, she figured. Flames danced before her eyes as she rocked, losing herself in thought. *Rainbow.*

She had named her the happiest thing her terrified seven-year-old brain could think of. Her only birthday present when she was seven. Rainbow was her only real friend in her whole world. *Dead*. Mother's very last present to her. *Dead*.

A funeral needed to be planned. It would have to be spectacular to pay homage to the sweet life of Rainbow. Perhaps her tombstone would be carved marble in her image with a bright rainbow jeweled collar. Her best friend, and only child would be the only attendees, but still, Jaspierre would spare no expense.

She supposed it was time to drop out of school. Kittens couldn't go to school. She'd hire a tutor to say they were finishing up at home. Hiring a nursemaid for the kitten would be horrible. No, no, no, Jaspierre was now a mother; seventeen and a mother. Nobody gets to touch the baby, but her. She had been contemplating it for a while. Only a few classes left until graduation, but still. She hesitated. Rearranging her schedule to accommodate feedings was a possibility. Graduating was one of the terms of her independence. She did not want to lose her independence. If it had been easy to quit, she would have already. She sighed and kissed her new best friend, completely ignoring the fact that she tied a boy in the basement.

JASPIERRE

CHAPTER

SIX

Lucas stood frozen. The big serval's teeth were pointy and ready, and he tried to back out of the bedroom.

Jaspierre leapt out of bed, a sword appearing as if from nowhere in her hands. She held it with both hands over her head and charged at him, swinging violently about; her voice was screaming and hoarse. He stood there, accepting his fate. *It was so sad,* he thought. *He almost had freedom.* Instinct took over and he ducked when she swung. She spun in a full circle, the blade catching on the bedpost, and sticking into the serval carving. She let go, leaving it there, sobbing.

Ikali stepped off the bed, hissing at Lucas, ears laid back. He stood between his lady and his enemy. Tessa stood by, meowing. Jaspierre touched the sweet cat's soft ears. "It was a nightmare. It's okay. I'm fine." Her voice was hoarse and sounded miserably sad. She turned to Ikali and saw Lucas. She was infuriated.

She grabbed the sword from the bedpost to pull it free. "What the hell are you doing in here!" Lucas instinctively wrapped his arms around her and gripped the sword.

"May I help you?"

Jaspierre slammed her elbow into his stomach before she processed what he said, and he recoiled. Then she spun around and kissed him, her whole body pressed tight around him. He was so confused, but he didn't care. He melted into her. Long before their kiss had finished, Ikali had enough and bit deep into Lucas's leg. Lucas cried out; he was certain she had changed her mind again and he was about to die. It could be worse than to die in her arms, though.

She looked startled. "Ikali! What is wrong with you!" Her voice was hoarse and yet, sounded amused and less angry. He turned and saw the sulking cat sit in the corner like a child. Ikali sat washing his paws as though he hadn't bitten anyone at all.

Blood trickled down Lucas's leg and he wondered if he should ask for a bandage, or if he should try to kiss her again. *This is Stockholm Syndrome,* he mused to himself. *Loving the person who was holding you captive, desiring to please them. That's what is happening.* She was scary, she was stunning. It was so much more fun than sitting and waiting for your fingers and toes to be severed. He would kill for her, live for her, die for her. What was the world was like now? Ten years had passed. But that was no longer his reality anymore anyway.

He slid his hands along her soft, curvy hips and squeezed them. "I don't want to bleed on your bed." He bit his lip nervously. Any request could be met with a knife.

She looked at his bloody leg and walked to the hall and came back with her med-kit. She cleaned it, and wrapped it up, and when she was done, she said, "What makes you think you will be on my bed?" She didn't check his chest wound. It was too embarrassing; that ruined stitch.

"My bed?" He grinned and tried to make her smile.

She did not smile. But she pulled him close. "No funny business." He was soon under her blankets, wrapped around her, two cats crawling under the covers, squirming annoyingly at this extra body in the bed. Nobody slept, and yet they were happy.

As the night came to morning, Jaspierre climbed out of the bed. Lucas lay there, wondering what kind of day it would be. He saw the sword still stuck in the bedpost carving. He grinned, stood up, and braced himself against the bed and pulled on it. It was stuck, but after a tight yank, he freed it. The blade itself was sharp and smooth. He wondered where it went. Jaspierre stepped out of the closet with waist-length curly brown hair and a dark bright blue dress.

"Can I ask you something?"

"I might not answer," she replied as she stared at the sword in his hand.

"Why, so many wigs and what not? Are you hiding?"

"It goes here." She took the sword and slid it into the tall serval carving with the stretched paw batting at an imaginary fly. The handle disappeared into the figure. "I have to go out today. I have an appointment."

They both knew that was hardly an answer. Truth was, Jaspierre didn't want to tell him how it started, but she knew she never wanted to be revealed. She knew what she was becoming.

She smiled at Lucas. "You need to feed the cats and do the dishes and what not. Feed Russell if you want."

And away she went.

Lucas smiled. He could wander around! This was gonna be...

She popped back in. "Oh yes, if you go too far, your monitor on your ankle will beep and you have ten seconds to come back or you explode. Have a nice day!" She vanished before he responded.

This was gonna be...

She popped back in again, her brown locks swirling, "Oh yeah, if you, like, call for help or communicate with the outside world, or any stuff, I'm gonna hunt you down and kill you. Just to be clear. No phones, no internet. Nothing. So, read a book or clean or whatever. I'll be back around noon for lunch." Again, she left before he even made a sound.

He couldn't help but grin. *She was nervous? It seemed so cute, this powerful, terrifying woman, nervous. She put a bomb in a tiny bracelet!* He chuckled to himself. As if he didn't know she would kill him if he messed anything up. Could he have a shower? He thought that was probably a bad idea with the 'ole bomb on his leg deal. He didn't want her to think he was trying to destroy it with water. Relief and freedom still felt euphoric. *Hello walls that aren't white.* He could explore, walk, see things, pet the cats, read a book. Nothing could damper this beautiful mood.

Time to explore. He had been released! He hoped the bracelet beeped loudly. What if he missed it? He tried to shake off the worry. Well, if he didn't hear it, it would be ten seconds of fun. Still better than the white prison. *Gotta feed those cats.* He walked through the hallway past a room with dusty exercise equipment. It was a full gym; weight machines, elliptical, treadmills, stair climbers, crazy machines he had never seen before. One wall was a massive mirror. The other was a screen. A whole wall was a screen. He wondered how to turn it on, when Ikali stood behind him. Ikali licked his teeth prepped to bite him one more time. Lucas swirled and evaded the cat.

Lucas hustled to the kitchen. He opened the four cans and plated them. Tessa leaped on to the counter, sitting and watching him while he worked. He almost tried to pet her, but it wasn't worth the risk. He set the plates on the fancy floor stand. The few dishes he loaded up and ran in the dishwasher.

Now it was time to explore, back up the stairs and past the gym and into the hall. He saw Jaspierre's room, his room, a long hall, twelve bedrooms, and four linen closets. He found the closet he had hidden in, it was strange to think of his boy self stuffed into it. All of the bedrooms had their own baths and massive closets. The last door was locked.

On the first floor, there was the library with the gorgeous fireplace and the prison. He walked around. The living room was massive. There was a playroom, with slides and rope swings. Perhaps it was for the cats? There was a ballroom and a small staff apartment area with four apartments. He found a game area with assorted games including basketball and pinball and ping pong. The rest of the house seemed so sterile. Decorated nicely, but it looked so vacant. Each room, grand and spacious but as empty as the others--furniture standing still in time, waiting for life.

Lucas hadn't finished exploring the house when he heard a noise. He walked a little farther, and he could hardly believe his eyes. The sounds of splashing water seemed so unbelievable. It was an elegant, majestic pool, complete with slides and a climbing net hovering over it. There were platforms floating on the pool. The water curled under a glass panel and into the outdoors. There was a small waterfall area, and at the top, Tessa stood. Lucas stared in amazement as the cat leapt into the water with a grand splash.

"You swim?" Tessa looked over and meowed and Ikali jumped off the netting and leapt on top of her. The two wrestled around, climbing and jumping. Lucas chuckled and laughed as he watched. Tessa crawled out, soaking wet, and shook, flickering water all over Lucas's legs. She picked up a stick and dropped it at his feet.

"You play fetch?!" He tossed the stick into the water and she was off like a rocket, paddling after it. These had to be some of the most interesting cats in the world.

As he sat and threw the stick over and over, he remembered Russell. It felt like a punch in the belly. Feed him. His stomach flipped again. A house plant withering away in prison, and all the fun sucked out of the playtime. He went to the kitchen, plating a sandwich and chips and a soda. Same old fare. He couldn't think of anything else to bring. At the fireplace he stared at the great white carved cats.

How does this thing open?

He set the plate and soda on the desk. Was it the paw? He tugged on it, and nothing happened. He pressed the tongue. Pulled the tongue. Then he pushed the ear. Pulled the tail. Nothing. He grabbed the other ear and gave it a tug. With a sweet click the door swung open. The staircase was pitch black. It's his fault. His wager. Russell is down there, and Lucas caused it.

Both cats were by his side, they hesitated though. He stood there. He didn't know how to turn on the lights. Also, he didn't want to go down there. His mouth was as dry as cotton. That scary, white box he had been locked in was down there. His toes had been snipped off his feet down there. Russell was down there, withering away like a plant. And Lucas was up here, safe and sound.

Jaspierre had said it was his choice. He could choose to feed Russell. Or choose not to.

He couldn't do it.

Would Russell feed him if it was the other way around?

He just couldn't do it.

His trembling hand rested on the marble

ear, and before he pulled it, Ikali walked down the dark stairs, meowing in a lost sounding way. His tail disappeared into the darkness, and then Ikali yelped. Then he was silent.

Tessa sniffed the air, and then walked down crouched low to the ground in a steady slinking motion. Lucas's heart pounded. He knew he couldn't leave them in the observation room. What would Jaspierre do to him?

Trembling he tiptoed down the dark stairs. He listened for the cats, and heard nothing. Scooting along, one hand sliding across the wall teetering on each step. He felt such dread.

Everything was silent. Not even the whisper of paw prints by soft feet. Russell was silent, no screaming or shouting, silent.

Lucas kept feeling with his few toes for the floor, sneaking down a step, and searching with his foot. He had forgotten the tray of food upstairs. He wasn't thinking about it though, as he touched the wall looking for lights.

Panic start to settle inside him. Where were those cats? How do I get the stupid light on? He turned and looked back, but the curve in the steps blocked the light from the open door. If only he had a flashlight. He kept pushing forward, and wondered if the lights came on to her hand print, like the doors. He found the floor and shuffled his feet along it. His hands petted the wall frantically looking for the light. His fingers found a switch and clicked it. The room came whirring on. The console lit up, the lights brightened. He looked around and saw Ikali sitting by his maze door, pouting and annoyed. Tessa was sitting by hers.

"I am sorry, I don't have a rabbit." He looked around and saw Russell on the screen looked asleep. The left arm of his shirt soaked in blood. He looked miserable. Lucas panicked. He almost chose to starve the man. Lucas flew up the stairs, then back down with the plate and soda. He felt terrible. This wasn't enough food for someone who was injured. He walked to the glass observatory, and looked around. There was no box to insert the food.

He stared at the huge console. It was so intimidating. What if he let Russell out? Tears suddenly choked him. He should let him out. Lucas was to blame for his capture, for Katie's death. He sat tears trickling, staring down in the window, consumed with guilt. Glanced at his unmade bed in his tiny room, then back at Russell.

"Hey, are you okay down there?" Russell stirred a little. "Can you hear me?"

"Who the fuck am I talking to?"

"Hi Russell. I am Lucas." Russell didn't respond to his introduction. Lucas impulsively said, "I... I am gonna try to release you if I can figure it out. There is a sandwich..."

"I'm hungry."

"I... I can't figure out how to get it to you. There are... a lot of switches and buttons."

Russell wept. "Let me out!" *Thump.* "Let me out!" *Thump.* "Let me out!" *Thump.* His cries grew frantic. He held the metal ring in his right hand and thumping it on the floor. "I didn't do anything! Let me out." *Thump.* "Let me out." *Thump.*

Lucas felt his pain, and his own tears welled up. Years of being locked up in that room played past him. The rhythm of screams and thumps reminded him of his own long silent years. He could hear the cries shouting what he himself never screamed. He sat with tears running down his face. *Let me out. I didn't want to be down there either.* He found empty words, "It's gonna be okay Russell."

Russell sobbed and thumped. The song of a broken man. Thudding and wailing. Beating and breaking.

Lucas stared at the console. It was too many choices. How could he possibly figure it out? Russell's beat sounded more and more like a slow clap. The kind that sent shivers of panic up his spine as nobody cheered. Applauding failure. Lucas stood up and went upstairs. He couldn't sit and listen any longer. He couldn't stand to listen to the beat of a man unraveling. Upstairs was quiet, and he glanced at the clock, it was almost one. He pulled food from the fridge, chicken wrapped in bacon. He wondered where Jaspierre was, and if his lunch would be too late.

CHAPTER

SEVEN

Jaspierre was sitting in her office at Kyller and Co. Most of the board members didn't even realize how important she was anymore. She rarely made a fuss and the board voted the way she wanted, by manipulating someone to bring it up and spearhead each decision. She sat at the head of the table, seemingly bored. *People talked more freely when they didn't know you were paying attention.* She operated this way when she was a child, she took a back seat and fired people for failing her. The system worked great. Today, there were no meetings and not too much to do. Medication deliveries were all on schedule and she was making lots of money as usual.

She only showed up so she could watch Lucas. What an interesting thing this was; letting her monkey run loose. She worked on her papers; companies were such a pain in the ass, but a necessary evil that had served her well. Their distribution circles were growing stronger. A new medication for cancer suffering patients had recently been approved and sales were through the roof. The notes from her team explained they had even added a few extra deliveries. The medicines were so lucrative. Anything with a prescription was easy to make big money on, after all, insurance would pay hundreds per pill. She watched him as Lucas found her cats playing in the water, and how he played with them. He was so handsome, so innocent and sweet. She would undress him the moment she got home. He was delicious. She watched how he didn't remember even the simplest things, like a light switch. *How cute he was, scared of the dark.*

She watched him while he promised Russell he would help him escape.

While the two men sobbed and the one man yelled, Jaspierre shattered her coffee mug on the wall. *That nasty bastard.* She stood up and grabbed her knife. This one was small, with a sharp curved blade. She slipped it from the armrest on her chair and stood up. *Time to get rid of that stupid freaking man. I never should have waited this long to kill him!* Took a deep breath, then slipped back into her high heels, smoothing her dark blue dress. She glanced into the mirror. Her long, curly brown hair looked professional. She fussed her hair a little, and then reapplied her lipstick.

Ready to kill. *Mother would finally be pleased.* She grinned. But then she remembered she would have to come all the way back to her office if she brought this knife. Better to use one from the house. She slipped the knife back into the armrest. There was a knock.

"Come in."

"Ma'am? I heard a noise..." The secretary paused as he saw the dripping coffee and the handle of the cup sticking out of the wall.

"I dropped my cup," she said with such smooth ease.

He held back a smile. "Yes, I will have this cleaned right up. Our stock is up ten cents today. Did you make a decision on the Zelyn account?"

Oh yes, she was at work. What a waste of time. "Tell them we agree. Also, if word gets out that I dropped my coffee cup, you'll be fired. Set up a staff meeting in two weeks, and a team meeting so we can go over the strategies for this years expansion."

"Yes, ma'am," he said.

She handed him a stack of papers she had signed. "Take this; I'll be back in two days. I shouldn't have come in today. It's my *vacation*." Her lying, angry voice seethed. She did as she pleased and everyone knew it. She never took an official vacation because she was always free to wander off.

She drove her dark red Mercedes at a fast angry clip. She thought about Lucas. *That stupid, useless man.* She had been thinking before he betrayed her, maybe they could stay friends. She'd let him out and nothing horrible would rain down upon her but that was not how it worked. *If you let them out, they would destroy you.* When would she learn? She remembered the last man who she let out and cringed. His angry hot breath pressed against her tiny face.

It was not a happy memory.

She slid the car into the massive garage, parking it with a click. She hung the keys on the board. Fourteen cars might seem excessive to some, but it was still half the amount Mother used to have.

She stepped into the house, and her beautiful kitties came purring up. "No." Her voice was low and scary. Both cats backed up and left. She walked in and pulled a long sword out of the marble staircase. "Lucas, what are you doing?" Her voice carried a sing-song rhythm.

She let the sword rattle on the floor behind her as she walked toward the kitchen. The sliding metal scraping on her marble floor made a nasty noise. She was careful not to scratch the floor though. *That'd be a pain to fix,* she thought.

Lucas pulled the chicken out of the oven. He was bent over with the hot pan in his hands when he heard her sing-song voice, and the metal dragging on the ground. *I should run.* Every bone in his body screamed it, but he didn't move. He would rather die than spend ten more years in that wretched prison. Hiding was a bad idea. Hiding didn't work. Facing her, though, might work. Last time, she might have hurt him, and his aching chest wound still bled. But she hadn't killed him. No doubt, she would kill him at some point. She had killed Katie with such venom, but it was swift and without warning. *If she warns me I still have a chance.*

It didn't mean he wanted to face her, though. He set the hot pan on top of the stove.

"I am almost done with lunch. I hope you like it." She walked in with the blade and stared at him curiously, with her head cocked.

"You will not have a chance to eat it." She swung wide, and he ducked out of the way, and took two plates from the cupboard.

Stay calm, stay calm. He trembled while he picked up tongs and started to plate the chicken. She was exasperated and swung again. He crouched down tight against the cupboard. "At least let me get the rice!"

He stood again and turned to the stove. "You'll be hungry after you slice me up. Might as well let me plate it."

Her rage built. "Stop," *Swing!* "**Plating.**" *Swing!* "**The food!**" Her swings were wide and terrifying, though he wasn't sure she was actually trying to hit him. The blade slammed down on the counter barely touching his fingertips.

He cried, "What have I done? What did I do? Did I make you angry because I fed the cats wrong? Is lunch too late? I can do better! Give me a chance! Give me a chance! Give me a chance!" His cries fell into the same rhythm of the other man and he stopped with a catch in his throat.

She pressed the tip of the blade into his throat and said one word. "Russell."

Then he realized she knew what he had promised Russell, and the color all drained from his face. "I have been in that room ten years." He held out his hands and he stood there, helpless and waiting.

The sad, sorry looking man stood in front of her. She had seen him sit, day after day in that tiny box of a room. *She* had left him there.

"If you let him go I will kill you both. I will hunt you down."

Lucas nodded, the blade still pointing into his throat. "You are gonna have to prove you are trustworthy."

She prodded him down the fireplace stairs with the blade at his back. Was he about to be locked back into his old prison? Terror stole his voice and he considered attacking her. *As soon as she is distracted, I'll have to.* He couldn't go back in there. He looked into the observation area and saw the sandwich and coke sitting there still. A few bites were stolen from the sandwich by a cat.

He heard the hissing sounds of gas as Jaspierre pressed buttons and pushed levers. She handed him garden shears. "Take all of them. Then move him to your room. When you are done, you can come back upstairs. If you won't do it, you will be down there forever." She took the blade, pressed it into the center of his back, and walked him to the wall, holding her hand on it. The wall slid and then the metal spiral staircase was visible.

Lucas trudged down the stairs and into Russell's room. She shut the door behind him with a crisp snap. She went upstairs and a few minutes later in Russell's room, two boxes opened. Lucas looked. One was an empty chute, Lucas recognized it; the trash chute. The other had bandages and a med-kit.

"The gas will last an hour or so," Jaspierre said.

Lucas stared at the shears in his hand, and looked at Russell. "Just the toes?" Or would he have to cut the fingers off too? If he obeyed her, he could play with kittens and make food, read books, and perhaps bone a pretty lady. If not he had to stay in a room with Russell forever. He didn't have to kill anyone, and for that he was grateful. Besides, she was right; he said he would betray her. He did have to prove himself.

He hoped it was toes.

"Yes, toes are enough." Her reply was crisp.

This is for you Jaspierre. This is for you. This is for me so I can have some life back. He often wished she would have killed him. *Living without toes wasn't so bad,* he reminded himself. He lived missing a good many toes, and it wasn't that bad. Russell would be fine. Russell lay unconscious with the metal ring in his hands. His left arm was bloody. He took off Russell's socks.

He snipped. The small toe was first, and blood seemingly poured everywhere. He grabbed the med-kit and regretted not looking at it first. Inside were two things. A propane torch, and a metal stick that had a wooden handle on one end and a flat metal plate on the other.

He turned the knob on the propane torch and it lit. He set it on the ground, holding the metal plate over it with one hand, and pressing on the toe stub with the other. He tried to stop Russell from bleeding out before he cauterized the wound. Soon, the plate was glowing red, and he pressed into Russell's foot with it.

Russell screamed. He wasn't fully awake, but he screamed in this drugged, dream scream. Lucas knew he would remember later, screaming himself hoarse, his raw throat aching when he awoke without his toes. Lucas had no idea how fragrant burning flesh was. His eyes watered, and the nasty stink made him gag. His stomach tempted to empty itself, but he resisted the urge.

His eyes watered. "You'll learn to walk again, it's just toes. I'm so sorry. I can't stay down here anymore," he whispered through his tears.

The second toe was much easier; the metal plate was already hot, and it was quicker without as much blood loss. Lucas cut off all the small toes on both feet. The horrendous stink of burning human flesh was pouring into his nose and throat. He kept choking as he tried to work.

Russell screamed and moaned deliriously as he worked. Lucas understood why it took her so many years to take six toes off of him. This was not a task that would be fun, even for a crazy person.

Jaspierre went upstairs and left Lucas and Russell. She placed her wig in her closet, dropping her clothes into the laundry chute. Further in the closet, she turned on the water to her oversized shower and stood there. She was so mad. What was wrong with her? She couldn't seem to kill Lucas no matter what he did wrong. Mother could have done it. Mother could have just stabbed him dead, or strangled or beat him to death. Her fingers scrubbed her flesh vigorously, skin turning pink. She did mean toes and fingers, but then she saw his sorry face standing there, with those sorry clippers. And here she was letting him do toes now! What next? Mother would have killed him. She kept scrubbing with a frantic pace. She might as well let him kill her. It was only a matter of time until he did it anyway. She needed to kill him now before he hurt her. How did Mother avoid these foolish emotions?

She slammed her sopping wet fist into the shower door. It spider-webbed with cracks. Now look what he did! Ruining her shower too. Enough was enough; she needed to swallow her doubts and get rid of him. He was back in the room with Russell; she'd turn the gas on and be done with it.

Instead, she burst into tears. Lucas was the only person she had. She wanted to keep him! Not put him down like a sick dog.

She stepped out of the shower, her raw skin almost bleeding. The glass cracked further as she moved, and it was time to leave before she ended up with glass in her feet. She didn't bother with a wig, bra, or panties, and put on a soft, ivory t-shirt dress. The whispered scent of burning flesh fluttered past. *Like Katie.* As she got closer, the stink was stronger, and she smiled. Lucas was a good boy. She stepped into the fireplace and walked into a hazy foul dungeon. With a few button presses, the air cleared and a sweet, clean, fresh breeze rolled into the room.

Lucas was sitting, his tired scrubs coated in blood. The toes were all in the bin. He sobbed, pressed against the door. "Please let me out please, Jasp, please."

Jaspierre wondered how long she had been

showering.

"Please let me out. I swear I won't help him. *Please*. I took all his toes." He tried to hold in his soft sobs. "I am so sorry. Please don't leave me down here. *Please*. I will do the dishes, and make you food. I will do anything you want. *Please*."

"You still have to move him to your room." She tried to sound cold into the microphone but her stomach twisted at the scene. Why couldn't she do this right?

He whimpered and stood up, and the door slid. He took Russell's ankles and dragged him down the hallway. His door slid open, and he was struck with terror. He did not want to go in. He shoved Russell inside. Then he waited for the door to shut. He realized Russell was still too far in the doorway for it to close. He took a deep breath for courage and he pushed him, as hard as he could with his foot. As soon as his foot was out of the way, the door snapped shut. He closed his eyes with relief.

He looked around, and the hallway was blank. Who knew how many secret doors there were. The one spiral staircase sat empty, spiraling up to a white blank wall. He waited, hoping for it to open.

Jaspierre watched as he shoved Russell into the room, trying to stay out. She almost caught his foot when she shut the door. But now he was in the hall, looking rather forlorn, and she had a choice to make. Let him up. Or press the gas.

Her hands hovered over the button. Gas him and put him back in his box. Let Russell face him for the toes. They'd work it out. *This is what Mother would do.*

Her fingertips traced the button. She had no backbone. She wasn't cold like Mother, she was weak.

If she opened the door, they could have a nice dinner, and she would tear off his clothes again. That was fun. It was, quite unlike any sex she had previously encountered. He was so desperate to please her and so sweet and loving. Maybe that was why she wanted it again. Thinking about it made her want to try again. He would be fun to have upstairs like the kitties.

Her fingers hovered, and she looked at his screen. He sat on the steps of the spiral staircase, his white scrubs wrinkled and bloody, and he stared at his hands.

This was no fun for her, leaving him down there, staring at his stupid hands. These last three days were the most fun, interesting few days of her life. She had a date, she had sex, she had romance, she had war. She had never had so many reasons to draw swords. What a good way to practice staying on her toes. She even had a new prisoner, hobbled and ready to play.

She pressed the button.

The door slid open, and Lucas flew up the stairs. As he stepped through the door, he froze. He waited for a knife to be plunged into him. He waited for her ambush. But she stood there, staring at him. Lucas whimpered. "I'm so sorry, I am."

She grinned. "Let's go get you cleaned up."

They held hands and walked together. He squeezed her hand with a sweet relief. She paused. Was she angry?

"When you decide to kill me, I wish you would make it quick," she said.

He pulled her close, "I will if you will." Then he kissed her.

She pushed him playfully and grinned. "You are covered in filth, and I just showered." She paused. "Fine, though. I will if you will."

"Let's not let it come to that," he said with warmth, and he had tenderness in his eyes.

Goosebumps crawled up her body. "We need to shower you off; you stink like burning flesh."

"So, um, before we do. Can I wear something other than white yet? And will this thing blow up when I shower?"

She laughed, "No, it is water tight. No harm; you can swim with it even. I don't have any other clothes for you."

They walked hand in hand and came to her bedroom. She started to take him through her closet into the shower, but remembered it was shattered.

She walked him to his room. "You have a shower and tub, towels, and soap too, I am sure. If it is all dried up let me know. I should go shopping soon. I obviously haven't had guests in a while." She paused, thinking. "You could come with and pick out clothes later?"

She left the room, and Lucas stepped into his bathroom. The place was spectacular. Absolutely fabulous. The shower was huge with tons of nozzles, and the tub was separate; jetted and big enough for five people. He dug around in the cupboards and found a bunch of small bottles of soaps. He turned on the water and jets for the tub, and tried to pour in a little soap from the tiny bottle. It was dried out like she had mentioned. He tossed the bottle in and let the water run.

While the water was running, he took off his clothes and looked in the mirror. It was strange to see himself. He stared at how old he had grown. His ribs were visible. When did he get so thin? He looked closely at the stab wound and saw it had a small stitch sewn. It was red and sore, and gaping. Keeping infection at bay would be a challenge. He shaved; he always hated having facial hair.

Eventually, the soap must have softened, because bubbles brewed. The soft lavender soapy scent got strong. The tub overflowed with foamy bubbles pouring out; he turned off the jets and turned off the water. The tub wasn't even halfway full of water, but the bubbles were pouring over the side. He laughed, but then fear flickered. *What if she got mad?* He tried scooping up the bubbles and putting them in the toilet. They did not flush, they swirled around on top of the water. By the armfuls, he put them in the shower. He found the little bottle in the bottom of the tub and it was empty.

He stood there, naked, bubbles in his arms, bubbles foaming from the tub, and toilet, and a big pile of bubbles in the shower. With a rap at the door, she opened it. Her nose was attacked with lavender, and she was mesmerized by the scene.

She stood there with clean scrubs in her arms and roared with laughter. Thank God this wasn't the thing that would get him killed.

"What are you doing?" She laughed so hard tears formed in her eyes.

"I... the... I tried to put bubbles in the tub," he stammered, giggling.

"But, the toilet too?" Tears streamed down her cheeks as she laughed harder. "Why in the toilet?"

He burst with laughter and he tried to answer. "I... I tried to flush them."

She laughed so hard she dropped his clean scrubs. "Oh man, you, you are something." She turned the water back on the tub. "Don't worry; the maid will be here in the morning, she can clean up whatever you can't flush." He kissed her giggling lips.

"Thank you." His naked, bubble-covered body; and her with the thin layer of t-shirt. She smiled and wrapped her arms around him, and they kissed again, sweet and firm.

"Good luck with your bubble mess. I'll go make us dinner." She broke away, and left the room.

He couldn't help but smile. He had never in all these years heard her laugh.

Jaspierre unwrapped the frozen pizza and set it in the oven she didn't bother to preheat. She looked at the chicken wrapped in bacon and the half made, cold lunch. Dumped it all in the trash and set the dishes by the sink. She set the timer and walked to her pool. The cats were sleeping. It was late, she knew. Probably should have had dinner an hour or two ago. It was funny how lunchtime merged into late dinner.

Thoughts of the boy upstairs covered in bubbles brought a smile to her lips. How he kissed her. She loved it and hated it all at once. Sex was too confusing and complicated, that's why she didn't bother. She didn't like to be out of control of herself. But he made her feel... different. Maybe it was worth the trouble. Or he'd kill her. It was so unpredictable.

EIGHT YEARS EARLIER

Jaspierre stood in the observatory, her chest pressed against the glass as she stared down. She was nineteen, and had just come home from a long work meeting. Her young body was dancing inside her. She felt so weird. Her eyes stared at the boy down below.

Lucas was lying in his bed under his sheet, eyes shut. He was squirming, and he looked so beautiful, unimaginably so. Panting and moving. He didn't appear to be having a nightmare, but she couldn't figure it out. She had never seen this before; this squirming, panting, eyes shut... whatever it was. They had hardly spoken since she locked him down there. She couldn't figure out when to kill him. But she liked to watch him. Sometimes, he did grand speeches, shouting and pacing. Sometimes he did push-ups. Once he appeared to be playing pirates. Another time, he appeared to be making a rope to hang himself. But he didn't even try to. Sometimes he cried, but she couldn't stand to watch.

He had climbed the rings in the walls many times, and once when she came to look at him, he was at the top, staring at her. She said nothing, staring at him. His face was furry and his hair was long, and he looked like a yellow monkey. She stared at him, right in the eyes, and he stared back. He then asked her, for grooming supplies, and more food if she didn't mind. She gave him a feast, more food than four people could eat and a little electric razor. He had been clean-shaven ever since. He was much more handsome with his fair skin showing. She always snuck stuff in while he was sleeping, terrified he would overpower her and kill her, but she kept putting off killing him. It was harder to kill someone when she wasn't enraged with them at that particular moment. She could chain him, like her mom used to do, but she liked letting him have freedom. She believed she was better than Mother.

But at this moment, she didn't feel like killing him at all. She wanted to see what he was doing. She wanted to know in ways that made no sense to her. Her body begged her, loudly; what was he doing? She pressed so hard against the glass she thought she would fall in. He made a soft sound, and she wanted to hear it again. Then she would know.

She made a decision, and walked down the small metal spiral staircase. She walked to his room and turned the key in the door, and the two latches on the outside. Then she turned the handle and opened it. He sat up.

His face was red, he was panting, and he was sweaty.

She stared at him, utterly confused. She

wanted to ask him. But instead she stared. Words stuck in her throat.

"I'm sorry," he said.

"Why?" she asked, even more confused.

He turned red, trembling.

Her skin crawled and demanded louder, why? *Why was he sorry? What was he doing?* She had to know. But she was scared to ask.

Tears welled up, and she backed up to leave. "Are you being bad?" she asked right before she shut the door.

He couldn't figure out what to say. He had hardly spoken to the girl. This was such an awkward start to conversing with a captor.

"I..." He hesitated. "I am, was, masturbating."

She stood there, her eyebrows wrinkled, with a frown. "I don't know what that word means."

What the hell was he supposed to say to her? How did she not know? "It... it is sex, I guess."

Her eyes grew wide. The door slammed and locked. Jaspierre knew sex. She knew it was horrible and painful. It was terrifying; never again would she do it. Never. No matter what.

But she couldn't shake how her curious body craved more. Her body was crawling around inside her in the most unpleasant, confusing way. His face as he lay in his bed with his eyes closed, his sweet peaceful face looked so pleasant. That one soft sound he made; she wanted to hear it again and figure it out.

It was because he was a boy. Sex didn't hurt boys. Sex made them monsters.

Somewhere inside herself she questioned. Lucas didn't look mean, not during his... sex. Masturbation. Whatever it was.

She went upstairs and by the end of the hour had made a decision to try sex one more time. She put on a sparkly dress and heels and went out to a club. Never before had she been in one. The noise was overwhelming, and she had not yet found any reason to drink. She liked to be in control of herself at all times.

The bartender was pleasant and recommended a strawberry daiquiri. Wasn't drinking supposed to make sex easier somehow? She sipped it, turned on her stool, and leaned back, pushing out her breasts invitingly as she sat. It worked, surprisingly well, and a young man came over with dark hair and asked her to dance. *This was how you got sex.*

And dance they did. She saw how other women pressed their bodies against men. Jaspierre tried it and intense, confused desire bubbled. She whispered in his ear she wanted to go back to his place, and he said, "Why wait?"

He took her to his van, and inside was an old dirty camping mat. She lay down on it, and lifted her skirt, and he said, "God, you want it bad, don't you?"

She didn't know what to say, so she smiled awkwardly. She couldn't admit she had no idea what she was doing.

He unzipped and pulled out his cock. It was different than she remembered them looking. Actually, she couldn't remember what the other one looked like at all. He shoved it hard against her and it hurt. She regretted this adventure, and he said, "Hang on." He spit on her. It was gross, and her skin crawled.

"Poor man's lube ha ha." He grinned.

He pressed his flesh against hers and he was inside. So weird, painful, good, and bad all at the same time. She squeaked in a new sound she hadn't made before. She thought of Lucas and his sound.

He moved around, back and forth, and it hurt. She squirmed and whimpered, and fear rose within her. She tried to back up and he kept chasing after her, his body pounding into hers. It hurt so badly. Pinned in the tiny van. Pain kept screaming inside her. She put her hands up to push him off of her, and he exploded. He pulsed horribly inside her. Just like the last time. She had no idea that part would happen every time. She punched him.

He was panting and confused, but seemed to not have noticed the punch. "Oh God, I am sorry I couldn't last longer; you were so squirmy. God, you are hot. Dammit. You are so tight. God. You kept squirming."

She hit him again harder.

"What the fuck! I said I was sorry."

Her eyes welled up with angry tears. "Get off of me."

"What happened? You started all of this, not me." Irritated, he got off of her. She climbed out of the van in a hurry. She wrestled her skirt down as she walked.

He zipped up and followed her. "Wait, please, wait." She kept walking, in a fast angry pace. He grabbed her arm. "Are you okay?"

She turned to look at him, and he saw the tears trickling down her face. He hugged her. "I'm sorry. I didn't know." And he kissed her forehead. He still didn't know. But he understood she was upset. And maybe he could screw her again if he got her to leave on a good note.

She drove a knife into his side and ran off.

She shouldn't have broken her rule. No sex. Not ever. It was a horrible thing.

She drove home full of regret, and then she thought of Lucas. Beautiful Lucas, and his soft face, and the sweet sounds. If she was lucky he would do that masturbation again. And she would watch up in the glass. *That* sex didn't seem so bad.

CHAPTER

EIGHT

Lucas came down the stairs in his nice and clean scrubs. His face was freshly shaved, and he couldn't help but grin about the bubble mess. There was a rich and delicious scent of freshly baked pizza. He walked to the kitchen where there was a pizza on the table, still warm, and an empty plate. Two pieces were already missing. He helped himself and wondered where she was.

He heard splashing and headed towards the pool. Ikali was on top of the waterfall jumping down on Tessa. He glanced around and saw and empty plate sitting by a chair. Sitting to eat his slice, he saw her.

She was standing upon the waterfall in her white t-shirt dress, soaking wet. Her dress clung to her and had become quite see-through. She had not noticed him and jumped into the water. She dove like a professional, barely creating a splash, and he stared at her as she moved under the water. It seemed like she might never come up. He finished his first slice and started on his second. He found he was nervous, watching for her. She shot out of the water as if fired by a cannon, and she laughed and cannonballed back in. The cats both jumped in after her and they wrestled in the water, dunking each other. She looked so sexy. She was smiling and laughing as Ikali climbed on top of her head until she went under. Then Ikali climbed on Tessa and the three of them were under the water.

Jaspierre popped back up at the side of the pool and stood up. Lucas stared; she wasn't wearing a bra or panties, and he saw everything under her white dress. She turned and saw him staring and she froze, her hair dripping and dress hugging her. He stared down at his pizza. She looked at him.

He glanced back up and tried not to let his eyes wander across her body.

She stood with such a devilish grin. He bit his lip and looked down. God, she was so confusing.

"So, you found dinner, I see. Took you forever to take a bath."

"Yes, I did." He kept looking down at his pizza. "Can I ask you something?"

"Alright."

"Do you want me to sex you or not?" He glanced up. "I just, I don't know. And I can see your tits. It's confusing. Please don't stab me for asking."

She was taken aback, but made no effort to cover herself. "I have never had a sexual relationship before. It's a little confusing for me." She was sure watching a man masturbate whenever she caught him wasn't the same thing as a relationship.

He was surprised. He assumed she had lovers. "Well, me too, obviously... I have been in your basement for the last ten years. Nobody before that. But, I mean, I have no idea what you are gonna do next. Don't kill me for asking for your body, okay? Because..." He stood and she saw his obvious bulge, "I would love to have it."

She squealed and kissed him. Her wet clothes soaked his. She pulled off the wet dress and helped him out of his wet scrubs. He stared at her nakedness, her beautiful tits, her round bottom, and all he could think was how lucky he was. They made love on the chair by the pool, and then went upstairs naked and giggling to her bed to make out and let their bodies dance together again. When they fell asleep, the cats crawled into the room and glared at him with disapproval.

* * * * * * * * * * * *

Russell woke up. He had no idea if it was day or night. He did know he was in serious trouble. His throat was raw and his left arm ached terribly. He was crammed into the wall. Now he had a bed. There was a small cubby open in the wall with a bottle of water and an apple. He felt like shit. His throat hurt, his arm hurt. His legs ached. He stood up and immediately fell to the ground. Shooting pain ran up his feet into the backs of his eyes. What the fuck? Stars burst through his vision. As it cleared he saw his missing toes. Screaming eventually gave way to sobbing. His toes were missing. Only a few were severed cleanly. His flesh was burned and black.

He sat sobbing for over an hour before he settled down enough to examine them. Apparently, his big toe on his right foot was too hard to cut off, and the skin cut to the bone at the base of the toe. But the toe was missing from the first joint forward. The left foot had the toe cut off at the first joint, no damage to his skin further down. Pain shuddered through him when he touched the toes or when he stood. Crawling was impossible. Bumping his toe stubs was not an option. He sat for a long while, sad and scared before he figured out a way to move.

Slowly, he shifted on his butt, keeping his missing toes in the air so they wouldn't bump anything. He scooted and saw the metal ring he had been holding left on the floor. Sniffling, he slithered back and took the ring in case he needed it. Then he crawled to the water bottle. He wore out. Crying was exhausting. Being angry took too much energy. He reached in above his head, his back against the wall, and took out the water bottle. He then reached back in and took the apple, resting his arm on the side. A painful prick. He yanked his arm away with the apple in his hand. He had cut his arm in a long, straight line across it. *What the fuck?* It looked like a razor cut. He shuddered. *Where the hell am I?*

He glanced at the bed. Was that full of razors? He shifted closer. It was a pain to carry the ring, the water bottle, and the apple, but he wouldn't have the energy to come back for them. He examined the bed. He looked at the bottom. Underneath the mattress, he saw something wedged. He didn't see any razors, but he kept waiting for a piano to drop. He slid out a brown leather tied in strings and women's silver panties. *What the fuck?*

He untied the leather and realized it was his own wallet, his own car keys, and two shoelaces. His own? This was a trap. Why the hell would they take his clothes and his toes, and then leave his wallet? He thought about Lucas, and what he said.

Had Lucas left the wallet for him? Maybe Lucas had a plan. Lucas'd get him out of here. But why the hell panties?

For all he knew, Lucas's empty promises were another razor-lined compartment.

He contemplated the water bottle and the apple. The apple tasted flat, and his stomach turned. Poison? Well, whatever. He ate the apple and drank all the water.

Then he slipped his wallet and the ring under the mattress. Getting into the bed would take skill. He positioned himself backwards so his missing toes wouldn't hit the ground when he lifted his butt. Then he pressed his hands on the side of the bed and tried to push up. He screamed. His arm! He knew it was aching, but who had time to think about a stupid arm while they were staring at the charred flesh where their toes used to be? Right under his bicep was broken, his... humorous. As far as he remembered, that was the word. Not as funny as it sounded.

The pain was unbearable, and he wished he would pass out. No such luck. He sat there, cradling his left arm. He saw blood dripping off his elbow and onto the floor. *Dammit dammit fuckershit*. The pain made him shudder.

He sat gasping with tears pouring out of him. The red-hot pain of his arm exploded into his eye sockets. He closed his eyes and tried to catch his breath. He could lie down on the soft bed if he could get there. He pressed his heels into the floor, and pressed the bed into his back on the right side. His broken left arm he held with his right arm. He pushed upwards, and his back slid against the bed. Almost up, when the bed shifted behind him, sliding across the room about six inches.

Russell couldn't catch himself and his butt slammed into the ground. There he sat and sobbed loudly, shouting out profanities. He tried again, pushing backwards on his sore ass and this time, leaned forward, pressing with his heels, trying desperately not to let his toe stubs hit the ground. His left arm dangled uselessly, and his right arm pressed into the mattress. The searing pain from his toes burned through his body as his ass touched mattress. He yelped and pushed hard with his heels. His butt was so far on the edge it was almost slipping off. He curled into a ball and cried with relief at having made it to a soft spot to rest. He wept until he slept.

* * * * * * * * * * * *

Jaspierre woke up with Lucas wrapped around her. He was naked as was she. He felt so flipping hot though. She woke up sweating and overheated. She kissed his forehead, and he woke up, stirring and moaning. His forehead was hot, and her annoyance at being too hot turned to concern. He was feverish.

She grabbed the med-kit from her bathroom. This one had all her feminine supplies in it, but also a thermometer and ibuprofen. She told him to hold still, and he made a crabby sound. She took his temp. 102. That, was bad.

She pulled the blanket down off him to cool him off, and then it was obvious. His chest was red. The puncture wound was oozing. The veins across his chest spider-webbed in a bright red road map.

Crap. Jaspierre could do a lot of things, but getting prescription antibiotics wasn't easy for anyone. She pondered. Work had lots of medications, but they weren't easy to steal. Even for the boss. It was a highly regulated business.

She got the med-kit from the hall and poured peroxide on his chest. He cried, and sounded distant and confused. She pressed on his chest and white bubbles and pus poured out. A lot of pus. She was horrified. All that pus so close to his heart was not a good thing. She contemplated what to do next. Time to go to work, time to be a thief.

She put on her long, brown, curled hair. Staring at her numerous dresses, she chose a black and white business jacket and a long black skirt. Today, there was nothing casual about it. She put on tall, black shoes. She looked ready to fire someone.

Her heels clicked the floor and she leaned over and kissed Lucas. He murmured. "Lucas, I need you to wake up." He stirred and opened his eyes. "I have to work; you my dear, need to wake up."

She clicked herself to the bathroom and came back with ibuprofen and a glass of water. "Take this."

He woke up more, and sat up and drank the water, swallowing the ibuprofen. "Look, when you wake up the rest of the way, you need to clean your chest again. He nodded, but his eyes were foggy and confused. "I'll write you a note."

She wrote a note, including the time and dosage for more ibuprofen. She set an alarm so he would wake up and take it, and left the ibuprofen and the cup full of fresh water. He was asleep again before she was done.

Out she clicked, her heels tapping at the floor. She left in a flurry, leaving the cats hungry, Russell was forgotten, and she completely forgot the maid would be there within the hour.

She drove off in her dark red Mercedes. It was her work car, her work persona. She stepped out of the car, dropping the keys with the secretary. She got up to go park it. Her office building was as magnificent as her home. Except her home was vacant and still, but this place was bustling with worker bees. Many of them thought they were in charge. The board met regularly, and Jaspierre led every meeting. But the reality was, nobody owned the company but her. She ran Kyller and Co as she pleased.

Today she ran an inspection. She called a flurry of staff and everyone was in motion. They gathered together and walked through the warehouse. "How many of these do we have? Where are they?" She stomped her pretty heels, and four men jumped, two counted, one ran and got paperwork. She picked up a box off the shelf.

"Ma'am you can't..."

She turned and glared. That box twirled in her fingers and she asked her nearest associate details. "How much are we paying for these?"

"Uh, about $5,500 per case, I think."

"How many in a case?"

"Five thousand."

"How much do we sell them for? How many on hand? This one is an antibiotic? Or a psych pill?"

The partners quivered in their boots as she drilled them, tossing the box on the shelf. Psych pill. Shit.

She picked up another one, twirling it in her hands. "How many of these are we moving? How could we sell more?"

One associate joked, "We could release new bacteria. That's a pretty powerful antibiotic."

Bingo. She turned and fired him.

Everyone froze. She sent them all on errands. "Max, go get paperwork for his firing. Lucy, find the foreman; this place is a mess. Frank, you better go get me numbers to back up how fast these are moving off the shelf. You, escort him out." She scattered them like the wind, and they all flew about to their orders. Soon, she was standing in an empty warehouse. She turned to set the box she was holding back on the shelf, and the entire case of antibiotics came crashing down.

Cramming her large leather purse with ten boxes, she stepped forward and fell into the boxes in a mess. People rushed back around her, hovering, helping her up. Her right high heel had pierced a box of pills, and it was clinging to her shoe when she stood up. She looked extremely pissed. Most of the boxes filled with expensive antibiotic pills had crushed under her weight. The entire case was a loss. She stood up, seething rage pouring out her, and took off her high heels, dropping six inches of height. She straightened her long skirt, now dragging on the ground, and leaned over and ripped the box from her shoe, throwing it deliberately at the crowd of people forming. Then she stepped back into her heels and again was tall, majestic and terrifying to all who surrounded her.

"This place is a mess. Get it cleaned up. Show me all these numbers again." She clicked her heels smartly across the floor and her entourage hurried and apologized repeatedly. A sly smile spread across her face, but then she checked it. She'd be smug later when she could leave. Now, she had caused drama, and now she had to stay and correct it. She clicked up to her office and proceeded to have meeting after meeting detailing numbers from the warehouse, and the foreman's explanation of how the box came crashing down. Reports were filed and signed, policies reviewed and refined. The office scurried at a fast pace.

Jaspierre demanded the security footage and watched it in her office while sipping coffee. The angle was perfect. It looked like an accident. Her fall into the pills looked perfectly legitimate. She had created the perfect accidental theft of her own property. She relaxed and smiled her smug smile.

There was a quick rap at her door, and her secretary stood there. "Ma'am, I wanted to check in with you. I also, wondered..." He paused. "Would you want to go out for a drink?" He was always looking for a way to get ahead.

She didn't even look up. "This is your first and only warning. If you ever ask me out again you are fired."

"My apologies." He froze nervously and tried to change the subject. "I heard about the warehouse incident. Were you injured?"

"Only my pride. It was time to shake things up around here; it seems things have gotten complacent. I think though, I am done for today. Send my car around, and I will be back tomorrow to see if everything is running top notch. Tell the warehouse to be prepared. Tell everyone else I am not done yet. See if that sets their motors running."

She stood, and her skirt swished. Her heels

clicked and out she went. Her keys were handed to her in mere minutes and she stepped into her red Mercedes. An associate followed her out. "I wanted to apologize for the..." She snapped her door shut, gave him the finger and drove off. Nobody would believe him when he told that story. In fact, he'd be fired for telling it in a few short days.

JASPIERRE

CHAPTER

NINE

While Jaspierre was off stealing antibiotics from her own company, Lucas was sleeping. He drove the car thump thumping over Rainbow, and looked up in time to see Jaspierre pull the scissors from Katie's chest. He stared down at his hands. He held the bloody snips and one of Russell's toes. Sweat poured down his back and he awoke sobbing. He was in her big bed, surrounded by the four serval carvings, naked, and under a sheet. The sheet was bloodied, and he wasn't sure he wanted to know why. He saw her note and reached over and grabbed it.

> **Hey,**
> *Off to get you meds. You are running a high temperature, and may be delirious. Please take two ibuprofen when the alarm sounds. Clean out your chest. It's badly infected, there is plenty of peroxide.*
> **Jasp**

The note was cute and her handwriting was sweet and curvy. She wrote him notes now! He read it again and wondered if he had missed the alarm. He looked the clock over. It was set to ring in two more hours. Okay, he didn't miss it. He went to his room, not daring to walk in her closet, and reviewed himself in his mirror. He looked like shit. His chest was bright red with spidery veins crawling across it. He pressed next to the gaping hole and pus poured out. It smelled foul, and he wondered if he could die of infection. That would be such a pathetic way to die after all these years: An infection.

Of course, if she had never stabbed him, he wouldn't have a puncture wound to be infected. She was getting meds. So hopefully she had connections. He stood there, still naked, pressing on the swollen flesh, trying to clear out the infection. It hurt to press out the pus, but at the same time as it drained, there was a small amount of relief. His chest deflated as the wound drained, and he cleared the worst of it. He turned to grab a towel to wipe off his chest as much as possible. Before he could, he heard a scream. He turned and saw someone running.

Oh my God. What now? He put pants on and went out into the hall. "Hello?"

He heard a strange noise and walked toward it. One of the back rooms had a long extension cord going into it, and he followed into the room. There he saw an older woman, changing bedding and talking to herself.

"A naked man! She let me walk in on him standing there with his dingle berries waggling about!" She fluffed pillows. "What is wrong with that woman! She can't even tell me she has a special guest!" She straightened the covers. "I come twice a week to clean. Change all the bedding, she says. Wash all the clothes she says. Dust everything she says." She shoved a pillow into the pillowcase. "And that locked room! Her mother's room. She won't even let me in it. Surely that is where all this dust is coming from." She fluffed the pillow again and set it on the bed lining it up. "A naked man! I can't even get his meat and potatoes out of my head."

She turned and gasped, staring at him standing there. "Who are you? How dare you stand there and sneak up on me!" He stood there, totally unsure of what to do. "What the hell happened to you!" She grabbed his arms, holding them open, and stared at his bloody pus-smeared chest. "Good God, you have an infection. You are so infected!" She threw her hands up in disgust. "You better go see a doc. Did she do that? She is crazy. Did she do that to you?"

He shook his head and said nothing.

"Why were you naked? Are you porking her? Is she your pork pudding? You shouldn't mess around with her. She is trouble. Serious!"

She threw her hands up again, prattling about. "I have work to do! I can't sit around and chat with you all day."

He turned to go but she was at it again. "Hey! Where are you going? What the heck!" He paused. "What is wrong with you? You can't say a darn word? Are you mute?" The hands went a-flyin' again. "I will clean up your chest and I won't say a word okay? Not a word."

He nodded. He couldn't seem to think of anything to say. Though, it seemed unlikely she would ever give him a chance to talk.

They walked back down the hall past Jaspierre's room, to his room, and she grabbed towels and a bottle of peroxide. "Good Lord, what has she done to you!" The lady pressed on his chest and pus bubbled out. "Was it one of those swords? I swear they are everywhere. I don't know what kind of ninja army she is planning on staffing here, but I sure won't clean it when they arrive!" She wiped with a towel, pouring peroxide on. He winced as it burned. "It's so deep! I keep thinking I see your bones, and then boom! It's pus! Disgusting white pus!" She poured the rest of the bottle on and wiped it away. "You didn't hear me talking about your hot dog and macaroni, did you?"

He didn't know what to say.

"Well, you shouldn't be flopping them about like that anyways! I am no young woman!

You'll give me a coronary!" She pressed a clean towel tight onto his chest. He felt so sleepy again. "Damn, boy, you are hot with fever. What the heck am I supposed to do with you?" She threw her hands up again in exasperation. "I gotta work; I can't get fired from this job. This is the only house I clean anymore, the pay is so good." She pushed him down and he found his head on his pillow. As she pulled the sheet up around him she kept chattering about. "You better go to sleep. You are white as a sheet; your body has work to do! And I do too! I'll check you if she isn't back soon. Not that I'd know where she's gone! She does as she pleases."

The chattering woman vanished from his sight, but the clickity-clack of her teeth and tongue never did seem to slow. Her voice murmured and mumbled along as she went. Lucas found he slept sound. He felt for a moment, as though he had been taken care of by his mother. Though his mother never talked quite as much, still, there was something sweet about being taken care of by a sweet old woman. He slept sound and dreamless.

He awoke to rambling noises. "If I hadn't stopped vacuuming to move the plug from one outlet to another, I wouldn't have ever heard it." She sat on the edge of his bed, with a glass of water and pills. "But I did. That cord doesn't reach everywhere! I wish it did!" She threw her hands up again melodramatically. "Anyways, so I hear it beeping along and I *saw* you were in her bed!" She handed him the pills, and pulled him up to sitting. "Your pus and blood on her sheets! I found your shirt in there!" She handed him the water. "I can't believe it! I don't know when she was last with a man. I certainly don't clean messes like this often." She motioned for him to swallow the pills, and he groggily obeyed. "You'd better be using a condom! I didn't see any in there! And I checked the bed and the floor and *everywhere*." She fluffed his pillow and pushed him back down as he swallowed. "You do not need crazy children! Get more cats!" She turned and grabbed rags and pressed his chest. Satisfied that there wasn't much pus in there, she smiled. "Well, it looks like we're getting ahead of it a little." She stood up and rambled off, words rolling out of her like steam out of a teakettle.

Lucas lay in his bed, took a deep breath, and closed his eyes. His chest hurt, and he tried to sleep again. He drifted off when Tessa jumped up on his bed. She looked miserable. She curled up against him and purred, but she hissed every time the cleaning lady walked past. *Tessa would prefer a filthy home,* he mused.

He petted her behind her pretty ears, trying to coax her to relax. Not much later, Ikali joined them, sitting on the end of the bed, staring into the hallway. Ikali bared his teeth, ready to fight. The vacuum passed by in the hallway. Both servals had their hairs on end, and Ikali's tail twitched angrily. Lucas went from safe in his bed to concerned that Ikali might find this particular moment an excellent opportunity to bite him. He tried to slide his feet to the side of the bed, but Ikali's giant paw slammed down on one of them.

"Ow! Hey. Let me out. I wanna get a snack." Ikali, raised his paw, staring at the sheet. Lucas tried to scoot out and his foot got bitten. "Hey!" Ikali, let go and Lucas leapt out of bed. He was so dizzy he almost teetered over. He had to sit back down and let his head rest. "Guys, I don't feel good." Tessa purred up close and pressed into him. He knew. "Are you hungry? I bet you are hungry."

He stood and tested his feet. He teetered to Jasp's room and, stumbling, he went down the hall. There she was again. Before she could get going, he asked, "What is your name?"

"Oh, I am Marcy. I know, a terrible name, but my mother was a drunk! I'm sure it meant something to her at the time. By God! Why are you out of bed! You are white as a piece of paper." She inhaled and was speechless for an entire second. "*My Lord!* What happened to your feet?" She threw her hands into the air and let out a yelping noise. "What on earth! Your toes are gone!"

Embarrassed, he took a teetering step

backwards. "I need to feed the cats."

"You! You don't need to do a single thing. Lie down and sleep. I'll feed those monsters." She grabbed his arm and led him down the hall, back to his room. "Have you eaten? Of course you haven't eaten. Just like Jasp to leave a guest unattended! I will give her a piece of my mind!" They stepped into his room, and she sat him on his bed. "What is with the toes? You never did tell me! They look mutilated!" Lucas smiled. As if it was ever his turn to talk. "I'll go feed those monsters and bring you up a snack. But no complaining!" She refilled his water glass and left it on the nightstand.

The servals did not come back in Lucas's room, so he assumed she made good and got them fed. He dozed off again, waiting for his snack. He awoke with Jaspierre curled in bed next to him. She slept on the edge of the bed in a black suit. Her heels were tossed on the floor. She looked to him, like the sweetest angel.

He kissed her, and her eyes flickered open. "How are you feeling?" she whispered to him.

"I'm fine when you are here. I am so... lost without you."

She smiled and rolled her eyes. He was still delirious and feverish.

She stood and took a box out of her purse. She read the directions and handed him two pills. "This is a strong antibiotic, so it should work.

Don't miss a dose." She knew he wouldn't because she wouldn't let him. She had ten boxes, but apparently would only need one box. Actually, two, if she dosed Russell. Might as well.

"I am gonna go give Russell a dose and his dinner." She kissed his forehead. He obediently took his antibiotic and went back to sleep.

She went downstairs and grabbed food from the kitchen on her way to the fireplace. She clicked the ear, and stepped down the stairway. Neither cat came running this time, and she glanced around curiously. Down the steps she went and unceremoniously clicked the box open, and shoved in the food she had grabbed. Carrot sticks and bologna and the pills. She put no effort into making the meal special because she didn't like Russell.

"The pills are an antibiotic."

And she left.

Russell shouted in response, but she had other things on her mind. Where were her cats? She walked upstairs and clicked the door shut behind her. "Tessa? Ikali!" Her voice rang out and nothing. She walked toward their playroom and peeked inside. No cats. She walked toward the pool, and she heard her.

"Marcy! I forgot you were here today." Concern rose within her. Had she seen Lucas?

"Good Lord, you frightened me!" Up went the hands. "I've been trying to clean up your mess down here." The rag she was using went attacking a chair. "Lord knows where you and your man toy have been getting it on." She wiped down the side table. "I found him naked! You hear that! His crown jewels sparkling in the sunshine!" She scooted the chair and table and turned on the vacuum, hitting where they were, and turning it off again. "Not that I am complaining. He sure seemed well equipped!" Up went the hands. Then she pushed the chair and table back in place. "I gave him the ibuprofen and made sure he didn't go hungry." Marcy paused and looked up at Jaspierre. "I also cleaned his chest. He needs real medication."

"That's where I was," Jaspierre replied curtly with a scowl. "He has medication now. Don't talk about him like that."

Marcy hesitated. "Are you sure? You might need girl talk after all that wang time. I know that with my first boyfriend, I couldn't wait to ride him again. Of course, I had lots of girlfriends too, so we went a-whisperin' about!" Up went the hands. "We compared notes, and parts even the big O's. Some men squeak and some men moan. You'd never believe it if I told you everything I know!"

Jaspierre stood there glaring, embarrassed hot anger building.

"Look Jasp." Marcy sighed. "Have you ever been with a man before? Come now. If you need to talk I will talk with you. I'm totally safe. Besides! I already saw what you've been blowing! He's got a nice one, and he's not too hairy of a man. I never did like a lot of hair on my men."

"I have warned you plenty." Jaspierre's rage roared to life. A blade in her hand before she even knew where she got it.

She raised it with both hands over her head. *"That is enough."*

Marcy ducked out of the way with unexpected skill. She slid one of the many hidden blades out of the nearby plant. "Oh? Come and get it." Marcy swung her blade and the two collided. Jaspierre glared exasperatedly.

She leapt up onto the chair behind her and swung hard again. Marcy ducked. "Jaspierre, come now. Be reasonable!" Marcy smacked the flat of her blade on Jaspierre's ass.

Jaspierre changed her stance and stopped swinging so thoughtlessly, making a quick sharp stab at Marcy's breast. Marcy swung hard to block and knocked the blade out of Jaspierre's hand. "You should hit the gym," Marcy smiled with her sword pressed against Jaspierre's throat. "You are out of practice." Jaspierre stood there, angry eyes burning into the older woman. Marcy lowered her sword. "I have to get back to work, and you have a sick man to attend to."

Jaspierre never took defeat well. She glared at her maid and considered stabbing her in the back. It wasn't worth the effort, and she turned and walked away. Marcy knew Jaspierre had a temper, they drew swords every few months. Most of the time, they sparred for fun. Marcy was getting good at it. After what had happened with Jaspierre's mother, she couldn't blame the girl. Nobody ever recovers from that sort of thing.

Jaspierre went back upstairs and sat next to Lucas. The vacuum hummed from the below and she was sure Ikali and Tessa were hiding from its racket. He slept a miserable, haunted feverish sleep. He moaned, cried, and complained. She tried to shush him, but there was no reasoning with him. In the quiet of the evening, she found herself thinking of Katie again. Why did she have so much regret? Mother would never regret slaughtering someone, especially when she was awful enough to kill a kitten. Mother wouldn't have cared about the kitten like Jasp did, though. After all these years, Jaspierre still was haunted by that moment. Those scissors plunging. It was the right thing to do. Mother, Chance, pretty much everyone she had ever met would agree she was right. She wished her emotions would remember that. Maybe she had waited too long to kill someone? Maybe she was too old and that was why it bothered her so much. Move on. Go do something else.

She went and got her leather notebook and reviewed. None of her previous plans were carried out. She drew a line through her list. Pitting Russell and Lucas against each other in the maze? *No.* Seeing which man would turn on the other first? Hmm. Lucas, she supposed since he had already cut off the other mans toes. She wrote notes, about Lucas's disgust, but his willingness to get it done. She wrote notes about Russell and his inability to handle captivity well.

She took notes and wrote, planning the next days experiments while she listened to Lucas and his feverish cries. Then she came up with a plan for Russell. She curled up and wrote about Marcy, and how she should be eviscerated. Then she wrote a particularly small note about how she agreed her temper was not under control.

Lucas was lost in dreams; his nightmarish memories flickered past him in a dance. They slowed. Jaspierre was in his room. He was lying on his white bed with his white sheets and his cock in his hand. She was standing there, in his room. She stood there, right before he had finished, asking him what he was doing. He asked her to come see, and she tiptoed in wearing a tight, teal dress asking what masturbation was, with her pretty innocent eyes. Then her silver panties hit the floor. He wanted her so badly. Her face was smeared with blood, and the kitten cried nearby. She tripped and fell walking to his bed. Then she looked up at him with those scissors left in the back of the woman she was stabbing, and she charged at him. Lucas screamed.

Jaspierre stopped writing, and glanced up at him. She glanced at the clock. Not yet time for more meds. She wondered, for the first time, what she would do if he died. They had been together for so long. Even though he didn't choose her, she chose him. She loved him, she supposed. That was the only reason she could think of for why she stopped trying to kill him. And taking his toes in the name of science wasn't pleasant. She considered her regrets about killing Katie. She had done it in such a fit of rage. Lucas was different she couldn't seem to summon up that kind of anger. Maybe it was because he seemed so vulnerable. Both Katie and he had killed her cats. They deserved the same brutal punishment. Mother could beat, maim, and kill emotionlessly. What was wrong with Jaspierre that she couldn't do the same? Her emotions controlled her, despite her efforts to ignore them.

Lucas was special. She leaned forward and kissed his forehead. She had been alone so long. She didn't want to be alone anymore. This was the moment she decided she would never kill him.

*** SIXTEEN YEARS EARLIER ***

Jaspierre was the quietest little eleven-year-old anyone had ever met. She never raised her hand in class. In spite of this, she did not miss a single day of school. She got excellent grades.

After school, she would bike home and change into a suit and high heels. Then she would pack her homework into a briefcase and take a chauffeured car to work. Her staff would open the door for her, carry her briefcase, and inform her of the details of the day. She would walk into her office, read papers, and demand the board sign them. She, being eleven, could not sign any documents herself, though in a pinch, she'd still sign Mother's name. The board did most of the heavy lifting, she was the yes or no person.

Mother had set it up this way years earlier so Jaspierre could easily run everything. Mother never did enjoy working. She was eager to pass the company on as soon as possible. Jaspierre had been attending board meetings since she was five. One of her first jobs as a five-year-old was to sign Mother's name to forms and paychecks. She'd practice for hours until Mother finally said it was good enough. Mother hated signing forms. She was expected to think and listen and ask good questions or she would be beaten. By seven she had learned quite a bit about running a company, and quite a bit more about how to avoid beatings. If Kyller and Co made more money, she got hit less frequently. It was an excellent motivator.

After her evening meetings, she would sit and do her homework quietly. Her secretary always brought her dinner. Her company was doing well. Everyone was so used to working with her, they rarely thought of her as a young child. It was screwed up, her working so hard, but whatever kept the honey flowing. Mother had fired any early protests to Jasp being present and making decisions.

After dinner, she would get in her chauffeured car and go home. Once she she climbed out of the car, her staff would carry her briefcase to her room and cater to her every wish. The house was immaculate, and the staff was enormous; eight gardeners, two maids, one chauffeur, one butler, and one full-time chef. The chef generally cooked for the staff, there were never any guests. The staff had been whispering that they hadn't seen Mother in a long while. But Jaspierre was often too tired to listen in at this point in the day.

Her only true friend in the world, a female serval, curled up on her bed every night, and licked her, and purred with her. She rarely had nightmares when Rainbow slept with her. Jaspierre pulled her cat close and held her. Tears bubbled down her face. "I don't know how long I can do this. The company is going fine, I am passing classes at school, but there are so many decisions to be made." She sobbed into Rainbow's fur. "I have no friends, except for you, Rainbow. Well, you and Chance, I guess, but he's kind of mean."

The cat licked her face and tried to console the tired, sobbing child. Lights went out in the hall, and Jaspierre stood up and peeked out. The staff had gone to their rooms at eight as always. She walked to her mother's room and stepped inside. The food cart sat with plenty of food. Jaspierre wrote a note, as she always did, typing it up on Mother's computer.

The spaghetti was disgusting. Never make it again. You better be feeding my daughter better shit than this. I am nearly at a breakthrough and will be traveling to Rome for the month of April. As always Jaspierre is in charge, and if I hear any of you have argued with her you, will be fired on the spot.

The note was unsigned. After it printed Jaspierre signed her mother's name. Then she sat and signed all of the paychecks for the next four weeks. She took the food and stirred it around, and set a plate on the floor for Rainbow to nibble.

Jaspierre ate the small fruit salad sitting on the desk while the cat ate a meatball. "I think this one is good. Sounds like her." Jasp smiled at the cat. "I think we should change your name. I'm not seven anymore. Rainbow seemed like such a great name at the time. I could shorten it to Rain... I hate when people shorten my name. I wish I could get a new name as easily as a cat."

She kissed her cat and petted it again. "I don't know, though. It is your *name*; that's an important part of who you are. Even if you don't like it... sometimes *especially* if you don't like it."

In the morning the chef made her pancakes. She ate with no enthusiasm. She hated school. It was the worst part of the day.

She took her packed lunch and rode off on her bike. She could take the car. And she did if it was too snowy or rainy. Taking the car made her stand out like a sore thumb. She would almost rather take the bus. But the last time she took the bus, Chance pulled her hair. Chance was a jerk, but also her only friend.

She pedaled her bike. Her mother had bought her a bike with a small electric motor so she could go at a good pace with little effort. Jaspierre hadn't ridden that bike in years, though. Instead, she was riding a blue bike that was old and tired-looking. The first time she saw it, leaning on a dumpster, set to go to the dump, she knew it was perfect for her. Nobody would call her a rich bastard with a tired old bike like this one.

That insult was the worst because she couldn't even argue. "You don't have a dad. That makes you a bastard." Well, it wasn't quite true, everyone had a dad. But she'd rather they thought she had no dad than hear the truth. The truth was far worse than anyone would have guessed.

She stopped thinking, and parked her bike, not bothering to chain it. Into class she walked, and sat quietly in her usual spot.

Her teacher called her out into the hallway. "Jaspierre, I have been trying to reach your mother. Parent teacher conferences are coming up, and I need to speak with her."

"Didn't you get her last note? She is going to Rome. She can't make it."

"Yes, I did. I need to hold a conversation with her." Jaspierre did not like where this was going one bit.

"What did you want to talk with her about?"

"Well, about you." The teacher paused, not willing to reveal more.

"What about me?" The little eleven-year-old was not in a business suit and could not fire anyone she didn't like. She was at school. She was frustrated.

The teacher looked at the small girl with concern. "Are you okay? When is the last time you saw your own mother?"

Jaspierre recoiled. She closed her eyes, clenching her fist. "*My mother is fine.*"

"When have you last seen her? As far as I can tell, she hasn't been at any school meeting, parent-teacher conference, or school sign-up or any event at all in years. She won't return my phone calls."

The blood rushed to her ears. She could almost see everything crashing before her eyes.

And it did.

Two weeks later, she was in court. She knew she was in serious trouble, probably about to go to prison for hiding that Mother was missing. Was that what they did to children? Maybe she would have to go to an orphanage. Or maybe they would send her to foster care. What if they sold her kitty?

"How long has your mother been missing?"

Jaspierre stood at the little microphone, reporters buzzing about. "I..." She paused. "I think you already know."

Jaspierre sat and looked at her hands.

The judge turned to Jaspierre. "But how could she be missing for three years? Why on earth didn't you tell anyone?"

Jaspierre looked up. "My mother taught me to run her- now *my* company Kyller and Co. We sell medicines, we help people. She set it up so I could attend the meetings, I have a great team of grownups who advise me. She taught me to fend for myself. I do not want anyone to mismanage my company, and my estate while I grow up. Nobody can do a better job than me. I have no family left." Jaspierre stood up, her face red and angry. "I would have filed for emancipation already, but I know it isn't typically granted to someone of my age."

The silence in the room was astounding. This small eleven-year-old girl would try to be emancipated.

"I have been on my own since I was eight. I have always paid for staff to take care of me. No pet of mine has died of starvation. No plant left un-watered. During the last three years my company has blossomed. It has grown fifteen percent every single year. Not one bill or paycheck has been paid late. An accountant did my taxes. I have gotten medical attention the one time I had strep throat. I *can* and I *do* take care of my estate, my business, and myself. If that isn't being a grown up, then what is? It has taken three years for anyone to notice I, Jaspierre have been running my home, my life, and my business. Everyone thought so far my mother was making these decisions. But it was me. And I did an excellent job! I am a wealthy woman. I do not want to end up a broke eighteen-year-old."

Jaspierre sat down, head held high. Cameras flashed and reporters scribbled notes.

The judge had no idea what to make of this. He had never even heard of someone who wasn't a teenager filing for emancipation. He cleared his throat. "Jaspierre, do you know where your mother is?"

"I know Mother," She tried to swallow the anger rising up. "My mother knew she would leave me. That's why she had me run board meetings at the age of five. That's why she gave me my office. That's why she showed me how to pay all the bills. She showed me how to fire someone and how to hire. "

"But do you know where she is? Has she contacted you in all this time?"

"Once."

"Where is she? What did she say?"

Jaspierre held back angry tears. "She asked me if I still had my cat she gave me when I was seven. If I was doing well, and said she heard the company's stock was up. She told me to stay in school. I heard a man snoring." Tears welled up and dribbled down her cheek as she spun the convincing lie.

"Do you know who your father is?"

"I don't know who he is," she replied both lying and telling the truth. "He might be dead."

"Your birth certificate says Jasper Pierre. Do you know who that is?"

Jaspierre had never read her birth certificate before. And terrified, angry tears poured out of her like a waterfall. "I don't know!" Her sobs echoed in the courtroom. "I am doing fine on my own. I am fine. Isn't that enough?"

The judge called for a break and asked Jaspierre to come to his office. He handed her a tissue. "Look, I can't emancipate you. It doesn't matter that you are doing grownup things; you need actual grownups to watch over you. But I think I have ideas on how I can give you almost what you want."

Jaspierre sat listening and wringing her hands. Once they finished talking, they walked to the courtroom, and she sat with her court-appointed lawyers, her court-appointed special advocate, her welfare worker. The team sat there, whispering together, ignoring the child altogether. One of them asked her what the judge said, and she waved them away.

"I have spoken with Jaspierre, and we will use a few programs to our advantage. First off, she will not be fully emancipated. We will treat her like a foster child, under her own care. She is, an extreme case, and I will require she meets with her court appointed special advocate, and her welfare worker once a month, until she turns eighteen. She will be required to meet with a psychiatrist once a week for the same number of years. Also, although I will allow her to live on her own and manage her own money, we are going to require other adults be in her home at all times. This can be staff of her choosing. She is required to maintain her grades, and graduate from high school."

Jaspierre sat dejected.

"Jaspierre, I know you feel like you have taken good care of yourself. But you are still an eleven-year-old child. I am concerned with all these grown up decisions you will have not had time for proper emotional development. That is why I am requiring so many check-ins with adults who can help you. The last thing I would like to note, while I do not pretend to know how an eleven-year-old child can run such a company, your work hours will be limited to ten per week, only increased to twenty per week once you hit high school. You are, first and foremost, a child. You can still have the reins of your business, but you may not work thirty to forty hours per week like you are doing now. Make friends, take a dance class if you wish. Try and be a kid for at least a portion of your life."

Jaspierre was hurt and angry. Her hours being cut was absolutely ridiculous. How could she run a company on ten hours a week? She supposed she would have to figure it out. She could do that, though. Worst-case scenarios were over. She wasn't emancipated. But she was her own guardian. She had to do all these pointless hours of meetings. But it could have been way worse, they could have found out about her father.

CHAPTER

TEN

Jasp slept in the chair next to Lucas. She checked his chest repeatedly and worked, and dozed the rest of the time. In the morning, he was still delirious, but he seemed like he'd rest all day. His fever was much lower, and there wasn't much pus left.

She left him a note saying she had gone to play with Russell. An idea for him came up and she couldn't wait to test her theory. She went down and made herself frozen waffles for breakfast and got Russell the standard apple and sandwich and coke combo. She clicked the ear of the serval, and her two cats came running along. They slipped into their boxes and she set out four animals for them to hunt. She mixed the maze up and then released the rabbit, fox, gerbil, and ferret.

She let the cats go and walked to Russell's room. What used to be Lucas's room. It was strange to see a different body down there, lying under those same sheets. She vaguely wondered if he would masturbate as beautifully, but she thought not.

His toes looked like they were bleeding some, by the marks on the sheets. Also his arm; his arm was bleeding quite a bit. She opened the dumbwaiter and found it said, "fuck you" in smeared blood. The two pills were still there.

She grinned. Oh yes. Russell was a spitfire. She sent down the sandwich and the coke. "Wake up, you dumb fucker!" She said playfully loud and sat on the rail to watch her cats hunt. She munched on her waffles like a sandwich; syrup and butter packed between the two.

Russell rolled awake and looked around. He saw the little dumbwaiter was open again. There sat food and the same two pills, and his message written in his own blood.

Russell debated if the sandwich was worth the effort. He was hungry, yes, but it hurt to get to the dumbwaiter. He should scoot the bed closer; it would help. But he wasn't up for shoving it around. He stared at his toe stubs; a few of them bled. They hurt today so extremely bad. His feet were red and swollen. "I need a doctor," he said.

"I can hear you even if you whisper. Just a little FYI to get us going. Call me the doctor." She sounded almost like she was singing.

"Doctor, I need to go to a hospital."

"Why don't you take your medicine?" Jaspierre giggled in a morbid way.

"I don't know what that is. I am not taking it."

She grinned and stared as Tessa found herself nose to nose with a fox. Tessa sniffed at the fox. The fox sniffed at Tessa.

"Doctor, can you give me something else to eat besides apples?" Russell said.

"Shhh, she found the fox."

"What the fuck are you talking about?"

The fox moved its tail, and Tessa jumped with surprise and ran off. Foxes were scary. Jaspierre giggled. That was one for the blooper reel. Ikali found the ferret and was carrying it around like a toy teddy bear.

Russell moved his sore, aching feet to the floor and he lowered to his butt. Then he crawled backwards toward the food. Jaspierre turned a screen so she could watch him while she stared out the window at the cats. As he squirmed across the floor, Jaspierre grinned. He got to the wall and pushed his back against it and pressed his heels into the ground, shifting his back up the wall. He turned to reach for the food, and Jaspierre snapped the door shut seconds before he reached in.

"What the fuck!"

"Sorry, a little bird told me you didn't like apples. So, tomorrow I will find something else for you to eat."

Russell let out an exasperated scream,."You bitch!" He sounded like he was ready to punch her.

"Can you move your left arm?" she asked.

He looked at the dangling limb. "No."

"How very interesting," She said. She heard the screaming of a terrorized infant, and turned back to her cats. The fox in the maze with them had the rabbit. Ikali still had the ferret. Tessa was following the gerbil. The two cats froze at the cry of the rabbit. Almost like magic they turned to the sound, teeth bared and pursued. The fox bit the rabbit harder, listening to the squeaky screams. The cats were not amused to see the fox with their rabbit. Ikali leapt on top of the fox, biting behind it's neck, running claws deep into the fox. The fox dropped the rabbit and turned to bite Ikali, and Tessa tore into the fox's throat. They both tore him to pieces.

"Excellent teamwork my dears." Jaspierre couldn't be prouder. The rabbit hopped away and hid, forgotten by everyone.

She turned to look at Russell, and saw his left, injured arm was limp and broken. It was still bleeding. His feet were red and raw. She sent a full box of antibiotics, three bottles of water, and a small timer down the dumbwaiter. Not a clock though; a timer. She didn't need to make it easy for him to count the hours and thus the days. No, not at all. But him dying of a pointlessly stupid infection was wasting everyone's time. She left the box for him so he'd read it and decide for himself. She didn't bother telling him he had a bathroom. Only if he was likable.

*** TEN YEARS EARLIER ***

Jaspierre went to check on Lucas. She always snuck his food in to him while he was sleeping. No easy feat. Sometimes, he slept while she was at school or work, and that made it difficult to get him fed. He was growing thin, and she felt bad. He had been in there about a month, and she couldn't seem to figure out when to kill him. She snuggled the soft little kitten as she bottle-fed it. His pale skin was on her mind. She fed the kitten while they sat observing the boy.

He was awake and sitting. He looked so hungry. The kitten finished its bottle and was snoozing. She had fashioned a little kitten-carrying sling out of a scarf she had. The kitten slept curled up in it, and she set the bottle down. Lucas stood and swung his arms around and stretched. Then he touched his toes and rubbed his shoulders.

He looked thin and achy. Jasp stared at him, and realized if she wasn't going to kill him, then something had to change. She couldn't let him starve to death. A better way to knock him out would help immensely. Then she could go in his room when she wanted.

She went down to Chef and announced her need for a midnight snack. He smiled at her and warmed her up leftover lasagna, complete with a side salad, and a delicious slice of triple chocolate cake. She grabbed two forks and said she would eat it in her room. "Two forks?"

"Dinner and dessert. What do you think I am, a heathen?" The chef smiled. "Also," Jaspierre continued, "let's have an extra bottle made up for the kitten from now on. He's been getting so hungry."

The chef replied, "Are you going to name him yet?"

"No, not yet. I want to wait until his eyes are open."

"Okay." The chef smiled and peeked at the little kitten in her scarf. "He looks like he is gonna make it. He is so improved from when you first had him."

Jaspierre preferred not to think about all of that.

"I noticed you have been going in your mother's room. Are you ready to go through her things?"

Jaspierre nodded. "I am seventeen and almost her size. Her clothes fit me. I... I don't know if I will ever wear them, but I have been looking through them."

"Did you want me to send someone to wash them all and tidy up?"

"No. Stay away from her room." Jaspierre's eyes flashed with hot anger, and he did not push the issue further. Jaspierre and the kitten went upstairs with the tray full of tasty food. She took the food down the hall to Mother's room, unlocked the door, and went inside. She set the food on the bed, and then turned around and peeked out the hall. Nobody was out there as far as she could tell. She locked the door and snuck down to the janitorial supply. The supply room had everything lined up in neat rows. Sheets, towels, blankets; her home was as well stocked as a hotel, despite the fact that she never had large groups stay over. She opened the closet in the back, and there they were. Small, portable beds designed to pop up for those rare times when the luxurious beds in the rooms weren't enough. She carried the bed under one arm, grabbing sheets, a blanket, and a pillow with the other. Her arms were full, but the kitten curled up safe in its sling. She carried the pile; nobody saw her or asked her what she was up to.

Once she was at the top of the spiral staircase, she took three trips, carrying the bed, then the bedding, then the food all down to the lower level, right outside Lucas's room. She hesitated. He was awake. It would be smarter to do this when he was sleeping. She should knock him out with the chloroform again.

But she kept her original plan. She went back up to her mother's room and took the sword out of the closet. Then she checked once more that the door was locked, stepped down the first step of the spiral staircase and shut and locked the door. Then she walked down to Lucas's room.

She knocked.

Lucas was startled and shouted, "Hello? Is anybody out there? I am locked down here!"

She rolled her eyes. "It's me."

He was quiet for a moment. "Why did you knock? I can't let you in."

"I didn't want to scare you. Don't do anything crazy." She unlocked the single lock on his door, and realized she should add a few more locks, in case. Mother always kept them chained, so she didn't need as many door locks.

The door creaked open, and a moderately hairy Lucas stood there. One month's growth of blond fuzz didn't seem to amount to much yet. She stood with the long, thin sword in hand. "If you try to run, I'll kill you."

"Okay," he said because he didn't know what else to say. It was their first conversation since he had been locked up.

"I brought you a present. Don't make me regret it." He stood uncertain what to do. "Come; you have to carry it in. It's not heavy."

He stepped gingerly into the hall. There

was nowhere to run to. It was a tiny hall with a few doors, and a spiral staircase up to another door. He didn't even know where he would go if he escaped.

Probably the staircase. But the staircase did not look inviting either. This might be a massive prison. He turned to see what she had brought. A bed. His stay was going to be extended. Maybe he could talk her out of it.

He took it into the room and came back and got the pillows and sheets and blankets. Then he took the tray of food inside. He rarely got to eat anything fresh and hot much less dessert. He set the tray down on the floor and set up the bed.

"This thing is great, thank you." He smiled at her. She stood there, big pretty eyes staring. It was a strange thing to be imprisoned by her. She didn't look terrifying most of the time. "I... I wanted to talk to you."

"Yes?" she answered curiously. She adjusted the kitten in the scarf as it let out a loud meow.

His eyes lingered on the kitten as he continued, "I know what happened with Katie; that... that was a terrible accident. I will not tell anyone. It wasn't your fault." He clicked the bed legs to a nice height. "If you let me go, you'll be safe, you know? I'm not gonna tell. I'm just gonna go to college and just ...forget this whole thing." The bed was complete and he put the sheets on.

"I... I would like to, if it's not too much trouble, be on my way. You've really been a great host."

The sword tip press into his back. "You are kidding me. You think I would let a murderer like you go?"

He stood and raised his hand. "I am sorry." He turned around so he could face her. "I am so sorry. It was an accident. Just like Katie."

She laughed. "Katie was not an accident. She killed my kitten. I killed her."

"Are you going to kill me?"

"Yes." Jaspierre lowered the blade. "Yes. I have to. It's only fair."

Lucas lunged at Jaspierre, grabbing her in a bear hug. The sword dropped to the floor while he tried to hold her still. She squirmed and kicked him, and they broke apart. She grabbed the blade and spun. Before it hit him, he held up something as he tried to block. As soon as she saw it she knew it was wrong.

But it was too late.

The blade went straight through the neck of the kitten Lucas had stolen. The tiny little head fell to the ground and Lucas screamed.

Jaspierre stood there, horrified. She dropped the blade. Her scream echoed through the room. Then she picked it back up and charged at Lucas. He tried to run, but she was so fast, and so angry. The blade hit his leg, slicing it. He knew he couldn't outrun her. His plan had been to hold the kitten hostage and get her to let him go. But now he was a dead man.

Jaspierre kept screaming. In blind grief and hatred, she swung again. Lucas easily ducked and charged at her, knocking her backwards onto his new bed. He lay there on top of her, wrestling the sword away. She howled with screaming sobs, punching at him. He held her soft seventeen-year-old self down with his slender nineteen-year-old frame and waited for her to settle down. After a few minutes, her angry fighting body softened below him, and he held her while she cried. In one hand he held the sword, the other he held her wrist, keeping her from beating him.

Try as he might, he couldn't hate this beautiful, soft girl he was lying on.

In a fit of foolishness, he almost kissed her. This sobbing, angry, miserable, beautiful, terrifying woman pressed tight against him. He wanted her to feel better. He had ruined her life. Her sobs turned back into anger and he stopped himself. He remembered. She would kill him.

"Stop, please, stop. Please," he whispered into her ear like a lover would. "Please let me go. I don't want to fight you. Let's not hurt each other. I am so sorry. I didn't mean for that to happen. Please. Don't fight with me. Please. Please let me go."

He let go of her wrist, he kissed her cheek, and he dropped the sword. Then he stood and backed out of his room. He raced up the spiral staircase, and it was locked. He checked the other doors. They were locked.

He stood at the end of the hall, tears falling down his face. Trapped. It all hit him; this was all his fault. He killed the cat, and that killed Katie, and then he killed this kitten. He deserved anything he got. Despair was winning.

The sword tip pressed into his back. "I will never let you go." He raised his hands and turned to her. His sad, miserable, sorry self walked back to his room with the tip of the sword prodding him the whole way. He turned to look at her before he stepped backwards into his room.

"I..." he stuttered. What did one say to a person in a time like this? "Thank you for letting me live." And he stepped backwards into his room, the door clicked shut, and he heard the lock.

CHAPTER

ELEVEN

Lucas being sick was a huge pain for Jaspierre. She spent a day checking on him and stealing meds. And she had played with the cats and Russell. Now it was another day and he was still sick, and she was kind of bored.

She wanted to talk with him. Well, she wanted to tear his clothes off and make him squeal. But, he was not up for it. He was still feverish, and he cried a lot. Crying men weren't much fun. It was pleasant to wrap herself around him and kiss him until he stopped. But, frankly, she was still bored. She spent an hour sword fighting with her training dummy. Then she tossed little throwing knives at targets for a bit. Still bored, and it was evening.

Time for fun.

She put on a bright blue short wig and party clothes. The fishnet stockings were nearly fully covered with her thigh-high boots. Her skirt was short and blue. Her black top was low cut, but loose, so her stomach wasn't too obvious. She put on bright blue earrings and grabbed a pair of hot pink glasses on her way out the door.

Time for fun.

She got on her little three-wheeled motorcycle and rode into town. Jaspierre drove to a tiny bar she liked to visit. Despite its weary look, it had plenty of prey to choose from. She parked and walked in. She walked up to the bar and winked at the bartender. He sauntered over and poured her a sweet tasty drink he liked to call party punch. She grinned and slipped him a ten. He knew she didn't drink booze and automatically made it a virgin. She'd bought the bar a while back and paid him extra to make her nights more fun.

"Anybody fun here tonight?"

"You mean besides you, sweetheart?" He smiled at her while another customer tried to flag him down.

She grinned and leaned forward, showing off her sweet rack. "Anybody?" She took a sip.

"I think you should be going for that guy in the suit or the youngster with the earring. Depends on your mood tonight. Good luck babe." He turned and spun bottles, pouring the next set of drinks.

Jaspierre turned around and stared at the crowd. The youngster with the earring looked like a dumb child. She glanced over, and this man sat there with a nice suit. He was drinking a clear liquid on the rocks, and he was sitting, bored. This bartender had a keen eye for targets; so if suit guy got boring she was gonna work the young one.

She sat down at the booth with the man in the suit. He looked up rather confused. "So, what are you doing here? You waiting for someone?"

The man shook his head, staring at this bouncy-breasted woman who was talking to him. Her look was not his style. But... it did look like fun. And he was out for fun, he supposed."I'm trying to burn time. I'm on a business trip, so I'm here for the weekend."

Sounded good to her. She laughed, and then invited him to play darts. "Wanna play for cash?"

He knew, as they got started, she was out for his money. But he didn't care. He bet her. His throws were okay, but hers were better. He swore she could make a bullseye every time if she wanted. She played darts three times a week, often at home by herself. It was one of the things she did to keep her skills strong.

Jaspierre never bothered to take all of someone's money. After all, she had plenty of her own. But she liked the competition. It was boring to play darts alone.

After the first two games, he had an idea.

"Make a bullseye, take a shot of vodka. I'll pay you a hundred bucks per bullseye."

She grinned. She never, ever drank, but she loved his idea of a game. "How much money did you bring?" The man laughed. "I'm serious. I wanna see the cash or no deal."

She realized the only flaw with this plan was that she would have to leave her bike and taxi home. Not her favorite decision. Who cared, though! She was out for fun. Fun, she would have.

She threw a bullseye, and he said, "That's one." And she drank a shot of vodka. She had forgotten what a terrible taste it would have. The burning down her throat stung her eyes. She felt the effects of the booze almost immediately. Such a lightweight, and well, she should have had dinner. She mentioned she had to pee, and went back and winked at the bartender on her way. He understood, and from then on, he gave her water poured from a vodka bottle.

"Two."

Drink.

She spun in a circle and shot another dart. "Three."

Drink.

"Four."

Drink.

She grinned; this was so easy. "Five."

Drink.

"Six."

She was drawing a small crowd now and the group was getting bigger.

"Seven."

Drink.

She winked playfully at the man who would be broke in a few more throws. "Eight."

Drink.

"Nine."

She slammed the shot on the table. "Last one boys!"

She tossed the dart and it hit smack in the middle.

The cheers were incredible, and she couldn't help but smile. The businessman pulled out his wallet and counted out ten hundred-dollar bills and handed them to her. Everyone was laughing and cheering. Except one man.

He was slowly clapping.

Long after everyone stopped, he kept clapping.

The bartender had cleverly cleared all the shot glasses and bottles already. So as far as Jasp could tell, nothing was in dispute. She turned to look at the man clapping, and recognized him.

There stood Chance Mickey Despoil. How could she ever forget him? In fact, she would pay to forget him. His brown hair was combed over where it had been falling out. He was still a little chunky, but she bet he was still quite strong. Her cheeks grew warm with anger.

"Slumming it, I see?"

It seemed unbelievable, but he was standing there in a cop uniform.

She wondered to herself who the hell would have made him a cop. She considered picking up a dart and slamming it into his eye. She said nothing; she didn't have to.

The men surrounding her, turned with venom.

"What the fuck, dude?"

"Leave her alone, she got ten bull's eyes in a row!"

"Hey now, what the hell is your problem?"

One by one they noticed he was a cop and grew silent. Chance stood there, ignoring them all, staring at the blue hair, and the short skirt. "You look damn nice."

She turned to the bartender. "I'm out; here's for my tab." And she pressed three hundred dollar bills into his hand. He nodded, and she turned, her long boots clicking on the floor.

Chance stood there, standing back, leering at her. He put his hand to his mouth, spreading two fingers across it, and stuck his tongue out, wiggling it up and down.

Jaspierre gagged. She walked out quickly. It didn't work, Chance followed close.

She walked toward her bike, and Chance pulled out his nightstick and shoved her with it.

"You seem a little too drunk to drive. You look like you might fall over and get a little bruised up any minute now. I should give you a ride home." He thrusted his hips when he said *ride,* and Jaspierre knew she was in serious shit. He shoved her harder with the end of his club, and she stumbled backwards. Her ass hit the dirt and fear rose within her.

She was uncertain what to do. Assaulting a cop would be a huge pain in the ass to fix. Of course, this was Chance. Here he was in his full glory. Who would believe her if she said a cop tried to rape her? Who would believe you if he did? If she hit him back, he might not tell.

She landed on the dirty gravel, scrambling backwards. He unzipped. He thought she was already beaten. But this would not be like the first time he tried this.

She lay back and pulled her skirt up a little, getting into position. "Good job, bitch. You are getting smart." He held his cock with one hand and the night stick in the other. "Fuck it off." He pressed the night stick on her head, pushing her face around as she sat there on the ground. "Take your pick: your nasty ass, your bitch tits, suck it. I don't care, fuck it." He pressed the nightstick into the back of her head, pushing her closer to his dick.

She pressed backwards and kicked her pointed boot directly into his balls. His squeal of pain was so cute. She hit him again as hard as she could, and he doubled over. She took his fallen nightstick and cracked it hard on his head, and he fell to the ground. She dropped the stick and spat on him. She got on her bike and rode away, flipping him off as she went. She drove fast. He was beaten, but not out. She was sure she would pay for what had happened. It wasn't long before the predictable sirens whistled behind her. She dropped down deep into town and parked in a parking garage. She waited. The sirens eventually came close, and whistled past. She was sure she had lost him. But it didn't matter. She left the bike parked and stuffed the wig in her purse, then she flagged down a cab and got herself dropped off on the wrong side of her property. Behind her grand home on one side of the wall was a trashy neighborhood. She trudged past the trailers, and then pushed vines and bushes away until she found her little gate. She unlocked it and slipped inside, pulling the brush back close. Then she locked the little gate.

Her house was still quite a walk, ten acres to walk across. She reminded herself she should park a bike near the gate to make it more pleasant. All that walking gave her a time to think.

She could hardly believe Chance was back in town. He was her never-ending nightmare. How the hell did he even get a cop badge?He was a scary man. Hell, she considered herself a terrible woman, but she was nothing compared to him.

She hated him more then she had ever loathed anyone. Almost. Almost anyone. She still disliked Mother more, even after all these years. She hoped Lucas was awake.

After about thirty minutes, she was near her house. Her aching feet trudged up the marble steps. She was tired. That was too much fun for one night. She tried to smile at her own joke. She locked the door behind her and set the security settings on full alert. They would stay on full alert until Chance was gone. Dead or gone; she didn't care.

She walked up the stairs. Lucas was standing in the hall leaning on the wall. "Oh! You're back." Before he said anything more, she was sobbing in his arms. He kissed down her neck and behind her ears, holding her steady with his firm arms.

She never knew how wonderful it could be to be held. Her whole body sobbed with sweet relief. She never knew. She had never been close with anyone. Her mother certainly had never held her. She had been alone for so long. So long. She said it before she could even stop herself. "I love you." She kissed him before he replied. She pressed her lips to his again, holding his mouth hostage with hers. He couldn't fathom what was happening, but he didn't care.

They parted and he slumped into the wall.

He was still weak. She led him to her bedroom. The sheets were clean and fresh, and she pulled Lucas down into her arms and they kissed again. His body demanded more, but he held back. "Are you okay, baby? What happened out there? Where is your wig? You have grass all over your boots."

She smiled. "You are so observant." She stood up and removed her boots and fishnets. Her legs were marked with x's all down them in little red lines. She dropped her skirt too, and was in soft white panties and her black low-cut top. "That stuff is making me crazy." He stared at her beautiful skin and patted the bed invitingly. "I saw Chance today. He... He is an old friend of mine. He tried to rape me."

"Has he done that before? Raped you?"

"Well, no no, I wouldn't say that. It was my fault. If I hadn't wanted to do it, I should have killed him. I mean, I should have known better. He's just um..." she said.

"It's not your fault." Lucas said, shocked. Why would she take the blame for something like that?

"No, it's not like, my fault. It's just that... Mother. Mother would never have allowed something like that to happen unless she wanted it. She was strong. She did whatever the hell she wanted. And I am just this weak loser who can't just kill someone and move on. I was supposed to kill you. You killed Rainbow; that was way worse than what Chance did. That's what any sane person would have done, and instead, I just kept you around." She bit her tongue, she was saying to much, being too emotional. "I... I shouldn't have said that earlier. I didn't mean it."

Lucas laughed. "That you love me?" He threw a pillow at her playfully. "Well then, I don't love you either! You beautiful, confusing, terrifying woman."

Jaspierre smiled and crawled back into bed. "Okay, fine, I might have meant it a little." She paused. "I have never been hugged like that in my entire life."

He kissed her. His body was hard and wanting against hers. A flash of fearful anger. She pulled back, and he bit her neck playfully. "Hey, baby, don't run away from me. It's okay. You are safe here."

"You'd say anything when you have a boner."

He blushed, and he whispered into her ear. "That's not true." He kissed her forehead and whispered in her other ear. "Don't listen to him; he wants you for your amazing body." He nibbled across under her chin, tickling her and making her squirm whispering into her ear once again, "I love you Jaspierre. I want to stay with you. I want to hold you. I love you, sweet dear."

She accepted and kissed him. She slid her

panties off, and wrapped her naked legs around him. He didn't tear his pants off and give it to her though. He kissed her and ran his fingers down over her. He held her ass, and squeezed it, whimpering at her. He slid his fingers down and touched her, until she couldn't help but cry out. He kissed her, and slid off his pants and pressed his flesh into hers. Her body was wet, and so ready.

There they lay, hearts pounding, two lonely bodies finding love for the first time. He kissed her, shifting, her whole body trembled with ecstasy. It didn't take long for them both to be crying out sweet sounds into each other's ears. She kissed him, and held him. Then he whispered into her ear, "Just let me love you."

She kissed behind his ear and whispered to him, "Lucas. I love you more than a little bit." He laughed. They snuggled up close for quite some time.

Eventually, he slept, but Jaspierre couldn't stop thinking about Chance.

CHAPTER

TWELVE

Russell woke up to the tiny alarm. He hadn't been fed in quite a while. He was hungry. Also, he stunk. He crapped in the corner because he didn't know what else to do. He was miserable.

His feet were swollen and red. His arm was oozing pus and blood. He took a little drink of water and turned off the alarm. Two more pills dropped down his throat. Pills didn't seem like a bad way to die. Either that or they would make him strong enough for whatever was next.

He rubbed his aching feet with his right hand. His left arm still seemed useless. It was so excruciating to move it, he stopped bothering to try. He set the little timer for his next dose in eight hours. He lay back down on the wet bed. Where had he gone wrong with his life? He regretted complaining asking her out. He curled up and closed his eyes and wished for sleep.

* * * * * * * * * * * *

Lucas stared at the woman sleeping next to him. This woman thought it was more sane to kill a person over a kitten than to let them live. What had she endured to mess her up so much? He kissed her and she awoke like magic. He said, "I think it's time for more meds..." He stopped as she sat on top of him. Her hands ran up his stomach and up to his chest, resting her palms on his nipples.

"I am sorry I stabbed you." She slid her hands to the wound, pressing. Only a tiny drop of pus pressed out; the rest was clear. "You, my dear, are looking much better. The infection has cleared out." She leaned forward and kissed him. "I'll go get your pills."

He held her hips firmly with his hands. "Two minutes?" he asked. She burst out laughing. It was such a new thing to have a lover. It was the most fun her little life had ever brought her. "I'll get it in one." She squealed playfully and squirmed, humping at him and giggling.

He stared at her and wished this moment would last. She climbed off him despite his protests. She was wearing only the now wrinkled black shirt, and he watched her ass as she walked off and got his medicine and water. When she came back, she was naked; pills in one hand, water in the other. He grinned at her. He took the pills. She climbed in between his legs and suckled him. He moaned and closed his eyes, lying back. When he opened them, he asked her to stop. Two large servals sat on the bed, menacingly staring. Ikali's teeth were bared.

"Oh, Tessa, Ikali! How could I have forgotten you!" Tessa hissed at her. "What is up with you guys!" Tessa refused to look over. Ikali's hair stood on end and he looked out the door. Jaspierre reached out and touched the cats, and they both hissed. She stood up and grabbed clothes from her closet; panties, pants, and a shirt. "Lucas, get dressed." Then she pulled out a sword from the bedpost.

She walked out of the room, sniffed into the hall, and looked around. She didn't see anything. She snuck down the hall farther, and looked into the grand hall entryway. She saw one of the lights was blinking on the alarm system. She turned and ran toward the pool, pausing at the doorway to listen.

She could hear splashing.

It was a big dog. It looked like a Great Dane to Jaspierre, but she wasn't sure. She had never seen one in person before. It was crawling around on the cargo net and appeared to be stuck. Both cats stood staring at the big dog on their toys, and their hair was on end. They both hissed in unison. Jaspierre was alarmed.

How did the dog get into her yard? How did he get on her property at all? Much less, in the outside pool, knowing, somehow to swim underneath the glass panel to the inside pool. It was wrong. *Wrong.* Paranoia sank in quickly. *It was too much like the dog knew. Or the dog was told. Is this dog from Chance?*

Jaspierre was standing there, sword drawn, frozen and waiting, deciding what to do next, when she heard a sound behind her. She spun around and pressed the blade against Lucas's chest. Then she lowered her weapon.

Lucas completely ignored the fact that he was nearly beheaded. "I didn't know you had a dog."

"I don't."

"Hmm." He stared at the scene, the two furious servals, and the one dog stuck in a cargo net. "So. You mind if I get him out?" He eyeballed her sword.

"I didn't know it was you. I thought it was an intruder," she replied. "I... yes, okay, get that stupid dog out of my pool."

She sat on a lawn chair, propping her feet up, holding the sword flat across her lap. She had thinking to do. How the hell did the dog get past her fence? It had a hot wire at both the top and the bottom. Barb wire at the top. The fence itself was rock and solid, except for four gates. One was the main gate, and the other three were hidden from the outside. All of the gates were padlocked.

She made a phone call. "This is Jaspierre,"

she said crisply, and waited while she was put on hold. Soon she was talking with the head of the company. "Your fence that you built me has a problem."

He sounded nervous; this was his biggest client on the phone. "Ma'am, that fence is as sturdy as they come. What appears to be the problem?"

"A dog got in."

"I will send a crew out in about thirty minutes to check the full length of the fence and do any maintenance."

With a click, her phone was off. She watched Lucas trying repeatedly to dislodge the dog from the netting. The pooch looked confused, but made no effort to growl or bare teeth. It seemed, though, as soon as he untangled one part of the dog, the stray tangled another. Jaspierre did not like dogs. They were so suspicious, tongues waggling. They had no depth. They were your friends no matter what. *That*, Jaspierre thought, *is the thing that bothers me the most*. It was too suspicious. Nobody loved you no matter what. Even her cats hissed at her this morning, to remind her.

Lucas fussed and laughed at the big mutt and kept petting him, and eventually he dislodged the soaking wet animal from the net. They both climbed out of the pool, and the dog shook, spraying water everywhere. He lumbered like a big dumb elephant, licking and fussing. He sniffed Jaspierre, and she hated him more.

"He has, a collar of sorts." Lucas stared at the knotted rope around his neck.

Jaspierre snorted. "Let's go put him in the animal barn. He doesn't belong in a house."

Lucas couldn't help but grin. "Can I keep him, Mom?"

She glared at him. "Don't be daft. I'd rather stab you with this blade than let you keep him."

He roared with laughter. "I'd rather stab *you* a few more times." He grabbed his crotch and winked, and Jaspierre smiled.

Lucas pulled the dog away from Jaspierre and whispered into the dog's ear, "She doesn't like you. I would not bug her. She has a sword."

Bells rang. Jaspierre was on her feet, and walked to the front door with her blade ready. She flipped open a panel and looked at the screen. There was someone at her door. She stared. It didn't look like Chance. Thank goodness for small miracles.

She pressed a button. "Who is this?"

The person looked around confused. "I am Jeff. I, uh, am with the lawn care company. We are here trimming bushes today, as we do once a month. I, uh, I need to talk with you."

She pressed another button and the door opened automatically. The first thing out the large, double doors was her blade. She pressed the tip against Jeff's throat. "Who sent you?"

"No, er. I-- I..." His shirt stuck to his skin from the sweat. "Nobody sent me. I just... I brought my dog today and I can't seem to find him."

"Lucas, bring this idiot's mutt." Lucas walked up with the dog and handed the tiny rope collar over to the man with the blade at his throat.

"Jasp, let him go..." Lucas saw the fire in her eyes and he backed down. He had no reason to get on her bad side. He stepped back inside and watched from the background.

"Your useless mutt interrupted my morning and broke into my house. He should be executed." Jaspierre raised the blade. Jeff froze, his eyes wide. "That said, Lucas has taken a liking to your ridiculously stupid dog. So I will let him live." She lowered the blade. "However, you are fired, your company is fired, and you will be hearing from my lawyers."

Flustered, Jeff said, "For what? Why?"

"For the damages to my pool, and because you should know better than to bring a freaking dog to my house."

The door clicked shut and Lucas smiled at Jaspierre. She didn't cut anyone this morning, and that seemed like a little miracle. "I'll start breakfast?"

Jaspierre nodded and was back on her phone. The calls were loud, and enthusiastic.

Lucas set to making a meal: delicious hash browns, eggs, sausage, biscuits.

"So, I have a question." Lucas looked up at her. "Are we gonna eat here, or is there a table?"

"Oh, uh, yes. There is a table," she said. "But, I mean, it's a tay-ble." She picked up the plate and her glass of juice. He followed behind with his own plate and cup. He didn't know what a tay-ble was, but he had a feeling it would be ridiculous.

And it was. The dining room was massive. The table was a giant crazy looped shape, like a long snake curling around in several directions. The table was delicate, yet solid wood. There was a built-in ornate table runner made of small wooden planks, each with an intricate carving on it. He estimated over a hundred people could sit at this long winding table. He pulled out a chair and sat down. She sat down far away at the other end.

"What? We won't sit by each other?"

She grinned and set the salt on the runner, and then pressed a switch. The table runner shifted and he realized it was a wooden conveyor belt. The salt circled around.

"Well, you didn't sit by the controls."

Lucas laughed. "You have the coolest things I have ever seen."

"I haven't been in here in years." Jaspierre looked around the crazy room.

*** TWENTY YEARS EARLIER ***

Jaspierre stood still with her hair in pigtails. She was wearing a floor-length dress. It was a lovely pink color and fit for a princess. Jaspierre had put on tiny, little, white high heels. She looked in the mirror. Her nanny stood there, fussing over her makeup.

"This is a big day for you. Seven years old."

Jaspierre didn't feel much like turning seven. "Is it time?" The nanny nodded.

She stood at the top of the marble stairs. The clapping started and soon it was a large whirlwind of applause. Jaspierre stood at the top, motionless and poised. Then as the cheering settled, she clicked down the stairs.

"Thank you everyone for coming," she said in a loud, steady tone. She smiled and waved at the crowd. "I do believe it is time for my birthday dinner. If you would all kindly follow me."

Everyone followed the child, and she sat at the head of the crazy, luxurious table. Jaspierre was tired of hosting parties. She wished, on this birthday of hers, her house was empty and she was alone.

Every seat was filled, and soon it was standing room only. There were only enough seats for the first two hundred guests. The table clicked to life, and food rode around the conveyor. The food always passed in front of Jaspierre before any other guests. She wondered where Mother was at. Probably kissing a gross man... or passed out drunk.

Jaspierre nibbled bread. After the first ten or so *happy birthdays* she was generally ignored. Guests spoke to each other. She was, of course, the only child at this party. She rang a little bell as the first round of food made it to the end of the table. Everyone settled in quietly.

She stood on her chair. "This year, I turn seven. I have been attending all of the board meetings, and I would like to thank each of you at our office for making it run so well. I appreciate how kind you all have been to me at my first year of running things without much of my mother's help." This was not strictly a company party, but she didn't care. She would say what she pleased. "I have big plans for this upcoming year, and I cannot wait. Seven will be one of the greatest years of my life." The crowd roared with applause.

"If anyone sees Mother, let her know I have a chair for her." She smiled wryly. The best way to get her mother's attention was always to make her a little bit angry. But not too angry. Jaspierre sat down pleasantly, smoothing her dress. She had wanted to dress more maturely, but her nanny said she made a better impression looking her age than looking like a high schooler. She tossed her little pigtails back and forth, and served herself potatoes and meat. The food crept by: rolls, meat, cheese, and fruit. She knew the food would be passing by for hours and hours. Desserts would be added to the lineup as soon as she was ready.

Cocktails too, spinning around the table. Jaspierre had tried one once, and the bitter taste was off-putting. She had no idea why grownups drank them so much. There was nothing pleasant about it.

Jaspierre always kept her eyes peeled for the gold-rimmed glasses. She had once told the bartender she had not had a single thing to drink for a party. She resented drinking water while everyone else drank something special. He said he would send out virgin drinks in gold-rimmed glasses, every tenth drink he made. Most of the guests had no idea and they would end up a little less drunk than they intended, but Jaspierre didn't care. Now she could sip delicious sweet punches with the adults, without that bitter, miserable taste ruining it all.

She lifted the gold-rimmed glass off the wooden conveyor belt, and sipped it. This was an orange and red swirled concoction. It tasted like strawberries and orange juice mixed with Sprite. The whipped cream and cherry were her favorite part. She took a sip, and random guests standing behind her shouted at her.

"You are only *seven*! No cocktails for you! What is wrong with you! Where is your mother!"

Jaspierre sat there, astonished as the woman ripped the glass from her hands. Jaspierre turned and glared. Hot anger flamed up inside her. She wanted this woman to die. It was *her* birthday. This was *her* party. She was feeding all these guests; she had planned the menu. She ran a whole company for an entire year! Who the hell was this stupid guest to tell her what she could and could not do? Before Jaspierre called security to send the guest packing, she saw the woman twist her head upwards and yelp.

Mother was here.

Jaspierre watched as her mother pulled the woman's hair down to her knees. The guest tumbled over backwards, yelping with pain. As soon as the woman was on the ground, Jaspierre's mother kicked her in the face. Then she walked over the lady's body while she moaned on the ground, her high heels piercing into her flesh. Mother sat at the chair next to Jaspierre. "Nasty whore should know better." She grabbed a glass off the conveyor belt that was orange and red and had whipped cream and a cherry. "Drink all you want, you little bitch."

She set the glass in front of Jaspierre, with its obvious lack of gold rim. Jaspierre knew her mother had no idea the gold-rimmed glasses had no alcohol. She surely would have fired everyone if she had found out. But, thankfully, Mother never paid much attention to anything anymore.

Jaspierre ate the cherry. "Thank you Mother. Having a good time?"

"What was all this bullshit about you looking for me?"

Jaspierre couldn't help but be pleased. "I *was* looking for you."

"Don't be silly. You weren't looking for me. You were schmoozing clients, or the board. You don't need me." Her dress was black, tight, and revealed most of her skin. She looked young and beautiful, but she was terrifying.

The woman on the ground behind them was ushered out and nobody spoke a word to Mother about it.

"Do you like the menu?" Jaspierre asked her mother. She had spent an entire week tasting dishes and picking cocktail combinations.

"The only amazing things in this room are me, that table, and you. The rest--the food, the décor, the guests-- are entirely forgettable." Her mother turned and smiled a sly smile. "I have a present for you."

Jaspierre tried to shake off the insult about the food. A present. It could be a trap, of course. Most birthdays, she got herself a present. This year though, she felt too old for presents, and instead gave money to the children's ward in the hospital.

"This year, you and I have great things planned! Seven is plenty old enough to think for yourself! Don't pretend I haven't noticed you are lonely, even with all these foolish guests you haven't scarcely spoken a word. So, this year, I have gotten you a kitten." She clapped her hands a butler showed up with a silver tray with a lid on it. Jaspierre was being served a kitten the same way she was served a boar's head.

Jaspierre lifted the lid and half expected the kitten to be fried with an apple in its mouth. If Mother had thought of that, she probably would have done it. But she hadn't, and her mother stood and clapped while the entire room joined in, clapping and whispering how beautiful it was.

The tiny kitten had big ears and spots and stripes. It didn't look quite like any kitten Jaspierre had seen before. She reached out to touch it, and the kitten hissed. The noise and being under a lid made the kitten uneasy. Jaspierre clamped the lid back on. "Just go put it in my room."

"Nonsense." Jaspierre's mother lifted the lid and snatched the kitten into the air. "This is a serval; she is a purebred, and one of the most expensive cats you can get. Twenty five thousand smackers. She will not go to your room."

The kitten meowed pitifully. Jaspierre took it from Mother's rough grip and held it. The kitten snuggled into her small arms.

Her mother continued, "She will make you a lot of money when she has kittens."

Jaspierre understood. This kitten would be put in the barn, not become a part of the family. *"No."* Jaspierre stood up. "I am seven now. I run the company, and I will keep my new kitten in my room."

She excused herself and went to her room with the kitten. She shoved the kitten deep into her closet, locking the door. Then she sat on her bed and waited.

Mother, predictably, came into her room moments later. She picked up her daughter and threw her into the wall. "Never disrespect me again." The scent of the bad drinks were on her breath.

"Mother. Hit me if you must. But if you ever hurt my kitten, I will kill you." Jaspierre's tiny angry eyes glared up at her mother in the tight black dress, and the painfully tall heels.

Mother smirked at the child. "You are seven, plenty big enough." Her mother proceeded to beat her until she bled. When her swings grew tired from the effort, she stood and straightened her dress, touched up her makeup and went back to the party. Jasp lay on the floor, curled up tightly, waiting for it to end. Then she dragged her aching, bloody body to the closet and opened the door. The kitten was tucked into the corner in the dark. Jaspierre trembled and crawled toward the kitten. It hissed at her. She held her hand out nervously, and the small kitten walked to Jaspierre and licked her, and sat with her and purred. The tired and beaten down child curled up with the kitten deep in her closet, too tired to even climb to her own bed five feet away.

"I am gonna name you the nicest happiest thing I can think of." Jaspierre kissed the kitten and whispered, "You will be Rainbow." She pulled the closet doors shut and they slept, hidden from Mother till morning.

CHAPTER

THIRTEEN

Lucas asked Jaspierre if she would show him how to feed Russell. She explained the controls and Lucas went down, clicking the serval's carved ear and darting down the dark stairs. Jaspierre stayed upstairs looking at her pool.

The pool was one of her favorite places. It was a difficult swim under the glass panel and through the pool to the outdoors. She had always thought it was an excellent escape route in case of fire, or if someone was chasing her. But not today. Today, it was much like she had created the perfect route for someone to sneak in and kill her. This had scared her too much.

Chance would do it. He would sneak in. It didn't matter if the fences were checked and fortified. It made no difference if it was a difficult swim. He would find a way in to rape her again, and possibly kill her. Chance was a dangerous man, especially now he was a cop, he had authority. He could find her when he pleased.

She stood there staring and tried to decide what to do. Close it off? Extend the glass to the floor? Add a secret panel? Replace it with bulletproof glass?

Closing it off was an issue, mostly because of the fluid dynamics to the pool. It would be a major redo to pipe around a solid wall. Of course, if it was a mesh wall, it would stop most anyone, and the water flow would be fine.

A mesh wall? How would she even make it secure? A padlock, she supposed. She was already tired of this nonsense. Surely there was a better way. Which type of war was she preparing for? Defend her home, or abandon it? Maybe she should just find Chance and attack him right now.

Both? Or all three. And Lucas. What was she supposed to do with him? Was he going to fight, or run? She realized it was time to make go bags. Weapons and clothing and wigs and whatever else they needed. Go bags. That was hardly all she needed to prepare. She grabbed her leather notebook and sat with her feet dangling in the water, writing lists for war. Chance was coming. He was going to break in and kill them. That was all Jaspierre could think about. That dog might not have been Chance, but the next person to break in *would* be Chance.

Lucas flicked on the lights and stared at the

massive control room. He sat down in her chair and slid around, running his fingers on each button and latch. Oh, and the sword. He wondered which lever it was. He tugged on one and it didn't budge. For all he knew, every knob was both a switch and a weapon. He looked for the button she had told him about. It was a black square button in the lower right console. When it was clicked on, it would turn red. Then all he would have to do was put his hand on the heat sensor. Red meant the heat sensors were active, and ready. So he clicked the square black button and it did, in fact, turn red. Now came the hard part.

Finding the sensor.

If he pressed his hand on the wrong spot, a different panel altogether would open. He needed the dumbwaiter. He had seen it so many times before. He would recognize the box, she promised. The wall was so seamless and smooth, he couldn't imagine he would find it. He went to the observation deck above the three rooms. It was such a strange thing to see Russell curled up on Lucas's own bed down there. Russell sat, as he had once sat, staring at his fingers, wondering how long he would be allowed to keep them. He was obviously in rough shape; pale and miserable. Lucas was watching his own captivity.

Lucas pressed his hand on the wall to the left of the window panel. Nothing happened. He rubbed his hands together and pressed a little lower. She had said that his hand would have to be motionless. He had to find the sensor and hold steady, or it wouldn't budge. Lucas had always thought it was fingerprint-activated, or perhaps even DNA-activated. It seemed funny to him it was simply a trick.

He pressed his hand into the wall again, a little higher. He waited, and wondered if he was even close. A half second before he moved, the door slid open. Without question, he knew it was the dumbwaiter. *Fuck you* was written in dried blood. Lucas found it surprising. Did Russell not understand his food was coming through here? Or that pissing off Jasp might mean his starvation? Russell seemed so angry. Lucas never had anger. He hated being in captivity, but most of the time, he agreed he deserved it. He did deserve it; he pressed that gas pedal and smashed her only friend. It started because he did it on purpose. He was a monster; he deserved no better than to lose ten years of his life in a prison.

Then there was that kitten. After his first murder, he took her tiny kitten and held it hostage and allowed it to have its furry little head cut from the tiny little innocent body. Accidental beheading. After all these years, Lucas still deserved anything he got. He was worse than her. She only seemed to kill when rage struck her, not because she could. He hadn't even been angry.

Rainbow, Katie, and that tiny kitten were all his fault.

She was as much a victim as he was. Sure, she didn't let him out of the room, but she also didn't hurt him, starve him, or torture him. Even the loss of his toes was his fault.

He shook off the memory and stared down at Russell. He was climbing out of the bed and backwards crab crawling, his left arm uselessly in his lap, over to the little dumbwaiter. Russell was different from him. It was obvious Russell had rage. He wanted to hurt her, not apologize. He would hurt her if he had the chance. This thought bothered Lucas so much.

He didn't speak to Russell, and he went back up to see what Jaspierre was working on. She was in the middle of writing in her notebook. He kissed her sweetly and asked her to come to bed. They went upstairs and took sweet solace in each other's sweet arms.

Lucas had made a mistake, though, as the black square button was still red.

CHAPTER

FOURTEEN

Russell miserably sat with his finished plate. The little panel with the food inside snapped shut as he had pulled the plate out. He looked around his prison. He was sitting next to where the dumbwaiter existed, though now it was a smooth wall. Shoving the bed closer to the food wall seemed like an excellent idea.

He stared at the smooth wall. There had to be a door. He saw blood smears on the wall. That must have been where he woke up with his toes missing. It was directly below the windows at the top where silhouettes sometimes appeared. At the moment, there was nobody.

He didn't know if he would ever be able to open it, but today seemed like a good day to try. The wallet, keys, panties, and the metal ring he tied around his waist and tucked in his pants. His feet hurt terribly, but he didn't feel like his spirit was as broken. He was gonna get out and make her pay. Hurt her if he got the chance. What kind of maniacal monster goes on a date with you, just to lock you up and cut off your toes! If only he'd listened to his dad, he could be coated in oil, working on cars instead of bagging groceries and meeting psychopaths.

He crab-crawled backwards, his left arm uselessly in his lap, to the wall under the windows. If only he could walk without that horrible burning pain running up through his body. He inched a little closer and rested, sitting with his back against the wall. Russell ran his right hand across the cold, smooth wall. Like glass almost. He pressed his feet tightly to the floor and slid his back up the wall. His weight on his feet, he paused, his hands spread out pressed against the wall. His left arm ached at the effort and it complained.

He stood there, panting for a few minutes. Then, he turned around. He let his bodyweight be held by his feet as he balanced himself with his fingertips against the wall. The pain wasn't so bad when he managed to keep everything next to his empty toe sockets off the floor, and all his weight off his left arm. He shuffled to the side gingerly. Exploring turned into a little walking lesson. He hit the wall on the right, and instead of turning down the next wall, he carefully spun around and went back.

He lost his balance on the way back and

yelped as pain crashed into his brain with such force that he lost his breath. His face pressed into the wall as he sobbed. Frozen in pain and sobbing with the agony, he didn't notice the door slid open. The pain was so intense, and the door was so quiet. He could now leave his room.

As the tears subsided, he opened his eyes. And then, he saw it. Freedom. He had no idea why the door had opened. He didn't care either, and he went into the hall. He hobbled and skip hopped as he tried to hurry without smashing his tender feet. In the hallway, he saw a smooth white walls, and a metal, spiral staircase leading to a solid wall.

He glanced around. There were probably lots of doors, hidden like his was. But the one at the top of the staircase seemed to be the most important. Up there was where the windows were. That was where she was. That was how she looked down on him. He painfully tried to climb the steps. He climbed one agonizing step at a time, pressing much of his weight into the railing with his right arm. His left arm clutched tightly to his chest; it was aching louder.

After a long while, he made it up the steps. He leaned against the door and listened. Nothing, no sounds. He waited, his ear pressed up close. His body ached, so he shifted to another spot, pressing his hand into the wall for balance. He heard nothing.

Helpless. He couldn't knock. She might hear him. He couldn't open the door; he couldn't even see the door. Frozen.

But he'd listen. Someone would come, someone like Lucas, and let him slip by. Adjusting himself against the wall, he listened. He continued for an hour and a half. Pressing his ear, shifting his weight, listening intently, and shifting his arms as they ached. He held his breath, eyes shut. It almost sounded like...

The door slid away and he fell into the room. He fell hard and instinctively tried to catch himself with his arms. His left arm smashed into the floor and it burst open. All ten stubby sores slammed into the polished floor. He crammed his hand into his mouth and stifled his scream. Wheezing from the uncontrollable pain he curled into a ball. Blood gushed from his ruined arm. He took a deep breath, and tried to hold in all the air. He begged his body to stop. *Just stop.* So close to escaping! *The pain must stop.* His body shook harder as he pressed his hand into his mouth tighter, stopping any sound from escaping. He lay there for fifteen minutes, then twenty, then an hour, until the pain became manageable.

He rolled over to his back and sat up, hugging his knees to his chest with his good arm. The left arm was useless. His missing toes dripped blood. He hugged himself one-handed, and tried to calm his screaming body. He looked around. It was dark. *Dammit.* The darkness was not his friend. After that white hall and the white room, his eyes felt like they would never adjust. Though they would. He sat there, curled up, and eventually, the pain tormenting his body slowed to a bearable throb.

He saw tiny lights, so he crawled backwards across the room. It was slow, with one arm useless. He bumped into a chair in the dark. It was a massive control panel. Who knew what it would control? He wasn't excited to touch any of the buttons. What if they released monsters on other victims?

Of course, one might be a light switch.

There might be one on a wall, though. He struggled with what to do next. He didn't want to tempt himself, and the only button he wanted to press was the one that let everyone go.

He crawled until his back bumped a wall. Flailing at it, he wondered if this was an excellent spot for a light switch. His hand grasped a strange corner. He blindly reached into the air with his good hand, and his hand rested on the bottom step. *Stairs.* He couldn't decide if he loved the stairs or hated the stairs. They were so hard to climb. But they might be a way out. He sat on one step and pressed with his right hand until he could lift his butt to the next one. Shifting up them backwards, painfully trying to spare his feet.

When he got to the top, it was another

dead end. He wondered if he could open this door by listening and staying still. He still wasn't sure how the other two doors let him go. It didn't appear anyone was opening them for him, though, since the control room was empty and dark. It also seemed like he was escaping. Behind the next door must be a trap; the moment he stepped through, death. But he had to try.

He stood up at the top, and he ran his right hand across the door and the walls. He found a small switch and he clicked it. The door swung and he was out of prison, and into... a library? *Oh yes. Her library.* He remembered her making him that drink. *That bitch.*

* * * * * * * * * * * *

There was a soft click at the front door, and Marcy came in. The alarm made a slight whoosh, and she hustled to click in her code. Why was it set on full alert? Jasp rarely had the alarm on full alert. She wanted to pretend it was a mistake, but experience told her Jaspierre did not make that kind of mistake. The young girl must be afraid. Of what?

She ruffled her gray hair with her hand. Jaspierre had been acting so strange these last few days. She did not like it. First off, who knew where she found that ridiculous man? Secondly, now she was on full alert. What kind of trouble was she in? Why didn't that naked guy have all his toes? Marcy locked the door from the inside with the key. She heard a light snoring noise upstairs, it would be best to start downstairs. Jasp was not normally home when she cleaned. Jaspierre went to work and stayed there all day and night it seemed.

The older woman walked to the kitchen. Of course now, with this new man, most of the dishes were washed instead of dirty. He must have taken over the cooking too, since there was at least four pans used. Jaspierre never was one to use pots and pans. She used the microwave or made a sandwich, and that was about it.

"That man with his junk hanging all over the place better be a good influence on her." She wiped down the cabinet. "At least she won't be so lonely!" Up went her hands. "Maybe she won't even stab me with a sword in the next few months." She grinned as she shined the next counter. "Of course, that's half the fun of the job! I wonder if that man's infection is better yet. And his toes! Lordy. His toes!"

Marcy finished with the counter tops, and unloaded and loaded the dishwasher. There were only a few dishes about. "Golly, if he keeps on a-cleanin' like this, I'm gonna end up outta a job. This kitchen only took me fifteen minutes. Fifteen!" Up went her hands. "He better not have vacuumed upstairs. Could you imagine!" She turned to go into the next room and let out a surprised scream.

The first thing she saw was missing toes. Stubby feet chopped off at the ends. They dripped blood and were raw and meaty. The white pants were smeared in blood and dirt. His shirt was wrinkled and the left half was soaked in blood. His left arm was bleeding still, with blood dripping off the shirt with a quiet plinking noise. His right arm held a sword.

He was wild eyed and panting. Marcy backed up, keeping her eyes on him, her hands in the air.

"Who are you?" His raspy voice trembled with anger. "You knew I was down there, and you did nothing. *You did **nothing!**"* His voice echoed through the quiet kitchen.

"Down where?" Marcy said, confused.

* * * * * * * * * * * *

Upstairs, Jaspierre stirred. The cats were both awake and their ears perked up. Ikali was on all fours, listening intently. He let out a hiss. Jaspierre stood up and grabbed her blade out of the bed. Something was up.

She clicked, and both cats followed her, downstairs, listening. Ikali stepped in front of her, sniffing and waiting impatiently. She stepped into the kitchen and saw Marcy. One eyeball was sliced and her mouth was cut straight across, her jaw hanging open. Blood was still pumping out of her. She had one other gash on her arm, and the sword still stuck in her like a pin in a pincushion.

She groaned when she saw Jaspierre.

Jaspierre grabbed her maid and held her. She was bleeding out faster than anyone could help her. Jaspierre tried to console the gray-haired woman. She made another noise, and then convulsed as she gushed blood. She died, choking on her blood as her lungs filled, her brain collapsing as it emptied.

Chance had broken in. Jaspierre's rage built into a whirlwind. "I decide who lives and dies. Not Chance. I will avenge you, Marcy," she whispered and turned, frantically looking around for the madman cop.

Uncontrollable fear pulsed with her heartbeat. Marcy was killed moments from where her family slept; Lucas, and her kitties. She called her cats, and they stood by her side. She fled upstairs, locking the four of them in the bedroom. "Lucas, Lucas!" She shook him awake, "Lucas. He is here."

* * * * * * * * * * * *

Russell crawled back over from his hiding spot. The front door was locked; he needed a key. He rummaged through Marcy's blood-soaked body and found a set of keys in her pocket. Stealing the keys he tied them to his drawstrings at his waist. Exhausted, his body hurt everywhere. His brain was sluggish. *Hide.* His brain ached. *Run.* Pain dulled him. He unlocked the front door once he found the key, and then he shut it, and relocked it. Under a bush pressed against the house, he hid and fell asleep.

*** FOUR YEARS EARLIER ***

Jaspierre stood in her newly built control room. She liked this much better. Now she had a maze for her cats to play in, and she had fortified and improved Lucas's room quite a bit. She added many dumbwaiters and the hidden doors. She hired Italian engineers to do all the work. They made her the most seamless, gorgeous, perfect walls. Their team developed the maze for her experiments. They never asked many questions about why she wanted such an elaborate, detailed project. But she paid them for their talents, and sent them back to Italy.

For one short week, she moved Lucas upstairs into her closet. It was interesting that, as a gorgeous twenty-three-year-old woman, the first man to stay a week in her bedroom was her hostage. She tied him to a ring on the wall with the chains her mother used to use. It was a strange thing to have a man so close. She barely spoke to him, though, he didn't speak to her much either. Until one day when she got home early and he was singing a song. She opened the closet and looked in on him, and he stopped and blushed.

"My apologies. I didn't know you were home."

"Oh, yes. I am. Your room is almost ready."

"Do I get a view now?" She shook her head.

"I figured as much," he said.

"Sorry," she said, and somehow they both almost believed her.

"Can I ask you something?"

"Sure, go ahead."

"Is there a way I could trade you for my freedom? A test? Is there anything I can do?"

"Like what?"

He sighed with relief; she didn't say no. She might even say yes. "Well, I was thinking we could bet on things, and if I win, I get to leave. And if you win, you... could...have one of my digits. Toes first, of course, I'd get to pick which one I am betting."

"I get your digit? Like... get it how?"

"Well, I dunno. Cut it off, I guess is what I mean. I have nothing else to trade with you. You love to experiment. I thought this might be fun for you."

She closed the closet door.

Lucas woke up in his room. Everything looked different and the same all at once. The rings in the wall still hung in pairs up the wall like a ladder. But the other walls were a new, smooth, shiny, and cold material. Her observation window was bigger, and grander. He had a new bed, much nicer than the wobbly old tiny cot he had been sleeping on. He looked under the bed, and his razor was gone. Jaspierre was standing overhead.

"Okay, first wager. You have one hour to find your bathroom. You find it, and you are free. You don't find it, I get a digit. Start thinking of your least favorite. No guesses. You either find it or you don't."

He didn't know what to think. He had never had a bathroom before. Mostly an awkward bucket system, of course. Finding a toilet meant finding his freedom.

He looked under the bed and around the room. The walls were white and blank. There was nothing. He was puzzled.

He climbed the rings to the top and looked at Jasp. She smiled and waved. He did not see any bathrooms. He climbed back down. He ran his hands along the walls; they were so smooth. His fingertips didn't find anything else. "Hot or cold?"

She roared with laughter. "I am not gonna help. I like having you here."

Examining the floor and the walls, he searched. He pressed his ear to the walls, and he didn't hear anything in them. He climbed the rings again and looked at the girl. "Come now; you don't wanna chop off my pretty toe. Give me a hint."

She flashed him a sweet smile and shook her head. He was so cute.

Sixty minutes came and went faster than Lucas would have liked. This game was so rigged. It was pleasant to have something to do. But it was unpleasant to have his toe on the line so to speak. He knew he could live without a few toes at least. Nineteen more guesses to freedom at least.

She told him he was out of time, and he climbed up the rings and looked at her again. "Try not to kill me when you take it, okay?" He flashed his smile and winked at her.

"Well, not tonight, but in a few days. I don't have... a way to remove it right now." Generally speaking, she wasn't looking forward to it. But it was part of the game, and the game was quite fun.

"Can I know where the bathroom is?" Lucas grinned at her playfully.

She laughed. After the flick of a button, the wall panel slid over and a tiny toilet and sink were there. The toilet and sink were both facing outward, so his legs dangled into the room if he sat. And he would stand in his bedroom to wash his hands at the sink. He could see a little package with a bow on it.

"How, how... that wall was smooth! I don't know how you did that. Magic, must be magic."

He looked at her. "Thank you. Then he blew her a kiss, climbing down the rings. He paused a few rings down. "Hey Jasp? How would I open it if I would like to use it when you aren't here?"

"Oh yes." The door snapped shut, and she pressed a button. A little red light was visible from behind the white wall. Just a faint glow. "Hold your hand there for fifteen seconds. That light is only going to last for two minutes, so don't forget where it is."

He scrambled down the ring wall. Losing his toes was part of the plan. The plan to escape. Plus, he now had a bathroom! And to top it off, she was smiling at him occasionally. So if he kept flirting, she'd keep smiling and let him go. She would treat him better if she liked him a little. It was a long-term kind of game plan. Plus, frankly, sitting around bored half to death for the last six years hadn't gotten him anywhere.

He pressed his hand on the light and tried to memorize the spot. The door popped back open in about sixty seconds. The hand print area was exactly as high as his nipple. Finding it vertically wasn't going to be an issue. However, finding it horizontally would be annoying. He paced the wall. Four steps. His room was nine steps long, four of them to the bathroom door switch. He opened the little box with a bow on it and found a new electric razor. *Nice*. He was so pleased with himself.

He marked the second toe on his left foot, right next to the pinky toe. So long, toe.

A few days later when he woke up and his toe was missing, he regretted everything. He sobbed at his deformed foot. The sheer agony to move about horrified him. He curled up into a pit of despair on his bed and kept thinking, *What did I get myself into?* For her part, Jaspierre did not enjoy it much either. Chopping off a toe was bloody, irritating work.

Neither of them spoke about making another wager for several months.

CHAPTER

FIFTEEN

Jaspierre took Lucas's hands and pulled him close. "He might still be in the house. He killed Marcy. It is time to fight. First, I will put you somewhere safe."

"Jaspierre, no, please, I want to help," he said, terrified she'd try to lock him up.

"He might *kill* you!"

"*You* might kill me *too*!" He grinned, and he pulled a sword out of the carving on the bed. "I'm coming."

She smiled. "Okay. But the cats have got to be safe."

"Absolutely, I agree. What is the plan?"

"Well, I guess... I guess we can leave them in here." She pulled out another blade from the bed. "Trade, though, I like that one better."

"Okay." They switched blades and locked the door behind them. They moved through the house silently, searching and looking.

Eventually, they made it to the kitchen. Lucas saw Marcy with her mouth sliced and her jaw hanging, and he retched before he warned his feet to move out of the way. He held back a sob. That sweet, chatty woman did not deserve this. There was blood smeared in the office, where the fight started, and ended in the kitchen. They didn't bother to check on Russell. They had bigger things to do.

The house was clear. They sat by the pool.

"I have been thinking, and I have a plan. Since he isn't here, I know where he is. He is taunting me, that nasty bastard. He breaks in to leave me a warning. So I am gonna go kill him. I'm sure he is waiting for me."

Lucas wasn't sure what to say.

"I am gonna need you to be my alibi, but it's difficult because you can't exist. But, I have these two cars. So, you are gonna be me. I have wigs, a dress, and the whole bit."

Lucas stared at her in disbelief.

"You are going to be me, and have my car and provide me an alibi. I was thinking like, driving around going to fast food joints, so you have receipts and are on traffic cameras and everything."

"Dressed like you, looking like a girl?"

"Yes."

"Aren't you afraid I will run away?"

She looked at him and smiled. "Nope."

"And while, I drive around and get a ridiculous amount of crappy food, you are going to be fighting for your life?"

"No. Not at all. I will kill him."

"How will you even know where he is?"

"I know he will be waiting where he... well, I know where. I am sure of it. Should have killed him years ago."

She stood as though that was enough to settle it all. "I'll go get the cars. You go find a dress, I guess."

Lucas couldn't find any words to respond. This was a horrible idea. But he knew he didn't have a vote.

She drove the first Lexus and parked it in front of the house, and then she drove the second one up to the front of the house. Russell woke up from the racket and stared at the two shiny black vehicles. She took the keys inside with her, though, and he waited. He could hitch a ride out of hell.

Why two cars? What the hell was happening? It was smart to wait. Hopefully, everyone was leaving and he could go back inside and find a phone, or if he had a chance, he would take the car. Walking out wasn't an option; his feet and arm hurt even more after he slept. Extremely weary, he waited.

Lucas was standing at the top of the stairs by her room. "I didn't want to let the cats out unless you were ready," he explained, while he stood there.

Jaspierre smiled and unlocked the door, letting the cats run free. Jasp and Lucas went into her room and into her closet. She picked a long-sleeved maxi dress, bright red. It had a high neckline. She pulled out a bra too, and the long, brown wig curled perfectly. She couldn't give him shoes, since his giant man feet were way bigger than hers. Then she pulled out a sparkly, large purse. She grabbed massive earrings and huge sunglasses.

"Well, hopefully, this will do." She went far into the back of the closet and came back with a pile of money. "Here is my credit card; you"ll have to practice signing like me of course. Cash too, but I mean, the cash is for places that don't take credit cards." She stuffed it all in the purse. Then she grabbed a backpack and picked a few blades to put in it, a taser, and a gun. "This is for me."

"I realized, before we get ready, we should take care of Marcy," she said. Neither of them looked like they wanted to do that task. "I'll go put this in the car. You can start dragging her to the fireplace."

She carried the bag outside and stood looking at both cars. "Hmm. Which one?" She looked at them and said, "Okay, well, this one for Lucas." She dropped the purse on the passenger seat. "I guess that means you are mine." She dropped the backpack on the other passenger seat. She walked to the back of Lucas's car and pressed a hidden button underneath the license plate. The plate now said XXX.

She went to her car and pressed the license plate on hers, and the plate now changed one letter or number every three minutes. She went back in the house to help build the fire.

* * * * * * * * * * * *

Russell made a decision. He watched her, and listened. *Lucas on the left. Lucas on the left.* He whispered to himself over and over. *Lucas on the left.* Lucas, the one who promised. He stood, light headed, and lumbered over to the two cars and he was about to get in the trunk of Lucas's car, when he had an idea. He popped the hood on Jaspierre's car. Hell, this plan would get him killed, but it would all be worth it if he survived.

He reached into the car and looked for the hoses. His father was a mechanic, so he knew what to look for. He pulled on the brake lines and one freed a little. Then, for a little extra insurance, he opened the car door and shifted the floor mat up a tiny bit, so it was barely on the gas pedal. Then he shut the door and hood of the car. He rushed back to his bush. That small amount of effort, getting up and opening and closing everything made him terribly exhausted. His left arm and his toes were bleeding and he found he was half-asleep again.

* * * * * * * * * * * *

Lucas said to her, "How did you know to burn Katie?"

Jaspierre looked at him with a confused expression. "What did you do with the bodies at your house growing up?" There was a long silence between them and he never did reply. They cleaned the kitchen with bleach while Marcy seared.

Once finished, they showered together. Jaspierre toweled off and turned to Lucas. "Well, time for your makeover."

Lucas pulled the bra on, and Jaspierre helped stuff it with tissues. Then they pulled the red dress on his thin body. He was quite taller than she was, and the dress fit oddly loose, but short. "Thankfully, nobody will see your legs."

"So, am I still gonna blow up?"

She grinned. "No, not at all." She took the ankle monitor off his ankle with the special screwdriver. "Just to be clear, you still have a tracking device in your back." He rolled his eyes.

She put dark maroon lipstick on his lips and kissed them as she finished. She helped him with the waist-long hair, and shook her head when it looked so much shorter on him. "I feel like you are part giant."

He stood in the blood-colored dress, makeup, and pink sparkly sunglasses, and he looked at himself in the mirror. It was a strange thing to trade out wearing white scrubs every single day for a dress.

He barely looked anything like her. But it would have to do.

"Now, the car has a push start and it's fancy, but I'm sure you'll remember how it all goes." She stood there, having changed into black leather pants, and a black leather vest over a tight green shirt. She was wearing green army boots.

"Aww, why do you get to wear all that fun stuff!" Lucas stared at her; she had a brown, long wig, and her lips were faint red from their kiss.

"I guess it is time."

"Wait," Lucas called her. "Jasp, I... what do I do if you don't come back?"

She turned back to him. "I will be coming back. If I don't, then take care of Ikali and Tessa. You go first; I have to grab a few more things. I will see you in four hours. Try to enjoy the drive, and well, the food too, I guess."

Lucas came out and got into his Lexus. He adjusted the seat for his long frame. This plan was total crap. He was thinking about how to push start the car. If he remembered right, he would have to put it in neutral, get it moving, then hop in, shut the door, and turn the key. He tried to put the key in, but all she had handed him was this bulky keychain. On the dashboard was a button that said start. *Oh, push start.* He pressed the start button and the car purred. He shut the door.

The door shutting woke Russell from his nap. He saw her brown hair in the car. *Shit shit shit shit shit.* He stared at the woman as she pulled out of the driveway, the sparkling pink sunglasses flickering light at his eyes. The second the car slithered out of sight, he dashed forward as fast as he could, and opened the car door, pressed the trunk button, and climbed into the trunk, pulling it shut.

Jaspierre fed the cats and kissed them both goodbye. She hoped she would see them again soon. Then she stepped out into the sunlight and got into the Lexus. She did not notice the tiny drips of brake fluid as she drove off to avenge Marcy.

Lucas drove for a full twenty minutes until he found the large town she had told him about. Lots of drive-thrus; take your pick: McDonalds, Arbys, Taco Bell. A dessert from each of them, for starters. Parking for a moment, he signed her name twenty-five times until it felt a little bit more natural. Then he got himself a milkshake at Arbys. It tasted so much sweeter than he remembered they would taste. He turned on the radio and realized he didn't know a single song. The sweet frozen milk cooled his throat as he drove, listening to the songs washing over him. He drove down streets and alleys and up hills. Tears ran when he saw children skipping rope.

The scent of grass clippings overwhelmed him. It was so terrifying to be out on his own. He couldn't decide if he was happy or sad. Sad for the years lost. Happy for the simple sweetness of having freedom. In all the time he drove, he never even once considered leaving Jasp for good.

Jaspierre drove an entirely different direction; she drove through the smaller town where she had picked up Russell. By the time she was about halfway there, she knew something was wrong with the car.

JASPIERRE

CHAPTER

SIXTEEN

Jaspierre's nose was bleeding. Her head was aching. The police car she had stolen had a lot of buttons, but it was labeled. It was also filthy. Porn magazines littered the floor.

She still couldn't believe her Lexus had accelerated like that. Chance must have done it. How could he have known which cars she would take? *Crap*. She'd have to get all her cars checked. So fucking irritating. How did he do that and still meet her at the lake?

Why hadn't she killed him! Yes, she had just smashed her car into a lake, and yes, she wasn't thinking clearly. But the whole point of this escapade was to murder him. Why hadn't she done it? She knew why. Killing Katie had messed her up. She wasn't like Mother, she couldn't handle it. She didn't really want to murder her childhood friend. Slaughtering people was horrible.

She flipped on the sirens and drove away faster. Cop cars were still flowing to the lake. Ditch this car soon. She tore off her wig and shoved it in her backpack. Up ahead, a green car pulled over to the right after seeing her lights flickering. She pulled in behind them and rummaged in the glove box and behind the seat. *Chance was such a bastard.* Behind a dildo in the glove box was a handgun with an ammo drum connected to it. Two extra drums sat underneath the gun. Everything was fully loaded. Under the seat sat a sawed-off rifle. She popped the trunk. It held a big container of zip-ties, a rocket launcher, four machine guns, and several bags of ammunition. She took the rocket launcher, and the only machine gun with ammo drums. She grabbed the duffel bag full of ammunition and rockets. Now she was set. Her backpack was slung on her back, a machine gun over her right shoulder, a rocket launcher on the other one, in her right hand was the handgun, and the other hand had the duffel bag. She had to tie her purse to her waist. She stepped out from behind the police vehicle and walked up to the driver in the car.

"Get out of the fucking car."

The little old lady climbed out and didn't say a word, pale and worried looking. Jaspierre zip-tied her hands together. Then Jaspierre dropped the duffel bag in the passenger seat, and set the rocket launcher and machine gun down. She pointed the handgun at the lady the entire time. She turned to the small woman and said, "Get in the back of the cop car. I'm sure they'll find you eventually." The woman obediently climbed in. She looked so relieved. Jasp turned off the lights and sirens and drove into the woods a little ways.

She walked back to the little lady's car and put the handgun on top of the pile of guns in the passenger seat. Then she drove away. Her nose had stopped bleeding, but the cut on her forehead was still dripping.

* * * * * * * * * * * *

Chance stood up. His car was gone. He heard sirens of more cops coming his way. Humiliating. His arm was throbbing where the little window hammer had slammed into it.

"Dammit, dammit dammit." He slammed his fist into the ground and he stood up. Should he go hide? He sure as hell didn't want anyone to know she had taken his car and hit him with a tiny hammer. "That bitch. That dirty bitch."

He stood and he saw a flicker from the car. The trunk pushed open a little further. Someone was in the trunk.

"Hey someone in there? I'm a cop. Come on out," Chance said.

The trunk creaked apart, and out stepped a bloody, wet Russell. He slowly and painfully climbed out of the trunk of the car. Chance couldn't help but smile. What the hell kind of present was this? He admired the man's missing toes, the broken and bleeding arm. This was too sweet of a gift to follow protocol.

The sirens squealed close now. *Better hustle.*

"Hey, what happened to you? What's your name, kid?" He grabbed the man's good arm and helped walk him to the shore. "Come on; let's go get you help."

"Russell." He could barely eek it out, he was so choked with emotion.

Russell sobbed with relief. A cop, somebody to help him. He couldn't even find words yet to explain what had happened to him. Tears fell from Russell's face as he mindlessly let himself be led by the other man. They walked together through the woods a little way, and they both heard the cops getting out of the car at the lake.

Chance drew a knife and pressed it into Russell's throat. "If you make a sound, you will die." He twisted Russell's right arm behind his back and kept the knife at his throat, and they walked silently through the woods, farther and farther from any real assistance. Russell was too weary to even try to resist.

Russell tried to think of something to say or do. He tried to imagine himself running away.

Tears kept trickling down his face as they walked. He was so tired. She controlled the cops, as far as he knew. He figured he would wake up back in her basement cell. Parts chopped off; his nose, his ears, who knew? His feet were bleeding terribly now, and he shuffled, limping in pain. The knife tightened at his throat, and he didn't even care anymore. Death might as well come. Captivity did not suit him. He stumbled hard and fell.

Chance awkwardly caught him. He realized this man he was dragging along had little left in him. Chance's own arm was bleeding rather profusely, and the steady ache was quite impossible to ignore. As Chance was starting to regret taking Russell into the woods, he saw a little bit of magic right before his eyes.

His god-damned cop car. He grinned like a fool, dragging along the miserable weak man at a brisk pace. *Fucking hell.* He stopped. What if she was in it? Was this a set-up? Russell collapsed. Chance hustled behind a tree and watched everything. He didn't see her anywhere. Nothing suspicious. He walked up to the car. Did she ditch it?

As he got up close, he saw a little old lady sleeping in the back seat. What the hell? He debated what he would do with her, but all in all, he knew in his heart what to do with her. He dragged Russell who was now out cold to the car, his bleeding, weeping feet banged against sticks and dirt as Chance pulled him along. He opened the door to the back seat and shoved the man on top of the little lady. She screamed. He shut the door and looked at the car. No keys in the front seat. No problem, though. He reached underneath and found his magnet key stuck to the wheel well where it always was.

He got in the car, and the old lady kept screaming. It was a good sign; he liked a woman with a little fight in her. It was convenient the more he thought about it. He could take his time with her, and Jaspierre would be to blame.

He pressed the button and closed the glass window between the front and the back seats, muffling the woman's screaming. Before he drove off, he radioed the station and let them know the girl who crashed into the lake got a ride home and she was fine. He popped on his lights, turned up the radio, and drove to his cabin.

* * * * * * * * * * * *

Jaspierre drove the green car down the road, trying not to draw attention to herself. She still had two hours left before she and Lucas would meet up. She glanced at the gas gauge; it was full. *Good. Nothing to fuss with there.* She drove away from everything and tried to clear her head. Her car was wrecked and sitting in that lake. Chance was one step ahead. She should have paused and killed him instead of driving off in that cop car. *What the hell will I do next?*

Mindlessly, she turned onto the highway and set the cruise control for fifty-five miles per hour. Getting pulled over was *not* on the agenda. She glanced at the large pile of bullets and guns on the seat. It seemed absurd to her. She had hardly even seen a gun in person before today, and now she had enough for her own goddamn army. Chance, though, had proven he wasn't just a sick pervert, but he was dangerous. *Seriously dangerous.* Why else would he have so many guns? She thought it would be easy to eviscerate him, but now she wasn't so sure.

The four-lane highway merged into a small two-lane road. She kept driving down the empty road. How the hell was she going to kill him now? Her face was flushed and anger was starting to build. She hadn't factored explosives and bullets into the equation; every altercation with him so far hadn't involved either. A few minutes later, a yellow sports car, clipping along at a fast pace caught up to her. Two yellow lines stood on their left. The young man in the car swerved back and forth behind her, peeking around to see if he could pass. There was now, of course, oncoming traffic. The road was always clear unless some asshole was trying to pass illegally. He swerved back behind her, pressing his nose into her car's ass as far as he could without clipping it. Jaspierre rolled her eyes. *What the fuck.* The last thing she felt like dealing with was an asshole on the road.

The hairs on her neck rose and she clenched the wheel tighter. *Don't do anything stupid,* she tried to convince herself.

The road curved up ahead, and as she turned, he swerved again, looking for a way to go around. He nearly smashed into a semi-truck coming the other direction. He veered back, over-correcting and skidding on the gravel. *Fucker.* Then he honked at her as if it was *her* fault the speed limit existed. She slowed down, and he honked again, swerving his car back and forth, tailing her, peeking around her car so he could pass on the double yellow as soon as he found room. *Fuck this shit.* She cracked; she never had learned to manage her rage. She saw nobody was coming at them for a while, so she turned her car hard to the left and slammed on the brakes. Her car skidded sideways and she prepared for his impact. He managed to stop in the nick of time, and the nose of his car was inches from her back door when they both squealed to a stop. Honking repeatedly, he opened his car door. He screamed profanities.

Jaspierre picked up the rocket launcher and stepped out of her car, pressing it tight to her shoulder. Without hesitating, she pulled the trigger, but the safety was on. He stared for a moment, and then slammed his car door shut, frantically trying to get into reverse. She looked at the gun and grinned. *Ah, so easy, right at her thumb.* Pressed the little switch and braced herself. The shot went right into the hood of his car as it started to back up. She would have flipped that irritating fucker off, but her ears and shoulder ached from the noisy gun. She set the rocket launcher back on the passenger seat, closed the door, and drove off. *That was a stupid idea, Jasp. So fricking stupid.*

Jaspierre skittered down the road in the green car. She couldn't help but smile. She didn't hear sirens. She would be long gone before any cops or ambulances showed up. Her shoulder ached from the kickback of the rocket gun. Her ears were ringing. But still she smiled. She could defeat Chance. She was untouchable.

CHAPTER

SEVENTEEN

Jaspierre dropped the lady's car off in the trashy neighborhood. She left it a fair six blocks from her secret fence gate. She took the guns and her belongings and left the keys on the seat with the window down. Hardly a block later, she heard it start up. She had tried to wipe her prints as best as she could, but, the best kinds of alibis were things like other people stripping and selling the vehicle.

At the gate, she was pleased to see it was locked. She unlocked it and then slipped through, locking it back up. The guns were heavy, but an ambush could be waiting at the house. So she trudged them along with her. She saw smoke pouring out the chimney and worried. But then she remembered. Sweet Marcy, burning in the fireplace. She trudged slower and sadder. She felt tired.

Lucas was watching the clock. It was time

to drive back. The car had a navigating computer in the dash. He wasn't sure he would be able to find the place without it. He pressed buttons, and thankfully home was a few clicks away. Soon he was listening to the sweet voice of a cute girl telling him to turn right and left, and stay on the road.

He turned down the radio and drove with silence, except for the sweet lady's voice in the computer. Admiring the houses as he passed them, he drove up to the fence. *The cat.* His memory demanded his attention. He slowed down considerably. Who knew where Ikali and Tessa might be? He slowed the car to a creeping pace, he felt so terrified. Heart pounding, he wanted to leap out of the car and run. His shirt grew sticky with sweat; all he could envision was her cats leaping out. *Thump, thump.* The crush of its body under the wheels. He stopped, closed his eyes and took a deep breath. *It is gonna be okay. Calm down.* He took another deep breath to slow his heart. Then he continued.

He got to the gate and wondered if he would have to get out and coax it apart. But as if by magic it swung open. It was so much more majestic than he had remembered. Elegantly sculptured bushes, the grand marble staircase. He stopped the car in front of the stairs. He got out and gathered up the last milkshake and the small bag of trash. He stared at the barn down the worn little path. What was in there exactly?

*** TWENTY TWO YEARS EARLIER ***

Jaspierre's hair was yanked and she tried to sit up before Mother lifted her from her bed by her hair.

"Wake up." It was a command by a terrifying woman to a little five-year-old child.

Jaspierre held back the urge to cry. Crying made it worse. "Yes Mother?"

"You need to come to the barn."

Jaspierre had never been in the barn before, but she never asked questions. "Okay." Mother let go of her hair, and she caught herself with her feet.

Jasp slipped on her boots and a coat-- it was a cold night-- while her mother stood there glaring. "Are you ready?"

She nodded and hustled and they walked out into the dark. Her mother took her hand and they walked along together. "You are five years old. When I was five, I was already running my own experiments. I'm afraid you are already sorely behind. I doubt you will ever be able to catch up."

She continued, "What kind of mother would I be if I didn't push you to become who you are? You are Jaspierre Kyller. One of a kind. Brilliant. You will be pushed to your limits in the next few years. So much to learn still. So much. But you are beginning. And you have taken no initiative!" Her voice grew sharp, and her grip on her daughter's hand grew painfully tight.

"Yes, Mother. I can do better. I will do better." Her voice was determined.

"Good." The angry grip relaxed a little and then dropped the small hand. Mother pushed the button and two large barn doors swung open. Inside, the lights brightened and she saw cages after cages. Big animals and small. The barn was so much bigger than she could have guessed.

They walked down the line and she saw rabbits, birds, rodents, and every farm animal she could name. Many she couldn't name. They were each in tiny wire boxes, crammed together. Food conveyor in front of them, poo conveyor behind them. In a small, horrified way, Jaspierre thought it was like the table for the parties. Except poo didn't conveyor out from behind the guests. *Thank God.*

"Pick something."

Jaspierre looked around and saw a nice little rabbit. It had black spots on its nose like a little mustache. "This one." She pointed and smiled.

Mother opened the cage and pulled out the rabbit. Jaspierre stepped close and reached for it.

"This isn't a pet, you dumb little thing." Mother snapped at Jaspierre and shook the rabbit.

It let out a terrible scream. "You have made an excellent choice."

"Pick a leg." Jaspierre stood still. She didn't like it one bit.

"Pick now." Mother's voice grew stern and angrier. She shook the rabbit harder, making it scream louder. "**Pick the fucking leg!**"

Jaspierre's tears welled up in her eyes. "The black one," she said.

"Haha, the black one. Let's go." They walked down the hall farther into the back room. The room looked like a hospital, with a flat stainless steel table in the middle of it, and bright lights up above. Jaspierre stood hesitantly at the door of the room, while Mother set the rabbit on the table and opened up a drawer. She pulled out a syringe and stabbed the rabbit, and soon the rabbit fell asleep on the table. Mother pulled out another drawer and set metal utensils on the stand lined with pink paper.

She turned and saw Jaspierre standing so far away. "What do you think you are going to learn standing way the hell over there? Come on; you can't even see anything."

Jaspierre nervously walked closer. "Fuck dammit, I forgot to wash up." Mother dropped the utensils and walked to the sink. "You too, you dumb little twit."

Jaspierre washed her hands along with her mother. They both took their time, Mother to be thorough, but Jasp was trying to stall whatever was about to happen next.

"Let me get him," Mother said and darted out of the room.

Jaspierre waited with the sleeping rabbit. She didn't pet it. She tried not to look at it. Mother wheeled in a little cage with a blanket over it. There were tubes coming out of the cage and hooked to bags of liquid.

"Well now, let's get started." Mother sliced through the skin all the way around the front right leg of the rabbit. Jaspierre gagged and looked away. "Come hold the light. You don't want her to die, do you? Hand me the clamp. No, not that one. The goddamn clamp." Jaspierre cringed and handed her mother the tool she was screaming about. She kept closing her eyes so she wouldn't see as her mother snipped through layer after layer until she found the bone, and after about an hour, the leg was cut off the rabbit.

Jaspierre's stomach lurched. She was relieved they were done. She asked her first question. "Are we going to stitch him up?"

Mother chuckled. "Are we gonna stitch him up?" she parroted back. Jaspierre, embarrassed and said nothing.

She left the rabbit with its leg socket clamped. She lifted the cover on the other cage and Jaspierre let out a terrified scream. The animal underneath was horrible; it let out a tiny cry.

"Jaspierre you shut your fucking mouth. Can't you see you scared it?" She motioned Jaspierre to come closer.

Jaspierre's lower lip start to tremble. Her stomach hurt. "What is it?"

"Oh, a little of this, a little of that." Mother was all smiles. This was her masterpiece. "However, the front leg is dying."

Jaspierre cringed and looked away again. She knew her mother would be so angry. Tears ran, but she ignored them and turned back.

It might have been one dog at a point. Its back had been peeled off and strange curly black fur was now growing on top of it. The head was brown and had smooth fur. The white right ear appeared to be from a lamb, sticking out from the side. A left ear was hanging low, as if from a rabbit, it was brown with a white tip. The tail was long and furry and striped, like a raccoon. Its legs were each from a different animal; the back left had a hoof they were a strange assortment of colors, and were each useless. Two of them looked dead, and the third was obviously rotting. Everything pieced on this animal was in different stages of rot.

The mouth and eyes were the worst part. The jaw had been taken off and replaced with one that was far too big. Lower teeth jutted out awkwardly. A feeding tube was down the animal's nose. But the eyes. The clear puppy eyes, whimpering for help. It was hard to believe but Jaspierre saw the tail move a little. That dumb damn dog was happy to see them. Mother reached in and petted the squealing animal.

"Was he sick?" Jaspierre asked, staring at it with confusion.

"Was he sick!" Mother parroted again. "No, we don't experiment on sick animals. That would taint the results." Mother used a syringe on the IV line, and the animal fell asleep.

"I was hoping he would learn to walk, but, these legs keep dying." She removed the left front leg. The skin fell off in slimy chunks as she worked removing the leg. This leg took even longer then the last one, and Jaspierre had to fetch her mother a glass of water while she worked. Mother hummed as she worked. Jaspierre was much quicker at handing the right tool at the right time now.

"*Oranges and lemons,*" her mother sang softly. "Clamp again. Say *the bells of St. Clement's.* The stitching needle. *You owe me five farthings, Say the bells of St. Martin's.*" She stitched the tiny blood vessels together. "*Here comes a candle to light you to bed,* hand me that clamp. *Here comes a chopper.* The needle again. *To chop off your head.*" She pressed gauze into the leg, wiping it out. "*Chip chop chip chop. The last man's dead!*" Mother smiled and finished stitching up the skin. Mother then pressed a few buttons and the little cage under the animal vibrated. "I have heard vibration helps the limbs heal faster. Blood flow increase, I guess." She turned and washed her hands thoroughly. "Well, I guess we are done for the night."

Jaspierre was so relieved. She was tired. "Mother, what about that one?" The rabbit without a leg lay on the table still asleep with clamps sticking out of it.

"Oh, throw it away. We are done with it." Jaspierre stared at the animal breathing on the table. "Wait, stop, before you throw it away, get my clamps and stuff. Then wash up. I'm sure you remember where the house is." Her mother got up and left.

Jaspierre stood there. Her tiny five-year-old body did not want to touch that rabbit. She sat with the dog animal and did not look at it or pet it. It was still asleep. She was tired. She wanted to go to bed. But she didn't want to throw the rabbit away. Or pull off the clamps.

Mother stood behind a mirrored window, watching her daughter, whispering to herself. "Pull the clamp off, you little dumb girl. Go on, go do it!" She couldn't wait.

Jaspierre stood up, and walked to the rabbit. It was breathing. She petted its fur. There was one large clamp, and it seemed to be holding a lot of those little tubes in the rabbit. Jaspierre opened the clamp. Blood sprayed out of the rabbit, draining its life all over Jaspierre's face and chest.

Mother cackled with laughter. Best prank ever.

CHAPTER

EIGHTEEN

The front door was locked. Lucas wasn't sure if he should try to go in through a window. He sat and waited, sipping at his milkshake. As he hit the bottom, he saw a figure walking toward the house. He couldn't tell who it was, but they were carrying a duffel bag and appeared to have a machine gun and, possibly, a rocket launcher. Lucas ducked behind a bush and hid quietly. As he sat he noticed silver by his foot. Panties? Why the hell were silver panties sitting here?

He peered out between the tiny branches and realized it was Jaspierre. She looked tired. Where the hell was her car? She could use help. Lucas climbed out of the bush. He realized, too late, he should have called out he was there.

The machine gun was pointed at him and she was already pulling the trigger. Her eyes grew wide as she realized it was Lucas. Jaspierre dropped the gun on the ground and sat down and cried.

"It's dumb luck I didn't know where the safety was," she said between sobs. "I am having the worst day."

Lucas hurried to her side and helped her up, holding her, and kissing her forehead. "Did you kill him? Are you okay? What happened?" He squeezed her and she calmed in his arms. "Let's go in and lie down and you can tell me all about it when you are ready."

Jaspierre stared at the man she loved. Him, in lipstick and sparkly sunglasses and a too short red dress. He was still perfection to her. He helped carry the guns and the duffel bag, and Jaspierre opened the front door with a code.

"Let's go shower." They went up to her room and they walked through her closet, and then they saw the shower was still shattered from when Jaspierre had punched it earlier. It had only been a few days ago, but it seemed like a lifetime ago.

"Uh, I guess we should use yours," she said. Lucas took off the dress and bra stuffed with tissues and was standing there in nothing but lipstick. Jaspierre couldn't help but smile a little. She took off her leather vest and pants and the tight green shirt. Lucas led her to the shower and he washed her. "Did you have fun getting food? What did you bring me?"

Lucas froze. "Well, er, I didn't bring

anything back. I kinda trashed it all, because I was trying to keep the car clean... I can make you dinner in a second, though."

Jaspierre nodded, and her weary eyes started to close. Lucas wrapped her in a towel and kissed her sweetly on the lips. "Do you want coffee or a coke? Or do you want to go to bed?"

Jaspierre looked up at Lucas. "A coke would be great."

Jaspierre put on a long, soft, flowing white dress, and Lucas put on a clean set of scrubs. They walked to the kitchen together, hand in hand. Lucas pulled her close and kissed her on the lips, and then turned to make her dinner. "What do you want to eat? Fish? Chicken? Salad?"

Jaspierre sipped on a coke and said she wanted a waffle. He grinned and looked for a cookbook. "Oh, well, they are in the freezer." He pulled out a large frozen waffle. He warmed it up in the oven with a dish of water to keep it moist. Then he sliced strawberries and bananas, and whipped cream. Her waffle was nice and hot; he layered the fruit, and then two scoops of vanilla ice cream, and the whipped cream piled on top.

She looked at the dish and back at Lucas and grinned. "Seriously, you have the best ideas."

"Come sit with me and you can eat and tell me what happened." Jaspierre and Lucas curled together on a large seat by the pool and she ate and explained the car wreck, and how she never even got to kill Chance. She burst out giggling as the caffeine worked it's magic, and she described shooting the rocket into the man's yellow car. Lucas couldn't help but giggle also.

As they sat and talked and discussed their day, Ikali walked up and hissed at Lucas. "Oh yes, let's get these two fed. How could I have forgotten?" Jaspierre sounded rather upset.

"I'll get right on it, ma'am." He saluted her playfully and hustled to the kitchen. He emptied the first can of cat food and Tessa appeared as if from no where. She meowed pitifully and pressed her body against his legs, nearly knocking him down. He hurried to open another can and Ikali was soon standing in the doorway, hissing with his teeth bared. Lucas hustled with the two remaining cans, trying not to be knocked down by Tessa or bitten by Ikali. The plates sat and the cats began munching enthusiastically.

Lucas had this terrible realization; he didn't know when he had last fed Russell. He plated a sandwich and chips and a coke. Hopefully, Jaspierre wouldn't mind him feeding the other pet. "Hey, Jasp? I was gonna feed Russell; did you want to come?" She came from the other room, carrying her empty plate.

"Okay, but nothing special like waffles for him, he doesn't deserve it."

"This okay?" He gestured to the plate he

had made, and she nodded.

She stepped between her cats as they ate and ran her hands down their backs. She caressed them. "I missed you guys."

She turned and walked to the library with Lucas following behind. The fire was still burning, but it wasn't hot. Marcy was not charred yet. Her skin, in many places, hadn't even blackened. "Dammit." Jaspierre threw more wood on the fire, and then more and more, until the pile of wood was as large as a couch. "This needs to be *way* the hell hotter or it's gonna take weeks."

"Can we still go down there?" Lucas asked. Walking underneath such a massive fire did not seem terribly pleasant.

"Oh, yes, it's not a big deal." She clicked the ear of the serval and the fire moved out of the way. "You can't leave the door open when it is lit because the fire will suffocate."

She stepped down inside and Lucas followed. The door slid shut. The lights clicked on. Jaspierre took one look and slid the sword out of the console. There was blood drips all over in tiny tracks. She glanced up at the monitors and it all came rushing to her in a big wild fury. She saw Marcy's face hanging askew where her mouth had been sliced apart. "You let him *out!*"

The blade pointed at a bewildered Lucas's throat. Lucas dropped the plate of food he was holding and the plate shattered as it hit the floor.

"He is out?" His voice rattled in a horrified whisper.

"Don't act so shocked. You are the one who did this. I should have known you were planning this all along. *You bastard.*"

"I... I didn't. I didn't do this. I didn't let him out! Why would I have done this! I took his toes!" Lucas held his hands out pleading with her.

She pressed the blade onto his still gaping and sore chest. "Down the stairs."

Terror rushed over him. He couldn't go back in his room. He couldn't do it. It didn't matter if it would be different, if it would be a kinder, better captivity with sex and delicious food. It didn't matter; he could not go back in that room. He took a step to the stairway, and as she followed he ducked and punched the back of her hand. She let go as she yelped, the sword skittering across the room. Jaspierre leapt on top of Lucas ripping at his hair, beating him with her fists, kicking him with her feet. Like Mother.

Lucas curled up tightly, waiting for the beating to end. He almost punched back, but he realized it would make his fate worse. *Don't fight her. Wait and she will grow weary, she can't keep this up.*

Jaspierre held his hair with one hand and punched his ribs with the other. Her toes popped when she kicked him with her bare feet, and she regretted not wearing her high heels. Mother wore heels, and they hurt like hell. Jaspierre let go of Lucas and stepped back. She closed her eyes and counted to ten. Mother was a monster. Jaspierre still remembered clear as day. Mother was a vicious monster.

Jaspierre had no intention of becoming like Mother. She opened her eyes and Lucas was standing; he looked ready to run at any moment. His eye was swelling, his nose was bleeding, he looked miserable.

"I'm sorry. Mother used to beat me, I promised myself I would never do that." She picked up the sword and slid it back in place.

He wasn't sure what to say. He hurt, but he wasn't imprisoned, and he didn't have to fight her. Weary relief washed over him.

She sat in the chair at the computer. She felt tired. It took a lot of energy to beat someone.

CHAPTER

NINETEEN

Chance reached under his seat to grab a gun; he didn't even care which one. People obeyed when they were at gunpoint. The lady and the man without toes were both fairly quiet in the back seat. They were probably worn out from all that screaming.

The bigger problem, was that the gun wasn't there. He wrinkled his nose. He opened the glove box. "Fucking shit." That gun was gone too. Now he knew he'd been robbed. He popped the trunk.

In the trunk, he found he still had a decent arsenal, but his favorite rocket launcher and machine gun were gone. "Dammit."

He grabbed a machine gun and shut the trunk. He'd have to figure out where she put his guns later. He tapped the window with his gun, and the old lady yelped. She was tear streaked and terrified. He open the door.

"Pick up that dumb mother-fucker and be a dear and help him into the house. That or I will fucking shoot you in the foot and still make you drag him inside." The lady stepped out nervously and shook Russell. He moaned and his eyes fluttered.

"Come on; I gotta get you inside," she said. He got out of the car, not processing anything happening. His weight on his feet was excruciating. What was left of them was swollen and bleeding. He yelped when his feet hit the ground. The little lady pulled his arm around her shoulders and lifted him the best she could. They stumbled to the house together. Chance kept poking her with the tip of the gun, Russell's crushing delirious weight pressed into her.

They went into the house. The house was filthy; porn magazines and movies littered the floor along with chip bags and candy wrappers. Chance kept them moving toward the kitchen. He flipped up a wooden panel in the floor and told them to go down the narrow stairs. It was a dirt cellar down there, filled with booze and not much else. The stairs were too narrow for the lady to carry Russell down. She stood helplessly at the top, trying to figure out how to maneuver him.

Chance gave her a moment, pleased with her struggle. But Chance got bored with the dilemma on how to get down a tiny flight of stairs with an injured man. He gave her a nice big shove with the front of his gun, and the pair of them tumbled down the cellar stairs with a loud thumping. rumbling crash. There was silence at the bottom and Chance flipped the cellar back shut.

* * * * * * * * * * * *

Helen and the man were pressed together at the bottom of the stairs. Helen had landed mostly on him. The wind was knocked out of her lungs. She lay there on top of the man, waiting for her air to come back. She closed her eyes tightly as the ache from the fall set in.

She tested her legs and they seemed achy but no other injury. Her left arm moved fine, but her right arm was still tucked under him. He was lying on his back, and breathing in a ragged, whistling sound. They were face to face; his stubbed feet were up three steps still. She pulled hard and slid her arm out from under him. Her arm hurt, it hurt. But it didn't appear to be bleeding, and she ran her hand up and down it. It didn't feel broken anywhere. It hurt.

She sat up, lifting her weight off of him. "Hey, are you okay?" she whispered, but he was silent. She took a small breather and stood, climbing off of him the rest of the way. Her old body creaked at the effort. She tried to look around, but it was dark. Only a small amount of light trickled down from between the floor boards.

She felt around the room; it was a small room lined with shelves. Probably bigger than her guest bathroom at her house. Helen fondled each thing in the dark; mostly bottles of booze, she assumed. That was not a good sign; it would have been better if it was canned goods or water. Then they could at least stay hydrated. Helen pushed her silver hair behind her ear. Booze certainly wouldn't help. In fact, all they could possibly do with it was drink themselves to death.

If she had known what would happen next, she probably would have tried.

* * * * * * * * * * * *

Chance walked to the fridge and cracked open a beer. He thought about his guns. Jaspierre had to have taken them. That little bitch. He chuckled to himself. She gave him a woman, and a tortured man. She was so full of surprises; now, wasn't she? The man he could save till tomorrow; the guy was practically comatose anyway. But thinking about having a woman in his house got his loins flaming with excitement.

He finished his beer and went back to the kitchen. He turned over the cellar door. "Hey, honey, I'm home. Be a fucking dear and come on up okay?"

She did not come up. He walked down the stairs and stared at the man still lying on the ground. His toes were all chopped and his arm was broken, the left arm. She crashed a small bottle next to his head. "Well well well, aren't you a little feisty?"

She grabbed another bottle to throw, and he punched her in the face. She was stunned and dropped the bottle. The whole room was spun. He grabbed her by the hair and shoved her up the stairs behind him. He shut the trapdoor and let go of her gray hair. "Take it off."

She ran. He ran after her in a terrible game of tag. She was faster and stronger than he suspected. They raced through the few rooms in his cabin and he caught her and body slammed her to the ground. She collapsed under his weight. "You are so damn feisty." He grinned as he pulled out a large knife. She was winded, but strong. She wasn't strong enough. He slit down the front of her shirt. Then he unbuttoned her pants.

She let out a sad cry. In her seventy-five years, she had never been so unlucky. She had never been attacked or raped or beaten. Helen had lived a quiet, happy life, marrying her best friend, attending church every Sunday, raising one beautiful little boy. She had never been in want for her whole life. She worked out, she was fit, but she was no match for a man.

He wrestled and ripped and sliced the clothes off her. She had stopped fighting. She figured he would blow his load and she would be back in the cellar. He slapped her, and she let out a cry. "There we go. I wanna hear it." As he pressed his body into her unwilling opening, he slapped her over and over again, making her cry. When he finished, he spit on her face. "I thought you would be more fun than that." He climbed off of her and left her naked, terrorized body trembling on the floor. Tears ran but she refused to make any more sounds.

* * * * * * * * * * * *

He came back five minutes later. "Now, I'd like to keep you around longer as my own personal sex doll, but you gotta see the bigger picture here. Jaspierre. She is the bigger picture."

Chance dragged her by the hair and tied her down on the table. Tied her waist, and each arm and leg separately. He already kind of wanted to fuck her again. He chugged another beer and sat staring at her still fairly firm older body. Shame, he didn't have that kind of time.

He went out to the shed and found the tools he needed, and back he came. First snipped off her pinky toe. She screamed and hollered and bled so much that he found he did have time. This time he fucked her in the ass. By the time he finished he knew breaking her left arm would be the best part.

* * * * * * * * * * * *

Jaspierre walked upstairs with Lucas. They didn't hold hands, but Lucas thought they were back on good terms. Jaspierre walked to the freezer and pulled out a bag of frozen vegetables and handed them to Lucas. He pressed them to his aching eye.

"That was so goddamn unlucky," Jaspierre said. "I mean, you fucked up majorly. You left that button clicked. I fucked up. I should have had them wired differently so the doors and the feeding doors don't operate at the same time." Jaspierre walked upstairs as she talked. Lucas followed because he had no idea what else to do. "But how fucking unlucky is it he leaned on the right spot on the wall for long enough? The footage showed he didn't even know how he got it opened and yet, he escaped. Then what? Then he must have killed Marcy. I don't even know why. Is he still here? Did he leave? Where the hell is he?" She paused on the stairs. "I was ready to kill Chance and he wasn't even here."

"Do you think he is still here?" Lucas looked around nervously.

"I don't think so. I think he would have killed the cats if he had been." Lucas nodded in agreement. "Thankfully, he should be easy to find." Jaspierre paused. "I don't want you to come in my workroom."

She walked past their rooms and to her workroom. Lucas wondered if they were on good terms again. Lucas went to his room and checked his chest. It was oozy but not pus-filled, thank goodness. Jaspierre showed up a few minutes later, dustier looking, and holding a strange looking computer device. "We can track him with this, sort of. We have to be close enough for him to be in range. I tried to modify it, but I couldn't get much farther of reach. I can find you, but he must be quite farther away. Definitely not in the house."

"How could he have even gone farther? When you chopped off my toes, it was hard to walk for weeks." Lucas put it together. "The panties! Behind the bush... I found silver panties. *Your* panties. I was trying to remember why they looked familiar. You left them in my room and I had put them under the mattress in my old room. He must have been behind that bush." He paused, and then he knew. "Which one of us did he hitch a ride with?"

"Well, he isn't still in your car, because I'd see his tracker. Did you hear anything while you were driving around?"

"Well, no... I would have noticed if someone got out. I was in the car the whole time. I didn't get out at all. Er, not even to urinate..." Another reason he dumped the trash before he got back.

"That means the only car he could have been in was mine." Jaspierre did not like the sound of that. Cops were driving up when she was driving off in the stolen cop car. Surely he would be on the news. This could be game over.

She found herself vaguely wondering if the old lady had been found yet, and what she told the police.

JASPIERRE

CHAPTER

TWENTY

By the time Chance was finished cutting off her toes the blood was pouring out of her. She did not survive the process. This was mind boggling to Chance because Russell was alive in his basement. He untied her left hand and snapped the arm on her virtually lifeless body. She made no cries, shuddered, then died. It was particularly annoying to him. He was hoping she would make it a few more days at least. One lousy orgasm and two halfway decent ones were all he got out of her. What a waste.

He rolled his eyes and left her naked body tied to the table. He grabbed a six-pack of beers and a leftover taco and sat on the couch and munched away. That old chick's death would be easy to pin on Jaspierre, if it came to that. But he wasn't sure how to best use Russell to his advantage. He turned on the TV and watched *CSI: Special Victims Unit*. That was his favorite

CSI because it always made him a little horny. Those victims really did seem to have special things happen to them.

He drank all the beers and belched repeatedly. It was a nice rest from all the effort he spent on the little old lady. He kinda wished he'd asked her name. Ah well. Too late now. He fell asleep on the couch. When he woke, he had an excellent plan for Russell.

He walked past Helen's body and squeezed her breast on the way by. He felt like a dirty homo because he kinda wanted to fuck Russell a little. Maybe he'd have her again; it's not like she was rotting. Maybe they could both fuck her. So many choices. Russell would inspire him to pick one.

He flipped open the trap door and walked downstairs. Russell was still lying there, his feet propped up on the stairs. He was snoring. *How cute.* Chance grinned at the man. He grabbed his feet and dragged him up the stairs carefully. He didn't want to knock him out. Russell woke up after the first thump of his head on the stairs. He was bewildered and couldn't remember where he was or what was happening. Chance dragged him and laid him on the kitchen floor. He flipped the trap door shut. Russell let out a little cry. A soft, scared, muffled cry as he saw Helen's stubbed feet sticking over the table edge. Chance knew right then and there he was gonna fuck. He picked

Russell up and sat him so he could watch, and he dropped his pants and climbed over the dead woman. Russell cried out weak, scared moans, and it was perfect. Chance hardly lasted. He loved the sounds, the feel, the death, the terror, the scared whimpering. The soft titties in his face. As he finished, he moved out of the way. "You wanna have a go?"

Russell made a terrified gagging noise. Chance grabbed his hair and dragged his face between her legs. "You wanna lick that?" He giggled as Russell gagged even harder.

"Alright, well that's enough of that. I didn't bring you up to fuck around, but we might later if you are nice." Chance let go of the weak man's head and zipped up his pants. "How did you piss off Jasp enough to have her rip off your toes?"

Russell's head hurt. "I don't even know. I asked her on a date. She said her name was Juniper."

"Hahaha, you tried to date her!" Chance roared with laughter. "That closed-legged nun doesn't date anyone, you fucking dumbass. Tell me more."

"Well, she said yes, we went out for dinner, it went well. She took me back to her house."

Chance nearly spit out the beer he was drinking. "You have got to be kidding me."

"No, I went to her house, and she made me a drink... And then... I don't know. She drugged me. I woke up in a prison cell. I tried to climb out, and I fell and broke my arm... She sprayed me with water... and I woke up without my toes."

"How did you escape this cell?"

"I don't know. The doors... I don't know.I killed her, cut her jaw right off."

Chance scoffed, and laughed. "Try again, you dumb shit. Who was driving the car you were riding in?"

"I..." Russell trailed off; his brain was fuzzy and blurry. "I am sure I killed someone... I remember how the sword felt in my hands. How it tore through..." He winced as he remembered swinging the blade around and it slamming into her open mouth. He meant to be chopping at her throat, but her mouth was so open and so big.

"Well don't leave out the details!" Chance smiled at the man, and clapped him on the back. "I wish I could have been there. I bet Jaspierre was not real happy to have you escape! Slicing up people! When did she throw you in the trunk?"

Russell swayed a little. He kept trying not to look at the naked old woman. He remembered her helping carry him, and sorrow grew withing him. His stomach flipped. She didn't deserve this.

"When! Think. When did she?"

"Oh, um, well. She... I got in the car by myself. But I was trying to get in Lucas's car... Wasn't I in Lucas's car?"

"Who is Lucas?" Chance felt pissed. Here

she was, whoring herself out to man after man like a bar of soap in the prison. Rub it on your dick and pass it on. She was a fucking slut. And even now that she was a slut she wouldn't give it to him in the parking lot? *What the fuck?* He was her first love! Russell slumped down, he fell toward the table and his face almost hit the woman's breast. Chance grabbed him by the hair. "Who. Is. Lucas?!" He emphasized each word with a painful, angry, whispering growl.

Russell lungs wheezed and he cried, "I don't know! I don't know. He said he was a prisoner like me. But I don't know! She let him drive a car."

"A prisoner like you?" Chance laughed and shook Russell's head, pressing it into the dead breast in front of him. Russell was too weak to fight. "Clearly, he was not like you." Chance's anger flared. Jaspierre had multiple lovers. But somehow, shaking Russell's weary face against a soft, wrinkly breast made him smile. "You know what would make you feel better?"

Russell shook his head. *He didn't want to know. He didn't want to know.*

Chance pressed Russell's face into her pretty tits and slid down the man's pants. Thankfully Russell, the man with a snapped arm, toes snipped from his body, and infection completely raging through his body, passed out long before he knew what was happening.

CHAPTER

TWENTY-ONE

Jaspierre and Lucas had watched the news and scoured the web. What they had found was nothing. This was good news because nobody knew Jaspierre was involved at all. Only a short story of the car in a lake was findable in the local newspaper. It barely even had two sentences.

However, the longer they looked, the more Jaspierre guessed the old lady and Russell were both with Chance. Besides being caught this was worst-case scenario. First off, Chance was fucking nuts. Secondly he could be interrogating them both and building a case against her so he could imprison her, imprison her in an actual prison.

Jaspierre rolled this around in her head. Or.

Or.

Chance was fucking nuts and he was holding them hostage. Did he think Jaspierre would come and save a random old lady? Or she wanted to have Russell back? Joke was on him; she didn't even like Russell. The old lady was different. She didn't deserve to be held hostage for no good reason.

He wasn't holding her hostage. He was raping her.

The thought turned her stomach.

*** THIRTEEN YEARS EARLIER ***

Jaspierre had long hair, past her waist. She curled her brown locks in a professional look, and then tied it up in two buns. Her hair was her favorite thing to mess with. She had learned and practiced curling and brushing it in so many different ways. Being fourteen was fantastic. She wore nice clothes, sure. But generally, she hired a stylist to find them. Her new clothes showed up every few months, with her wardrobe refreshed and delightful. She was wearing a soft, yellow buttoned shirt, and a short blue skirt with sweet pink flowers.

Her favorite, was tossing her hair up in the perky, playful floppy buns. She looked so bright and cheery and sweet, but also not quite as childish as pigtails. No need to look childish anymore. She was fourteen; the world was hers. She was rich, and for the first time in a long while she was a little bit happy.

Last week had been downright excellent.

Chance had been out of school for the whole week; he was on vacation. He was always harassing her. She even had time to try to make new friends. Usually he interfered with everything. He was all right; he was her only real friend, but he was so possessive.

She left her massive house and climbed on her bike and rode to school. Zone out and fly down the road. The ride was kind of long, now that she was in high school. But eight miles wasn't bad once you did it twice a day. She even had slimmed down a little. Her sweet little body had blossomed breasts. This was an unfortunate thing for her to have. They seemed uncomfortable, unruly, and over-sized already.

She zoomed along pleasantly and coasted the last little downhill area and parked her bike in the rack. She finished locking it up, turned, and her face fell. There he stood. He was like an annoying little brother who couldn't seem to let up. "Miss me?" he said as he stared at her breasts.

"No. I wish you were still gone." Jaspierre stuck her tongue out at him.

He winked at her, and she blushed a little. She waved at one of the girls she had talked to last week. "Hey, who are you waving at? What? Am I not good enough for you anymore?"

"You were never good enough for me to begin with." She playfully stuck out her finger and tapped it on his nose. He tried to bite it.

She laughed and they went inside. They hassled each other class to class. He pulled her chair out from under her, and she stole his pencils. He maneuvered himself so Jaspierre would sit by him, always between her and any other students if he could manage it. He liked her. And he didn't like to share.

It was lunchtime. He had been waiting for this all day. He had been gone a whole week. That entire time he only thought about one thing.

Jaspierre.

And now, it was lunchtime. The best time of the day. He grabbed her hand and told her to come along. She tried to say goodbye to the girl she was talking to, but he dragged her out in the middle of her sentence.

"I wish you would stop. It's not a big deal if I have other friends, you know."

"Oh, I don't care if you have other friends. Come see what I got."

"I think you do care. I think you're jealous. You're always jealous."

"Jasp, I'm not jealous. Come on!" He dragged her along faster and soon they had walked a few blocks to his house. She didn't normally come to his house. In fact, she had only been there a few times for dinner. He had never been to hers.

"What do you want to show me? Something from vacation or whatever?"

"Yeah, it's back here in my room." They walked into the house. It wasn't small, but it seemed absurdly tiny to Jaspierre, having grown up in a mansion.

They stepped into his tiny room. Jaspierre had never been back here before. The walls were all covered with black paper. His bed was made and his dresser was tidy. "What do you want to show me?" She felt nervous.

"Sit down." He led her to his bed and she sat down.

"How long is this gonna take? I don't wanna be late for class..."

"Heh, don't be silly Jaspierre." Chance picked up a small box from behind a little chair. "This is what I got for you."

She opened the small box and inside was a little golden necklace that said "*Mine Forever*." Jaspierre stared at it with a little bit of childish excitement. This was the first time a boy had ever given her anything special. It was a moment she would remember forever.

Chance took it from her hands and chained it around her neck. He ran his hands down her shoulders, and touched her hair. She felt fluttery and confused. He got up and locked his bedroom door, but she didn't notice as she admired the little golden heart.

"Thank you. That was so sweet of you." She stood, and his face fell.

"No no no, wait. I... Jaspierre, I... I want." His words faltered. "You know I like you. I love you even." She looked nervous and he continued. "I do. I love you. You're my first love. I... I just got you something nice. And I wanted you to... let... to..." He stuttered. "I want to see your boobs."

She was kind of confused. They were embarrassing. "I ... no. No, I mean, I like the necklace. It is so beautiful. But I don't want to show you my boobs... They are hideous."

He trembled and stared at them again through her shirt. "Let me see them." She sat there and turned red. She didn't take off her shirt.

"Let. Me. See." He balled up his fist in an angry, tight clench.

"I don't like this." Jaspierre stood up and tried to go, and Chance smashed his fist into her face. She fell back onto the bed, both startled and horrified. *Mother. Just like Mother. He is just like Mother.* She needed to get out of there, but before she could regroup, he was on top of her.

"I spent a *whole year* saving up for that necklace." His hot, angry breath pressed into her ear as his hands fumbled at her shirt. "You *owe* me. When I do nice things for you, I expect you to repay me!" He tore the buttons from her shirt he pulled it so hard.

She let out a tiny yelp. Then she steeled herself. As soon as he saw them he would stop. She told herself this would be over soon. Like when Mother wore herself out punching and kicking, it would be over.

She couldn't have been more wrong.

His hormonal teenage body screamed for more the second he saw them. Sucked them, bit them, and gripped them with his hands. He slapped one and watched them dance. He tore off his own shirt, his chubby boy body pressing skin against hers.

She froze, scared. She yelped when he slapped them. It was like he was lost in another world. He hadn't looked at her since he had ripped her shirt open. Just *them*. He stared at *them*. They were even worse then she imagined. They turned him into a monster. He lifted up her skirt and tried to pull down her panties.

"No! Stop it. *Stop it!* You already saw my boobs. That's enough! Let me go!" Her body squirmed and she tried to stop him from taking them, but he was much stronger than her. Chance pulled on the little chain necklace and she choked. She tried to pull it, both of her hands struggling to release it off her neck and he punched her face again.

Dazed, she fell back onto the bed. He slapped her breasts again and giggled. He pulled off her panties and she stopped fighting. He was so scary looking. Then he took off his pants. His body was strange and foreign. She had never seen a penis before. Her heart was pounding and she was absolutely terrified.

"Touch it." He took her hand and pressed his erection into it. She touched it timidly and he made a groaning moan. "Fuck. I can't wait for all this."

He pressed her legs apart with his knees and he pushed hard into her. It hurt. She let out a cry. It hurt so much. She had never felt pain like this. It ran up her body and made her shudder.

He heard her scream and his hands gripped her hair like handlebars. He humped into her harder, pulsing. After he finished he laid on top of her. He kissed her neck. "I can't wait until we do it again. I'm so glad you showed them to me."

She made a horrible noise. *Again? Why would they do that again?* "I have to go." She left her panties and tried to hold her shirt shut as she walked to the door. Fumbling to open it, she had to release her shirt and her breasts hung freely. She unlocked the door and ran. Her strong legs carried her all the way home. Her bike was left at school.

"Mine Forever" was still imprinted against her neck when she got home and looked in the mirror. Panic and horror set in, and she grabbed a pair of scissors. She lifted them above her heart, ready to plunge it into her soft breast. But she froze. Mother would have slapped her for stopping. She stared at herself in the mirror and

angrily scissored through her brown pigtail bun. Then she cut off the other one. She hacked away in big chunks what was left of her hair while she sobbed. One of the maids was cleaning and heard Jaspierre.

"Honey, aren't you supposed to be at..." A gasp of horror ended her sentence. She stared at the girl in her torn shirt and ruined hair. Jaspierre started to shut the door. "Wait... wait. Let me help you."

She cut off all of Jaspierre's hair, as short as it would go, while Jasp sat and sobbed. The maid helped her ice her blackened eye, and change her ruined shirt. "Don't tell anyone. Don't you tell a soul," Jaspierre whispered with angry hate through her burning tears.

"Well, okay, but everyone is going to know this isn't a proper haircut."

Jaspierre sat quietly in her clean clothes.

"Burn those." She pointed at the clothes. "And... get me a wig. I don't want anyone to know I have cut my hair... and tell everyone I have the flu. I am not coming out of my room for a few days."

The maid did so. Never once did she even ask what happened.

Jasp curled up on her bed, miserable and sad. Her crotch hurt. Mindlessly, she fiddled with the necklace on her neck before she remembered what it was.

CHAPTER

TWENTY-TWO

"Well, I think I should man the machine gun, and you can take the handgun and the rocket launcher." Lucas strapped the machine gun to his chest. His face was still swollen, but she hadn't blackened his eye thankfully.

"But... you... you can't come. I'd never forgive myself if you got injured. I know we have a kind of fucked up relationship, but you are the only real relationship I have ever had. You're it for me. You are the only person who could ever love me." Jaspierre wrapped herself around the man and slid the machine gun off his shoulder. "I can't risk it."

Lucas ran his hands around her face, kissing her. "I love you Jaspierre. And I am sorry, but you need my help. I'm coming with." He pulled the machine gun back on.

She slid her hands down his body and kissed him back harder. "Since when have you ever been the boss?" She pressed her body up close, her heart beating faster.

"Jasp." He stared into her eyes and held her face. "Trust me, and let me come with you. Let me help keep you safe. Please." Jaspierre pressed her body invitingly against his.

"We don't have to go quite yet..."

He kissed her. "Are you gonna try to get me upstairs so you can drug me? Baby, you know I want you. I always want you. You are so damn fine. But let's go learn how to shoot these guns, and go catch Russell."

Jaspierre pouted. He did know all her tricks already, didn't he? She was, of course, going to ride him like a pony before she drugged him... It didn't matter, she guessed. "Fine, I won't drug you. This is getting ridiculous though. You are so much harder to boss around now that I let you out."

He grinned and winked at her. "But it's a hell of a lot more fun this way, isn't it?"

She did have to admit it was a hell of a lot of fun.

They went out and shot several rounds into a bush for target practice. They figured out how the safety on each gun worked, and how to load them. The rocket launcher was surprisingly the easiest one to load, although they didn't practice shooting it. Once they had figured it out, they loaded up the car. Jaspierre set the license plate to spin one letter or number every five minutes.

"How on earth did you get that kind of thing?"

Jasp laughed. "Well, I like to build things. Especially things to avoid detection. Once I realized I had plenty of wigs and I.D cards and what not, I collected more things, in case I ever need to hide, or... whatever. I mean, I know murder and locking people up is a little bit illegal."

Lucas said, "What?"

"Yeah," she continued, "You know, like speeding; everyone does it, but you gotta be careful not to get caught. That kind of thing."

Lucas stared at her. There was a long pause before he could think of a reply. "I don't think murder is as common as you think it is. Are you ready to go get dressed?"

Jaspierre nodded. "You go make us protein smoothies. I have a feeling we will need all the energy we can get. I'll go get clothes."

She walked up the stairs and into her closet. She changed into tight jeans and a snug blue tank top. She didn't bother with a bra. When fighting Chance, they were an excellent weapon swinging about. She realized how much easier all of this would be with a holster.

She also looked at Lucas's scrubs and realized they were a terrible idea to fight in, plus he would need real shoes.

Lucas came up with the smoothies. "Strawberry? Or blueberry?"

"Strawberry definitely." She took a sip. "Okay, we have got to go shopping. You need shoes and pants and well, clothes. And I am gonna get holsters."

She slipped on black, flippy, short hair with bright green tips. "What color do you want?" She pointed at the shelf of short wigs. He cringed. She rolled her eyes.

"Look, you need to be memorable. Without the wig, they won't recognize you. Easy to change who you are." She pulled an orange and black wig down; it was striped almost like a tiger. She tucked his blond hair into it, and then cut the hair to look more boyish and spiked it up.

Lucas looked cool, he supposed, but also, nothing like himself.

Jaspierre put dark eyeliner on them both and threw makeup remover wipes into a bag. She gave Lucas a second pair of socks. "I don't know what shoes will work, but we are gonna have to make do. You are gonna have to be able to run."

Lucas nodded and they finished packing up the car and went into town. They first stopped at a small leather-working shop. They did custom leather pants and holsters and saddles, and anything else. Jaspierre got a hip holster strapped across her waist and around her thigh. The hip holster came with three long knives. She preferred swords, but today, she carried a gun. She found an ornate leather piece. This one fit almost like a vest in the back, and the front clipped above and below her breasts. This was an ornate piece designed for costume play. It held rounds on the right side and a gun on the left. Her breasts were pushed and lifted in such a way that they were hard to avoid staring at.

She walked over to the salesman. "Okay, I want this. I need it modified to hold my guns. Can you have it done in an hour?" He stuttered and stared at her breasts. She snapped her fingers at him. "Can you?"

He nodded. "Lucas, did you find something?" He stood there in his white scrub top and a pair of loose-fitted leather pants. They also looked kind of costume-oriented. They had lots of cargo pockets, and fit tight in the ass, but loose everywhere else. The pockets were all detailed with fancy scrollwork. "Do they fit okay?"

He nodded, and the pants and the holsters were purchased. Lucas didn't need a strap for his machine gun since it already had one.

They left the shop so Jaspierre's holster could be adjusted to fit her gun. As they were leaving, Lucas heard the man behind the counter whispering to someone, "She spent ten grand and didn't even blink."

She picked up a t-shirt for him at a random stand they walked past. The shirt was black and said, "Catch me if you can." She turned to him in the street and slid her hands up his sides pulling the scrubs off of him playfully. He felt shy with his naked skin in the street, but her lips pressed against his and he couldn't find a reason to care. She pulled it on him, her body pressed up against his. Her hands ran across his back and down his sides and then she pulled it into place. He looked delicious in his leather pants and snug t-shirt.

"Hot damn, you two need a room." Jaspierre flipped off the man and they walked into the custom shoe store.

"He needs custom shoes. He's missing a bunch of toes." Jaspierre said it as though it was the most normal thing in the world. "We need them done in a half hour."

"Okay," he said.

He stripped Lucas's sock and the misfit sandals he was attempting to wear. "What happened to your toes?" This was clearly not a birth defect. The pinky toes and the big toes remained, and between them were obvious scars.

"Cat bite," Lucas said so calm and cool. Jaspierre burst out laughing. He winked at her, and she sat with him and held his hand. The shoemaker might have giggled if he had not been so busy figuring out a plan on how to make these shoes so fast. All in all, it took him forty-five minutes, which she spent snuggling with Lucas. She tipped the man an extra five thousand dollars. Lucas walked up and down in the shoes and he grinned. "Not too bad."

They walked past the t-shirt stand and Lucas playfully squeezed Jaspierre's round delicious bottom. "Didn't I tell you two to get a room?" The salesman hooted and hollered at them.

Jaspierre spun around, grabbing Lucas's hands and running them up her body and onto her breasts. Then she flipped off the salesman with both hands, still on top of Lucas's hands. The salesman cheered and whistled and laughed.

Lucas kissed her behind her ear. "I love you, Jasp." She looked up at him and winked and they walked to the leather store. She put on her hip holster with the three long knives. It was black and contrasted nicely with her jeans. The shoulder holster fit her guns, and the odd barrel ammo packs perfectly. Her breasts were impossible to avoid staring at now. And that was the point.

Lucas stared at her. "Damn, girl. I kinda don't want you to go out like that."

She looked at him. "I think it's going to give me an advantage or I wouldn't do it."

They walked to the car. "Dammit Jasp, I just, I..." He pressed her back into the car and kissed her. He ran his face down her body, kissing at her nipples poking out from under the thin shirt. His hands held her hips with a firm grip, and he kissed her on the lips again, then pressed his face into her ear. "Mmm. You. You are something special." He squeezed her hips with his firm hands and pressed his bulging leather against her.

She bit her lip and stared at him. Her hands slid up his sides and landed on the short orange and black wig. She pulled it off. "I should have left you at home," she whispered into her ear, biting it and purring. "You're a terrible distraction."

He took off her wig and kissed her again. "Tell me to stop, then." He nibbled into her neck and kissed it.

"May it never be." She kissed him again and they opened the door and got into the back seat.

He slid her pants down just enough in a soft caressing motion, pushing her knees up. He pulled his down a little and slid in. She whimpered, her body folded up underneath his. He kissed her hard and thrusted into her, staring into her eyes. She bit her lip and cried out, as he leaned in close and pressed his cheek against hers and they came together in sweet harmony.

They kissed again. He held her face in his hands. "Come now, enough; we gotta go murder," she whispered into his ear and he giggled.

"Mmmm, never enough of that." He slid his pants back up and playfully smacked her bare ass.

"Yes. Yes, never enough." She giggled at him and slid her jeans up. Soon she was driving out toward the lake, looking for Russell. Lucas held the little tracking computer on his lap. He kept staring over at her, her short hair, her determined eyes, and he kept thinking how she needed to be loved. She needed it. He didn't even care about being captive anymore. He wanted her. Her and nothing else.

CHAPTER

TWENTY-THREE

Chance was singing in the shower. He washed his body and sang boisterously. He had been having the best day ever. He washed the wound on his arm. It was amazing to him how little it was bothering him. He thought about Jaspierre's big titties and how her green shirt stretched tight into them. *Damn she was fine.* It was a shame she never gave him a chance. He thought about the man he had tied to the table leg. Obviously she was into seriously fucking great stuff. His toes were gone, his arm was broken. It was a beautiful thing to find a woman so into this. He thought about how kinky she had been on their first time. How her hot gasping noises whimpered in his ear while he pulled on the necklace. *Kinky little slut.* She put it all out, but then she had been a close-legged bitch the rest of the time.

Russell woke up to loud, drunken singing.

He kept his eyes closed; he didn't particularly want to know what would happen next. *Just kill me. Just kill me.* His bleeding stubs throbbed and he opened his eyes. There was blood everywhere; it was all over the floor. He was sitting in it. His scrubs were coated with blood. His feet were dripping. He made a horrified little squeal, and then closed his eyes.

This is it. I've bled to death. No wonder I feel so weak, he thought to himself. Tears welled up in his eyes. He blinked them back and realized he could still move a little. *How can I move with all my blood outside my body? Shouldn't I be dead?* He stood, his hands still tied to the table leg. On the table was a dead woman. She was beautiful, and old. He stared at her face, and he looked at her broken arm, and her naked breasts, and her severed toes. *Her blood.* The realization hit him. He stared at her, and he was overcome with guilt. If he hadn't tried to run, she would still be fine.

He sat back down in the blood. Too miserable and weak to even care. He sat down and he heard the tiniest clunking noise. The singing in the shower continued as Russell felt his scrubs. The metal ring was still tied to the string on his waist. His keys were still tied up too. But the wallet was missing. And the panties, although he didn't know what they would have been for anyway. He sat there depressed, and wondered if trying to escape was even worth the effort. Things could always get worse, he had been learning. How the hell could life have done this? A short week or two ago, he was bagging groceries and going home to look at porn and play with his Xbox. Now he was a broken man. His arm was useless, his toes were gone.

He sat in drying blood and closed his eyes again. Death would be best. Then he heard the singing and wondered how long until the cop came back. He wanted to live, to escape. He did. He pulled out his keys and tried to snap the zip-ties. He snickered when he realized he could lift the table leg a little and slide them off the leg. They weren't tight at all with the table leg gone, and Russell slipped them off his hands.

This was too damn easy. But he didn't care. Where the hell could he go? He wished to himself that he hadn't left the antibiotic pills in his room.

He was weak. This might not be all his blood, but some of it was. He went into the pantry and sat down and waited. There were mostly chips and granola bars. He opened a box, munching quietly. If nothing else, he might be able to gain energy.

Chance came out of the shower and put on clean clothes. He trimmed his nose hairs and took his time putting on lotion and deodorants. Smell his best for work. He picked up his keys and hollered, "Have a nice day, honey," before he left, clicking the door shut. He locked it up. He knew

Russell was still tied to the table without even looking. That man was so weak and disoriented, it hardly even mattered where he left him. He wished the lady had made it a little longer. She was a lot of fun. Now he had two corpses to screw. One was simply, slightly warmer than the other.

Russell heard the front door shut, and he froze and waited. His mouth was full of granola and he sat and waited; he dared not chew or swallow. After ten agonizing minutes he finished his bite. Then he finished his granola bar. He was thirsty. He stood up and walked back into the kitchen. Her dead, naked body greeted him. It was hard not to look. As she lay there, he felt like he was watching a morbid porno for a moment. He was thirsty. But he couldn't seem to find a cup. He opened the fridge. There was a lot of beer, but he thought being fuzzier would not be a smart move. A small Gatorade sat in the door; who knew how old it was. He sipped and tried to figure out what to do next. He was so foggy and lost.

He wanted an omelet and looked for a pan. A sawed-off rifle greeted him from a large metal pot. Russell couldn't hold back his excitement. He picked up the rifle and checked if it was loaded. It was. He pressed it under his chin and smiled brightly. *Freedom.* He stopped. What if he shot that cop first? *A good idea. Yes. A great idea.*

He sat back into the pantry with his Gatorade and ate another granola bar. He fiddled with the metal ring while he sat. He slid it up and down the gun. Up and down his arm. Up and down the other arm. "You, my friend, have seen it all. My toes, my capture. You broke my arm." He sipped the Gatorade. "I'd try to escape but it won't work, and I'm too damn tired for it anyway." He looked up and saw vanilla wafers. Could you get those for me?" He Frisbee-tossed the ring at the cookies and the ring bounced off the box and fell back on his lap. The box teetered, back and forth and flipped forward down through the air and onto his legs. "I can't believe that worked." Russell kissed the ring and tied it back to his pants. He rested before he opened the cookies.

"My arm is ruined. My feet are ruined. I'm never gonna be the same. And I don't even think I can escape. I'll get out of here, and then they will find me again."

He took a few cookies out. His scrubs were dirty red. Pus was oozing in his arm and leaking off the back of it. His temperature was around 102. If he had known he might have tried to do something about it. But he didn't know, and he felt terrible, his brain muddled with fever and infection. He ate more and rested.

Chance drove in his cop car, meandering down the road to work. All he could think of was her. Lovely Jaspierre, his childhood sweetheart. She always made him be his best, truest self. She made him feel like the man he had always known he should be. He thought about the necklace he had given her. *Mine Forever.* He wondered if she still had it; what a silly thought. Of course she did. She loved him; he knew it. She was a little fucked up since her mother left her. That kind of shit would fuck anyone up.

Chance puttered down the road when he saw her. She was in the car coming up the other lane. She had her hair short, and a boy in the seat next to her.

What was she doing way out here? He didn't know, but he knew he was about to find out.

CHAPTER

TWENTY-FOUR

Jaspierre looked over at Lucas. He had found a faint signal from Russell. They were driving farther into the middle of nowhere, and that did not feel promising. Lucas pointed out the window. "I think he is that way."

She slowed the car down and they looked for a road on the right. So far it was trees. She didn't like this one bit. "He's got to be with Chance."

Lucas nodded, even though he didn't know what that meant. Chance to him, at this point, was a description, nothing more. "We've got to be getting close."

Jaspierre turned the car into the small dirt road. It was probably more like a driveway than a road. She slowed down. There was a small wooden cabin up ahead. No garages. No cars either. She stared at the building. Everything in her body cried out this was a bad idea.

"Lucas, I want you to stay here. I'm gonna go peek in the window." Jaspierre climbed out of the driver's seat and snuck up to the window. The scent of rotting flesh mixed with chips and beer was strong. She held back a gag and peered inside the window. The lights were off. The house was littered with trash and porn.

No people, though. She scooted around the corner of the building to the next window. She saw feet with no toes. Small, feminine feet. Sadness filled Jaspierre. It had to be the poor old lady. Jaspierre had never imagined she would have ended up with Chance. She wouldn't have left her in the car if she had realized.

But she hadn't. That woman's death was squarely on her shoulders. The amount of blood loss surely killed her. With any luck, it did... Jaspierre didn't like to imagine the woman would have survived it. This was her fault. Corpses, but no life. She pressed her ear to the door and listened. She heard the click of a gun being cocked.

She listened quietly and didn't hear anything else. She turned to go back to Lucas, and her heart stopped. There he stood, his eyes wild with fear and his arms behind his back. He had a hand pressed over his mouth and nose. A gun was pressed to his temple. *Chance.*

The cop stood there with a leering smile. "So you thought you'd come to my house? I can't wait to give you the grand tour." He stared at her breasts and licked his lips.

Chance's eyes burned into her, but she couldn't think of a thing to do. She stared helplessly at Lucas. The sweet man who had made love to her. Who had stolen her heart. The man she loved. She cringed. She knew she would do literally anything to save him. Anything. And what she would have to do would be horrible.

She held her hands up and surrendered. "Toss your weapons." She did, tossing all but one small knife still in the holster.

Chance smiled and opened the door, ushering them inside. The three walked into the living room and the two were forced to sit on the couch. Chance was practically skipping. Jasp was here, in his house. Shit. He should have cleaned up a little. Chance glanced around his house at the littered chip bags, porno magazines, and the blood on the floor of the kitchen. The blood was smeared into streaks and swirls and he realized Russell was gone.

"Shit." Chance spit on the ground. "Dammit, and I was ready to have so much fun." He tied Jaspierre's hands behind her back. He pressed his crotch into her face while he tied her. He held back the desire to fuck her like a bunny; that man on the loose could be causing all sorts of problems. He wanted to take his time with her, not be worrying the dumb, toeless fuck would jump out of a closet and shoot him.

"Dammit. You get me so hard." He held her chin with his fingers, lifting her mouth toward him. "Remember when we were kids? That first time. God, it was so perfect. You were so coy and shy." He ran his hands into her short hair. "Shame you cut your hair. That's okay. It'll grow."

She sat there and didn't move; no reaction. She would be raped. It wasn't a shock. She was prepared for this, she was ready. All she needed was to get her knife out so she could give it to him when he gave it to her. She was waiting for her moment to shine. *This was her time.* This was when she would turn the tide; she would become someone newer, stronger, better. She wasn't one bit scared.

Chance went into the kitchen and stared at the old naked woman. She seemed like such a pointless thing to fuck around with. He had Jaspierre.

Heh, damn, he was easily distracted. *Stop thinking about fuck and cock and dick dipping, and instead think about that toeless man. Where the hell would he have gone?* Chance flipped up the cellar and looked down inside. He didn't see him. He looked at the blood and it looked like he might be in the pantry. Well, easy enough. He opened the door and stuck his head in. He remembered his earlier fear he'd get shot from the fucker in a closet. Chance clicked on the light, ready to jump back.

Well, two things were obvious. One, the guy had been sitting in his pantry a long damn time. The blood was pooled and smeared, there were granola wrappers everywhere, and his Gatorade bottle was sitting empty.

It was also obvious he was gone. He was mother fucking gone. How far could he even walk with his feet mangled? Chance stepped outside into the cool air. He saw blood and started to follow it.

Jaspierre and Lucas sat quietly on the couch. Terror washed over Lucas. This, this he didn't deserve. It wasn't his fault; this wasn't captivity he could learn to endure. It was a nightmare. The love of his life would be raped and tortured in front of him. He could not bear it. He had to save her.

"Jasp, we have got to get you out of here."

"What? No, I'm so close! I've got a knife. I'm gonna kill him. God, I can hardly wait. That sick fuck." Her soft, whispering voice sounded so confident and excited, she squirmed, trying to reach the knife with the tip of her fingers.

"No, babe, no. He's gonna rape you." Lucas choked on the words. "You... please. We have to get out of here. We can kill him later."

"Lucas." Her soft voice sounded so calm and firm. "I'm going to kill him. I can't stop now." She turned her body toward him. Mother would be delighted. Her first real, guiltless kill. "It's gonna be okay."

It wasn't going to be okay. But he couldn't help but believe her. She was beautiful and strong. She was terrifying and sweet. She was almost all-powerful. A mastermind of her own making. "Jaspierre, my sweet love," he said staring into her eyes as she stared back. She was working her blade through the zip-ties.

Chance dejected he couldn't find Russell, stepped back into the kitchen.

Lucas kissed her nose. "Please marry me. Please. When this is over, please be my wife."

Chance's hairs on his neck rose in fury.

Both men stared at Jaspierre. Her pale skin flushed a sweet red. She kissed Lucas and, as they parted, she whispered, "Absolutely, I will marry you."

And for a split second, Jaspierre was the happiest she had ever been in her entire life. Her nemesis was about to die. She was about to be married. Her life felt complete right before the bullet leapt out of the gun and into Lucas's face. His head seemed to explode. Brains and blood splattered out where his eyeball used to exist.

Chance's voice rang out like a second round of gun-fire. "That *sick fuck* wanted to *marry* you!?" His voice shuddered with horror and rage. His body was still trembling. "You said yes? You said fucking **yes**?" His voice was building louder and louder. His heart was pounding.

Jaspierre was dazed. She stared at the only person in the world who had ever given her love. His mangled bleeding mess of a face. She reached her untied hand out and touched him. She felt it. In that moment, the tiniest touch of his body. Snapping inside her. She knew she would never recover. Never be the same. She was newer, stronger, better. She stood up and stretched, cracking her neck.

Then she turned around and stared at Chance.

Chance was still screaming with rage. "Why the *fuck* would you say yes?! We just got back together. We *just* got *fucking* back *together!*" His words rang out, and his body was so full of rage he could not stop shaking.

She planted her right foot on the couch and stepped up, launching herself into a flying leap at Chance. He dropped his gun when she stabbed the small knife into his stomach. She hissed and drove it in deep. He barely knew the pain, fury still surged within him. Her hot body pressed against him made him want to fuck her and kill her and fuck her all over again. He licked her face and shoved her body between him and the wall. She pulled out the knife and stabbed him again in the side. He slammed her harder into the wall, crashing her skull against it.

He gripped her hand with one of his and

held it up above her head. His hips pressed tight into her body, holding her against the wall as he pulled out his cock with his other hand. Jaspierre was dazed. Her head was aching, but her heart was aching more. She kneed him. His grip on her hand weakened at the blow and she had a chance. She stabbed him again hard in the shoulder. He shuddered with the pain and she threw her weight into the knife. He fell backwards, slamming his head into the wall.

Out cold.

Jaspierre kicked him in the balls for good measure.

Then she turned and looked around. The cellar door in the kitchen was open. She figured there was booze down there. She walked down the tiny steps and came up with four large bottles. She dumped one on Chance. He lay there, still unconscious. She chugged from the next bottle and smashed it in the kitchen.

She avoided looking at Lucas and shattered another bottle towards him. Drinking from the last bottle, she then poured it to the back door. She didn't want to walk past Lucas. A match. *Fucking shit.* She went back into the kitchen and rummaged in the drawers. She found a box of matches and walked out back. It took her a few tries but she got it lit, and the flames ran through the alcohol and tore into the house.

NINETEEN YEARS EARLIER

Mother came down late for breakfast. Her hair was pinned up like a movie star's, but Jaspierre barely paid attention. She pushed at her scrambled eggs with her fork and couldn't seem to get any bites in her mouth. Her small eight-year-old body was frustrated. Rainbow was safely locked in her room so Mother couldn't hurt her. But it seemed unlikely the kitten would make it to a full-grown cat. Mother was not nice.

But even that wasn't bothering her at the moment. Mother poured herself orange juice and sat down on the edge of the table. Her floor-length robe was white and had feathers sewn down it. It swirled as she moved, her tight, sexy, white silky lingerie peeking out from underneath it. "What's a matter with you, kid?"

"Mother," Jaspierre started. She wasn't sure if talking to her mom about this was a good idea. "I have this friend, Chance, and he is kind of mean sometimes."

"Mean how?" Mother sipped at the juice with amusement.

"Well, he's..." Jaspierre paused. She didn't want to explain it. Chance was mean-- sometimes he kicked her, sometimes he hit her. He always pulled her hair. But sometimes he was nice too. He picked her flowers once. "He keeps asking me why I don't have a dad, and I... I don't know what to tell him."

Mother set down her glass with a giggle. "Oh, is that it? And here I thought I would have to beat the shit out of this little Chance. You want to meet your dad? Let's go."

Jaspierre dropped her fork. *What?*

"Come on. Don't tally." Mother's white heels clicked on the floor as they walked. Jaspierre looked down at her dress. It was yellow, but it wasn't special.

"Should... should I change?" Meeting her dad sounded terrifying. *How was he even here?*

Mother turned to her daughter and smiled. "Oh, he's gonna love that you wanted to meet him."

She clicked her heels up the staircase and they walked down the hall to her room. "He is in your room?"

"He is in your room?" Mother parroted back and opened the door. Jaspierre rarely went in her mother's room.

They went into her room and stepped through her closet. Mother pulled a little latch and a secret door swung open. Down they went, down a spiral staircase. At the bottom of the stairs was three doors.

Cold fear crept up Jaspierre's skin. This could be a prank. *Or worse.* Mother was a monster. She closed her eyes and counted to ten.

"Jasp! Come along." Mother opened the last door. Jaspierre didn't want to know any more. "Come. Now." Mother's voice took an edge Jasp knew all too well. She walked forward.

As she peered into the room, her small mind could hardly comprehend what she was seeing. "This is your daughter." Mother's heels clicked, and her feathered robe swirled dramatically as she revealed Jaspierre.

Jaspierre's eyes grew wide and she covered her mouth. She closed her eyes as quickly as she could, and let out a tiny terrified whimper.

"She is beautiful." A soft, deep manly voice filled the room.

"You fucking monster." The low, nasty, raspy whisper rang in Jaspierre's ears. A different voice, a second man.

She opened her eyes again. A thin angry man was chained to metal rings with his hands up above his head. He was naked. His feet were standing on two metal rings attached to the wall. He was like that puppy. His skin was not his own. His toes and fingers looked like they were dying. His teeth were in pieces. Jaspierre trembled and could hardly speak.

"Thank you for letting me meet her," the other voice rang out again. The nicer one. Jaspierre turned to the sound, and saw a second man. He was muscular and handsome. His face was nice, and left untouched by surgery. Yet his fingers were different colors, and one looked dead like the leg they took off the dog. His back was a completely different skin than his front. He was chained to the wall. All he wore was a small towel tied around his waist.

"Jasper." Mother looked at the skinny man on the wall. "She looks like you, don't you think?"

"Fuck you." He urinated in front of them.

"Which one is my father?" Jaspierre struggled with this. "How... how long have you kept them here?" Her body trembled.

"Jaspierre, don't be dense. *They* are your father. Right Pierre?" Mother licked her lips in a naughty smile.

"Hello" Pierre's warm voice sounded sad.

Jasper's coarse rasping sound gurgled out of him, "*You named her after us?*" Disgust rolled out of his mouth like smoke.

"Jaspierre, go on up. That is enough for now." Mother's robe slid off her shoulders and she hung it on a small hook on the wall. She walked over to the wall in her tight silky lingerie where Jasper was and climbed the rings, heels and all. Pierre turned toward Jaspierre.

"Go quick, please, dear child." And he turned to follow Mother. Jaspierre ran out and sobbed in her room. Her father was a monster. A monster made by Mother.

Three days later Jaspierre snuck into Mother's room with a large tray of food. She looked for the latch and clicked the door.

She tiptoed down the spiral staircase, careful not to drop any of the food. When she got to the bottom she walked to the last room. It wasn't locked, and she opened the door.

"Are you hungry?"

Pierre stood up. "Where is Severina? Where is your mother?"

"Do you want to eat?"

Jasper called out from the wall, "*You feed us, but then you have to fuck us.*" His angry, hoarse whisper scared her so much she nearly dropped the food.

Pierre chided, "Hush, you idiot; at least we get to eat today."

Pierre didn't move any closer to Jaspierre. "Don't listen to him. Can you bring it to me?" He stood frozen in place with his hands held out, like someone trying to coax a frightened bird to hop a little closer.

"I..." Jaspierre trembled. She handed him the tray. "I want to let you out." She whispered to Pierre, and stared into his oddly colored eyes. *Were they even his eyes?* Jaspierre shuddered.

"I don't think that is a good idea," Pierre whispered back sadly. Mother would kill them all.

"I have to," Jaspierre said, her tiny eight-year-old self did not budge. "I cannot leave you down here. I cannot do it."

She held out the keys and Pierre unlocked the chain at his ankle, unwrapping it from his waist. He handed them back to her. "Tell her I took the keys from you by force."

Jaspierre couldn't think of anything to say, so she nodded. Pierre grabbed two handfuls of food-- green beans and turkey-- and fled. Jasper let out a sad howl.

"*Don't leave me! Let me go! Please let me go!*" His voice was still hoarse. His cries were muted like a dog who had been debarked.

"Shhhh," Jaspierre hushed him. "How do I unlock you?" He was scary. But leaving him down here was wrong.

Jasper whimpered, "*Up here, you have to climb.*"

She hesitated. He was naked and scary. His skin was falling off his leg in a big, dead patch. She didn't want to go near him. "*Please. Please.*" His scared voice gave her strength. She started climbing. She had to go around his leg. Her left foot was directly under his naked penis. Her right foot was pressed close to his knee. She tried not to look at him. The right half of his chest was covered in hair. The left half had pink, smooth, hairless skin that didn't look like it belonged.

There was one lock at his waist: the chains from his waist and feet and hands all led back to his waist. She unlocked it, her hands trembling with nervousness. "I'm sorry my mother did this to you."

"*I am sorry too.*" His hoarse voice felt so close on her face. She climbed down as he freed himself from the chains. He dropped to the ground behind her. His face was set into a fierce look. She turned to get him the tray of food, but before she could even pick it up, a chain was crushing her throat.

"*You are the devil's spawn and you must die!*" His words rang into her ears as she helplessly choked. A tiny child against a grown man. A man filled with hate. Her body was desperate to survive.

"Jasper!" Pierre made a horrified noise from the doorway, racing into the room. He punched Jasper in the face.

"*If I didn't know any better, I would think that you loved her. You sick fuck.*" Jasper released the girl and swung the chain, smashing it into Pierre's soft face.

Jaspierre collapsed to the floor.

Pierre ducked Jasper's next swing and charged into the man's stomach. "What if I did?" He punched Jasper's face and he fell to the ground.

"*She is a fucking sociopath. She keeps taking us apart and putting us together! I will fucking kill that bitch and her spawn!*" Jasper screamed his hoarse, broken voice at Pierre. Pierre took the man's head and slammed it into the floor over and over. Jasper lost consciousness, but Pierre couldn't stop. He had years of pent-up fury he couldn't stop anymore. He beat and punched and pummeled the man's skull until his brain leaked out.

Jaspierre watched it all, curled into the corner of the room. She couldn't even sob yet. She was so frightened. Pierre relented. He sat there in his small towel, eyes shut, his body still trembling.

He wiped his hands on the towel. "Are you okay?" His voice sounded soft and warm again. But he looked like a monster to her.

Blood pooled between them, swirling into the drain. Pierre stepped over it to the small girl. "I didn't know you were going to let him out too, or I would have stopped you. I am so sorry. Are you okay?" He held out his hand, and she cringed.

He bent down close to her. "I'm not going to hurt you." He held out his hand again.

Her tiny little body sobbed frightened wails. He scooped her up off the floor and, for the first time in her life, she was hugged. He held her and kissed her forehead. "I am so sorry." He carried her out of the room. Then he walked her up the spiral staircase to Mother's room. "I am so sorry, Jaspierre." His voice sounded so warm and sweet. "Where is your mother? I... I don't want her to..." He was uncertain what to say. He didn't know how Mother was with Jaspierre, but letting him and Jasper out would ruin it.

He stepped into the empty hallway, still carrying the child. He couldn't put her in Mother's bed. "Which one is yours?" He brushed her hair from her face.

She pointed, tears still streaming down her face. He opened up her door and stepped inside. A small cat jumped up from under the bed. He tucked the two in together.

"Can't you stay and be my daddy?" Jaspierre whispered.

"I can't."

"Please?"

"I can't. I am so sorry Jaspierre." He kissed her forehead and that was the last she saw of him.

CHAPTER

TWENTY-FIVE

The boozy scent burned Chance's eyes when he opened them. It took him a moment to figure out what was happening. He heard the first match spark. The flames were faster than he was, and he barely made it to the front door when flames engulfed his body. The meaty scent of flesh roasting filled his nostrils. He flung the door open and rolled back and forth in the dirt driveway, putting out his burning flesh. *Dammit. She was so fucking fun.*

Jaspierre walked around to her car. Burning him alive; it wasn't enough. She knew it. She wanted more blood. She found herself humming as she opened the car door and started it up. *"Oranges and lemons."* Just like Mother sang. *"Say the bells of St. Clement's."* She coasted down the road. *"You owe me five farthings, Say the bells of St. Martin's."* As she drove, she saw a ragged, bloody man standing on the side of the road.

"*Here comes a candle to light you to bed,*" He waved his arms back and forth. She slowed and stopped. As he saw her, he stumbled backwards, trying to flee. "*Here comes a chopper.*" She smiled and climbed out of the car with the little knife. "*To chop off your head.*" Russell tried to run, but his limp, feverish miserable body had nothing left. He tried to protest as she slit his throat. "*Chip chop chip chop*" She took her time and severed his head. "*The last man's dead!*" Jaspierre stood, her jeans and her shirt covered in Russell's blood. Mother would be so proud. Russell had something in his hands. She turned and looked closer and saw it was her metal ring. She smiled to herself, and picked it up to take it home. Seemed like she was going to need it.

She climbed back into the car and turned up the radio and drove home. She finally freed herself from those emotions that had held her back. She finally understood Mother.

JASPIERRE

JASPIERRE

A Note from Mixi...

Thank you for reading Jaspierre. *I'd really appreciate a review if you aren't too busy!*

Keep your eyes peeled for the sequel: **Jaspierre's Descent-** Where Jaspierre looks for her father and finds Mother.

If you enjoyed this novel and haven't yet read **Landlocked Lighthouse**, *you might want to give it a try- Here is a little excerpt:*

I called her a few times, but she didn't come running. She slinked up, her teeth bared at me as I held out my hand. A large chunk of fur was missing from the side of her neck, and fresh blood dripped from it. *Crap.*

I gently petted her, and she never stopped growling. There was a stick in the wound. I don't know if she ran into a tree and then bled all over, or if she started out injured and then got a stick in the wound. Either way, it was not good. I carefully pulled on the stick and she let out a snarling yelp. It didn't gush with blood, so hopefully, it hadn't hit anything that couldn't heal. I pressed my left knee against her head and my right one into her shoulder and I pulled with all my strength. Quick was better than slow when you had an angry animal in pain. She snarled, struggled and nearly bit me and the blood was quickly pouring. I pressed both my hands into the wound, slowing the flow, and she cried out. I counted to ten slowly, her body writhing under mine and I tried not to cry.

By the time I got to ten, she had stopped. No more growling, no more yelping. No wiggling or struggling. For a moment I thought she was dead. I lifted one hand, and the blood poured again, so I pressed hard and counted to thirty. Finally, at thirty seconds, the flow wasn't as dangerous. She wouldn't bleed out if she could hold still long enough for it to mend. That would be a challenge. I slowly took my right knee off her shoulder, still pinning her head with the other knee. *You gotta let 'em up slow or they'll bite.* That's what great-grandmother always said. Didn't matter what kind of animal, you let 'em up slow.

The wound was definitely a puncture from the stick, and it looked like she had been chewing on it, or caught the stick on something while she ran. It was a mess. I should clip off all the fur from around it and wrap it with something. Hell,

I couldn't find our food box, it seemed unlikely I'd find the box of medical stuff.

I let up her head. She gazed at me with her big, doofy eyes and licked my hand. Back to her old self, it seemed. We slowly walked back to the house together. Thankfully, we made it back without her wound bursting and pouring open. I gave her a little bowl of water and she drank, then immediately fell asleep.

I never did examine the stick she had in her neck or I would have noticed it was carved to a sharp, barbed point.

I am currently living on an eight-acre peach orchard, running a small pie shop. Between pies, I typed out this novel. This is the first book I've ever written, and I hopes you enjoyed it. I have three kids, eleven cats, and two dogs. If you want to hear when my next book is out, sign up for my newsletter.

Thanks so much!

Mixi J Applebottom

Feel free to contact Mixi directly at:
mixijapplebottom@gmail.com
or visit her blog at: mixijapplebottom.com
Join my email list:
mixijapplebottom.com/booklinks